AF439928

With a tightly woven plot, great characters, and full of thrills and chills, you'll enjoy Remembrandt.

— MICHELE ASHMAN BELL, AUTHOR OF *A MODEST PROPOSAL*

In this clever and fast-paced young adult novel, Robin King delivers a perfect mix of suspense and romance. . . . Alexandra's eidetic memory will reel you in, and her double life will keep you guessing until the end.

— BROOKE HARGETT

What a great debut novel! Author Robin King keeps you intrigued as you try to figure out the puzzles Alexandra is faced with. . . . I would highly recommend this book to young adults and adults alike.

— WENDY MALLATT

When I read Remembrandt, *I didn't want the story to end. I loved the setting, intrigue, surprises, adventures, and romance . . . I'm happy to hear that the experiences and friendships won't end. I'm looking forward to what happens next. I recommend this book to the young and young at heart alike.*

— KAREN LUBEAN

VAN GOGH GONE

THE ART OF ESPIONAGE
BOOK 2

ROBIN KING

THE ART OF ESPIONAGE SERIES

Remembrandt
Van Gogh Gone
Memory of Monet

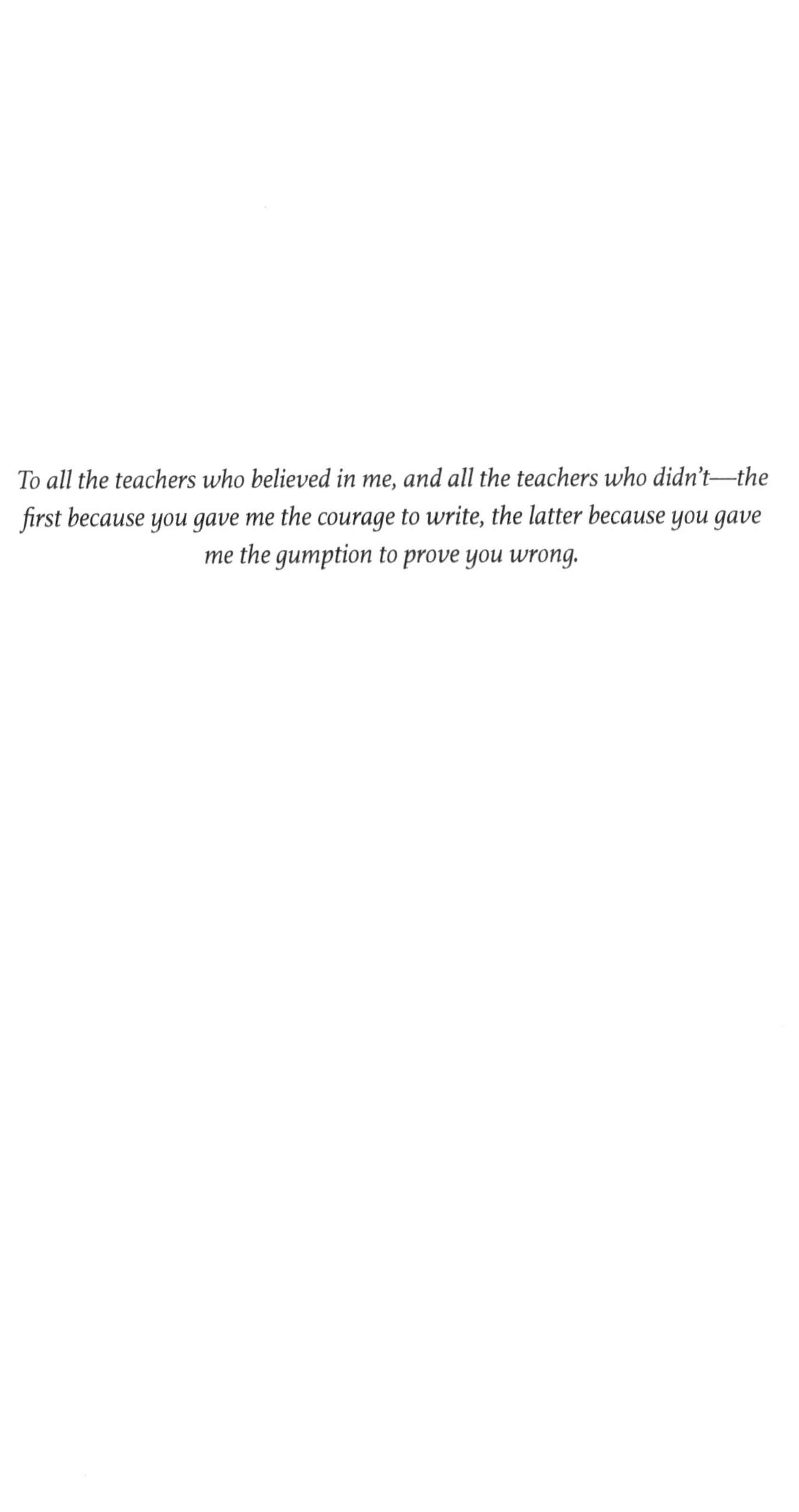

To all the teachers who believed in me, and all the teachers who didn't—the first because you gave me the courage to write, the latter because you gave me the gumption to prove you wrong.

1

BASICALLY

I clutched the polished steel table to keep my hands from trembling. A dim light glowed above, but it brought no warmth into the frigid room. I instinctively reached toward my jacket pocket for the phone that wasn't there. No phone. No electronic device specially made by Millard. No handler giving me directions in my earpiece. Nothing. All they left me with were the clothes I'd put on that morning. At least I still had the use of my hands.

I pressed my back against the cold metal chair and crossed my arms in front of me. I wasn't sure how long I'd been in the small space, furnished only with a table and two chairs. After about two hours, I stopped keeping track. I knew it was all part of their game— get me agitated, make me think too much about the things that might happen when they returned.

I knew I should be searching my mind for ways to escape an enclosed fifteen-by-fifteen-foot room, or maybe how to react to a hostile interrogator. Instead, I flipped the pages of the English 301 notes shelved in my brain. It kept my mind calm and relaxed my body. Besides, if I got out of this in time, I still had a test on Monday.

The lock clicked in the door. I sat up straight and tensed my abdominal muscles. It was now or never. *Don't let them get to you, Alex. You can do this.*

The door swung open loudly. Peering past the tall man standing there, I tried to catch a glimpse of where I'd been taken. They hadn't removed the blindfold until they deposited me in this room. I spied a dim hallway before the door slammed shut behind the guy.

He wore a tailored gray suit—not at all what I was expecting from my interrogator—and a scowl on his face. Although he looked about twenty-five, his swagger reminded me of an overconfident teen. He threw a manila folder onto the table in front of him, close enough for me to reach across and snag it. The words from the interrogation chapter in The Manual filled my mind. *"The basic rule in interrogations is for respondents to reduce the amount of harm they are likely to experience, particularly in the long term. Do not anger an interrogator."*

I stared at the folder for several seconds before I vowed to keep my hands clenched in my lap, hidden from the man's view. If he wanted me to see what was in the folder, I would wait for his permission. His chair screeched across the concrete floor as he pulled it out, and then he took a seat directly across from me.

Adrenalin pulsed through my body. Hopefully I would remember everything I'd been taught—no, not remember. My memory was never a problem. The challenge was putting my knowledge to use while my heart almost pounded right out of my chest.

"Kak vas zovut? Kto vu?" he said in Russian.

I ignored his command and studied his closely trimmed black hair, the same color as the thick stubble shadowing the lower half of his face.

"Kak vas zovut?" he repeated in a more demanding tone.

I kept my shoulders relaxed and stared blankly at him.

"I know you speak Russian, so you can stop the act, you filthy spy." The interrogator's perfect English didn't surprise me, but I raised an eyebrow at the slight British accent. "I also know all about the 'barrier technique,' so you can stop the silent act. Now tell me your name."

My eyes widened. So this was how it was going to go. Fine. "Dana

Laxer." I gave him my false name, an anagram of my real first name, Alexandra.

"And why are you here?"

"To visit my cousin," I lied.

His mouth twitched at the corner before he tensed his square jaw. "Who is that cousin?"

I made up a name on the spot. "Hermia."

"Why were you here visiting her?"

"I . . ."

He cut in, "Before you answer that, give me your hands."

I hesitated.

"Now!" he yelled.

I jumped at the anger in his voice and pushed my hands across the cool surface of the table. He snatched them and turned them over so my palms faced the ceiling. The top of my ring collided with the tabletop, sending a clang through the room. He moved his hands until his index fingers rested on the veins at my wrists. My blood pulsated against his grip.

"I am an expert in lie detection." He pressed his fingers deeper into the tendons in my wrists, sending a shooting pain through my arm. I didn't flinch. "So no stories."

Great. Just great. Now what am I supposed to do? I stared past the man at the dreary gray wall behind him. I searched through my mind for any information I had on passing a lie detector. Though The Manual only had a short section on the subject, I'd once seen a documentary on a man who had learned to beat the test. I fast-forwarded to his main tips and listened to them in my mind.

"Now, tell me again, what is your name?" The interrogator pushed his fingers deeper into my wrists.

I watched a scene of calming ocean waves in my mind while I replied, "Dana Laxer."

"What color are my eyes?" His face focused on mine, an expression of complete concentration.

A bit my tongue, hard enough to draw blood, but kept my face complacent. *I hope this works.* "Brown. Your eyes are brown."

"How old are you?"

I bit my tongue again before I replied. "Seventeen."

"Seems a little young to be working on your own."

"Is that a question?" I started to narrow my eyes at him, thought better of it, and relaxed my face muscles once again.

"Why are you here?"

William's face flashed in my mind. Those soft brown curls falling onto his forehead. A small smile playing across his face. Eyes that reminded me of the blue skies of summers back home. "To visit my cousin, Hermia."

My interrogator cleared his throat. "Why are you visiting this Hermia?"

I listened to the documentary man's words in my mind: *For lies to be the most convincing, they must be founded in truth.*

Truth? I should have just picked the name of someone I knew. Hermia? Why the heck did I pick the name—wait, Hermia? My mind raced at double speed.

I took a deep, calming breath. "Well, Hermia's dad wanted her to marry Demetrius, but she was in love with Lysander. Her dad told her if she didn't marry him, he would send her to a nunnery. So they decided to run away together."

A deep burrow formed between my questioner's eyebrows. "What does that have to do with you?"

"On the way out of town, they ran into Helena, who used to be engaged to Demetrius and is also Hermia's best friend. Helena was still in love with Demetrius, who left her to try to win over Hermia. Then Oberon, the fairy king, got involved and messed things up— well, actually it was Puck who messed it up and then—

The man's nostrils flared. "Stop!"

"What?" I said as innocently as possible.

"We are getting nowhere with this. Obviously you're not going to give me any real answers this way." He licked his lips. "But we have other ways of getting at the truth." He stood up and removed his jacket. The sleeves of his fitted white dress shirt clung to the muscles at his biceps. He threw the jacket on the table on top of the folder and kicked his chair. It landed on its back against the side wall. Then he whipped the table out from under my arms and slammed it against the door.

My stomach gave a lurch and I swallowed hard. Before I could say anything or move, he kicked at my chair. I managed to lean forward and find my footing before I followed the chair to its final resting place in the corner of the room. I straightened as tall as I could and planted my feet shoulder-width apart.

His hand came at my face. I swiped it away with my palm. A crushing weight pressed my stomach with such force that my body flew backward and hit the wall. A loud crack sounded in my head as my skull met with brick. I stumbled to the side. *What the heck is he . . .* A blurry leg was coming for me again. I fell to the floor. I wasn't sure if it was the dazed feeling in my head or my attempt at ducking. Either way, he yelled when his foot slammed into the wall behind me.

I scrambled up, grabbed the chair in the corner, and swung it at his back with all of my strength. He turned just in time to catch it in his hand and pull it away from me. He swept it at my legs. I jumped up in response and hit my hip against the table. Through the pain in my head and hip, I pulled the other chair from under the table. I swung it up from the ground like a hammer thrower. It clanged against the chair in his hand, which then flew from his grasp. I took my chance and pitched my chair at him. Metal met with flesh and he barked in pain, stumbling to the wall. A flood of triumph washed over me, and I relaxed my stance.

The anger in his eyes ignited and I nearly dropped the chair. He launched himself forward and ripped it from my hands, then propelled it across the room. His shoulder met my chest like a wrecking ball against a building and I fell to the floor, his body sprawled on top of me. I wrapped my legs around his middle and my arms around his neck and squeezed. His face pressed against my neck while the heat of his heavy breathing misted on my skin. I squeezed harder.

He grunted and tried to speak, but I now had my chin pressed against his windpipe, something Sensei Itosu had taught me just last week. I pulled my chin back just enough to allow the guy to talk. I wouldn't stop unless I heard the word.

"*Milost',*" he croaked.

"What?" I said into his neck. I'd heard it, but I wanted to hear him say it again.

"*Milost'.* Mercy."

I released my arms from his neck and slowly relaxed my legs. He rolled to the side and onto his back. His wheezes and coughs filled the room until they changed to ragged chuckles.

"I can't believe you, Alexandra," he said hoarsely.

I rose to my feet and peered down at his sprawled-out body. Sweat and tears dripped down the side of his handsome face and onto the floor. A wave of satisfaction and relief washed over me. I offered my hand down to him and laughed.

Smiling, Daly grabbed it and pulled himself to his feet. "I have to admit, you stayed in character the entire time. I almost thought you'd lose it with the age comment." He took a step forward and winced.

"Hey, that was a low blow, even for my handler, who is supposed to be prepping me for a real interrogation," I said. "What was with the chair, anyway? You could have given me a concussion, not to mention broken bones when you started swinging it." I touched the back of my head, where a goose egg had already formed.

"You're the one who made the interrogator mad with that Shake-speare stuff." Daly brushed off his dress pants.

"Wait, you knew it was Shakespeare?"

"Any bloke who took high school English knows *A Midsummer Night's Dream.*" He rolled his neck, and a few cracks sounded from his spine.

"Yeah, but probably not a Russian terrorist." We lifted the table and moved it back to the center of the interrogation room. Daly picked up his crumpled jacket and the folder that had somehow managed to remain closed. "What was that British accent anyway? And *bloke*? No one says that."

"Did you like that? I thought I would test out my English charm.

So how was it?" He said that last part with the accent. Honestly, he could have passed as British, but I wasn't about to let him know that.

"Not very charming when you started yelling."

"I can't believe I didn't catch that Hermia comment sooner." He leaned against the wall near the door and stretched his arms. "You're getting good at that chin choke, by the way. My vision was already blurring when . . ." He cleared his throat.

"When you said mercy. See, wasn't that idea of mine a good one?" I reached down to pick up a chair, but it had lost a leg in one of our throws, so I left it where it lay. I placed the other one at the table, still waiting for Daly to respond to my question. I glanced in his direction and found him studying me.

"How did you beat my lie detection?" he asked. "I thought for sure I'd sense something with that cousin comment, but there was nothing different than your other responses. And then with Oberon, I waited for a change in pulse or breathing, but—"

"Maybe I need to teach you a thing or two." I tapped at my temple.

The door opened to a beaming Professor Golkov. His nearly white hair hung in short waves on his head, a few wisps of gray streaking through the top. I'd noticed that around the other agents, he usually maintained a professional demeanor, but with me, Golkov often let his guard down. Maybe it was because we had met when I enrolled in one of his Russian classes, or because he'd worked with my mother before she died. Either way, he felt like family.

"That was quite a show you two put on in here." Golkov winked at me.

My face got warm. "You were watching that?"

The wrinkles at the corners of his eyes deepened. "Of course. The two of you are often the highlight of my day." He and Daly laughed.

I bit the inside of my cheek, and this time it wasn't because I was trying to beat a human lie detector.

"I know some of this training might seem silly"—Golkov motioned for Daly and me to follow him out of the room and down the hallway— "but we really are training you for any possible situations you might encounter."

"I know." I elbowed Daly in the arm. "Sorry about the cousin Hermia bit. It was just the first thing that popped in my head."

"I couldn't even sense the lie, Golkov." Daly slowed down as we reached the end of the hallway. "Had I not been listening to the words, I wouldn't even have noticed. She's good." He patted me on the back. Since I had joined The Company three months before, that was probably the first time Daly had given me an actual compliment. Not that I didn't think he had confidence in me—I just felt like he was always wanting more.

We stopped at a door at the end of the dim hallway. "I wouldn't expect anything less," Golkov said as he punched a few numbers on the keypad, numbers that my mind automatically memorized. The door beeped and he turned the handle.

We stepped into the brightly lit gymnasium used for the training of operatives. After all this time, it still astonished me that Brown University, unbeknown to them, housed the expansive headquarters of Golkov's secret organization, The Company. Had I known before fall semester that my Russian professor's "real" office was twenty feet below ground, I might have enjoyed some of my boring classes a little more, imagining the exciting things happening underneath me.

Footsteps pounded on one of the treadmills in the corner of the gym as an older male agent I recognized ran at top speed. A pair of agents in black workout attire were sparring to the right of us, their huffs and grunts a pleasant reminder of my fight with Daly back in the interrogation room. I replayed him saying "mercy" several times in my head as we walked across the black cushioned flooring of the gym. I got a brief glimpse of Millard, my techno-savvy gadget creator, on the second floor. A five-foot-wide deck surrounded the top half of the room. The metal railing with a glass enclosure allowed me to see into Millard's office above, along with several handlers' offices, including Daly's.

"Do you have the file?" Golkov asked Daly. I always thought it was funny how Golkov preferred paper files over the electronic ones that could so easily have been accessed on a phone or tablet.

"Yes, our next mission details, right here." Daly held up the manila folder he had brought with him earlier. His gray suit jacket was still draped over his other arm. I reached for the file, but Daly snatched it away and jogged up the metal steps in front of us. "Not just yet." He waved it in the air.

"I knew I should've grabbed that earlier," I said under my breath.

"Daly's right. You're not quite ready for the mission." Golkov held onto the railing as he moved up the steps.

"What? It's not like it's my first one. Can't I just see it for a second or two?"

"Ha!" Daly tucked the folder under his arm. "We both know what one second with your eyes means."

I rolled my eyes. Daly and Golkov knew about my photographic memory, but I'd never told them what my father and William knew. My mind didn't just take pictures of pages—it recorded my memories in exact detail like a movie. My eidetic memory allowed me to re-experience everything I saw, heard, tasted, smelled, or touched. Having perfect recall had its advantages, but sometimes I wished I had better control of it.

I looked around the gym for Sensei Itosu, an expert in karate and meditation whose training had helped me make it through fall semester. He was nowhere in sight.

"So when do I get to see it?" I motioned to the folder under my handler's arm. A look passed between Golkov and Daly, one that made me even more curious about my next mission.

Golkov smiled. "Once you pass your Russian 500 test on Monday. I hear it's a real humdinger."

"Fine." I resigned myself to a boring weekend of studying.

"I need to discuss a few things with Millard. I'll see you on Monday," Daly said before he continued up the second level of stairs. Golkov and I exited the gym and entered The Company's offices. After being locked up in a small room for several hours, I found the offices' glass walls almost comforting. At least I had passed today's test.

"I hope you will find some time this weekend to relax your body and your mind," Golkov said. "I know the last few months have been rough on you, with the Moscow mission, and resting your injured leg." As if in response, my leg faltered on the polished black floor of the glass corridor. My stitches from the four-inch gash had long since healed, but my mind flashed to the rooftop of the warehouse. I could smell the smoke and feel the rain pelting my skin.

My first real mission as an operative for The Company should have been simple—collect information about a missing agent and bring her home. I got the information all right, then found the nearly lifeless agent, saved her, and soon after blew up the lab that housed a toxic liquid created by Red Eye, a Russian terrorist organization. Of course, that was followed by finding out that my trusted chauffeur, Elijah, was actually a double agent working for Red Eye. All in a day's work.

"How is that leg of yours today?" Golkov asked as we stopped a few feet from his office. I stared past him and through the glass walls to an operative tapping the thin computer screen on her glass desk. "Alexandra?"

"Yes. I mean, my leg is just fine. Everything healed great—only a thin scar to show for it."

"It's fine if you aren't ready for the mission. There will be others. We can wait a month or two, maybe in February when—"

"No," I cut in, surprising myself with the intensity in my voice. "I'm ready." The truth was, I needed a mission, a distraction. Just being in the interrogation room, even though I knew it was just a test, had drawn my mind away from memories I desperately wanted to forget.

"Good, good. Well, I'll see you on Monday morning. Early tutoring session, say eight in my office?" I glanced over Golkov's shoulder to his office and tilted my head slightly. "My other office, I mean." He gave me a playful smile.

"Sure, Professor. See you then."

He continued into his glass office and sat down at his desk, his pen already scribbling away at a notebook in front of him. Behind him, the wall-size electronic display fluttered with a constant stream of information on a rectangular checkerboard of screens—operatives on current missions, world maps, weather displays, communication grids. I peeled my eyes away and headed to the exit.

One retina scan and a dark basement stairwell later, I found myself blinking at the sunlight shining through Marston Hall windows. I waved to a few students I recognized. They stared at me as if I was strange and I looked away. I may have seen their faces many times on campus, but they didn't know me.

I made it about ten feet from the steps of Marston Hall before I noticed him standing against a leafless tree.

William.

I could replay his smile a million times in my mind, but seeing it in person sent a swirl of anticipation through me.

His face was flushed from the cold, his blue eyes were a bright glimmer of light in the dreary winter's wake. A few brown curls peeked out along the edges of his navy stocking hat.

"Hey there," he said, moving across the Quad in my direction.

"Hi." My voice came out suddenly shy. I crossed the sidewalk and stopped at the frosty grass.

"What happened?" he asked.

"Hmm?"

He reached out and touched my arm, sending an electric thrill to my center. "Your sleeve."

I looked down at my arm and found what William was touching. A rip in my jacket ran from the top of my shoulder to about halfway down to my elbow. *How did that . . . Wait.* I knew exactly how the tear happened. *That darned Daly!*

"Yeah, I think I must have caught it on something." Like maybe Daly's grip, or a metal chair being thrown at me.

"At least you don't need stitches this time." William reached his arm around mine until his gloved hand found my fingers. He led me down the sidewalk.

"Yeah." I cringed. I wouldn't have been able to hide the stitches, let alone the limp from my mission back in November. It was the first real lie I'd had to tell William. I really wasn't that clumsy, but I'd told him I had tripped and landed on some glass. At least the glass part was true. The fact that it had come from the windows of an exploding building—an explosion I'd caused— never left my lips.

"I'm wondering if you need a bodyguard." He laughed.

"I've got you, don't I?" I hit my hip against his. He let go of my hand and wrapped his arm around my waist.

"Which is why I've got a request." He cleared his throat.

"A request, huh? If it involves listening to Dr. Red and Devin doing a karaoke duet again at your house, I think I'll just hang with Casey."

"Hey, my roommates weren't that bad," he said. I paused on the sidewalk and looked at him with a raised eyebrow. "They were pretty bad, weren't they?" He let go of my waist and pulled at his hat. "No, in fact, I'm thinking kind of the opposite."

"The opposite?" I said. He reached for my hand again and we continued toward my dorm.

"Yeah, I was thinking maybe we need to go on a date."

"We've been on lots of dates." We ran together several mornings a week, studied and talked in Spanish between classes, and I'd been to his house every week for the last month for William Wednesday, where he made dinner for his roommates.

"I mean without roommates or university students hovering around us—like just the two of us." He kicked a skiff of snow on the sidewalk. A memory from last fall flashed across my vision, when William was still my Spanish professor. I'd nearly accepted that we could only be good friends, since we didn't want one of those tricky student-teacher relationships. But then he told me he couldn't be my teacher anymore. I played the memory of our first kiss again for probably the hundredth time.

"Alex?" William squeezed my hand and brought me back to the present. Anyone else might have questioned my distraction, but he had known about my eidetic memory for a few months and had accepted the way my mind worked.

I cleared my throat. "Sorry. I think I'm up for running in the morning. Seven at *la linea de meta*?" We usually met at our "finish line" near Blackstone Park.

William stopped at the steps of Wayland House and let go of my hand to face me. "No, Alex, I mean more than a few miles from campus and without our sweaty running clothes on."

My mouth fell open. *Did he just say what I thought he said?*

His eyes went wide. "No, that's not what . . . you know that's not what I . . ."

A laugh bubbled out of me. "I'm sorry. I know you didn't mean without our . . ." Suddenly, my face felt hot.

He let out a frustrated breath. "Can't a guy ask his girlfriend out on a romantic date?"

Oh. I grabbed his hand and pulled him toward me. "Did you just call me your girlfriend?"

"What else would you be?" He ran his fingers over the small of my back. Even through the layers of jacket and his glove, heat traveled up my spine.

"I don't know. Spanish student, running partner, girl in need of a bodyguard?"

He pulled me into him until we shared the same breath. "So will you?"

"Hmm?" Standing that close to him and those long eyelashes had all my attention. I reached up and touched a curl that fell across the middle of his forehead. I tugged at it and let go. It bounced back up against his hat.

"Go on a date with me?" His chest rumbled against me as he spoke.

"Mmm-hmm." I nodded.

"Good." He erased the distance between us and didn't let me ask any more questions.

2

SCARS & SECRETS

"Do you want to talk about it?" Tanner asked.

I got into the front seat of his Buick and huffed. "What?"

"About why you have a crease in the middle of your forehead."

Tanner turned the key in the ignition and the engine sputtered off. My brother and I sat outside of the karate studio near Wenatchee Valley College, where I was taking spring-semester classes. Though I'd finally gotten my driver's license, we only had one car and he often picked me up after my karate class.

"No." I buckled my seatbelt and reached to rub out whatever crease he was referring to.

"You know I can just tickle it out of you." He started to bring his hand toward my ribs.

"No!" I shouted loud enough for anyone in the parking lot to hear and pushed his arms away. We both knew he could have easily taken me in any tickle war.

"Then out with it," Tanner said.

"Fine." I shifted in my seat. "How do you do it?"

"Do what?"

"Hide stuff from people around you without it bugging you?"

He jiggled his car keys back and forth with his hand. "If you mean not telling people about you being Little Miss Polaroid, it's no big deal. Personally, I think it's kind of cool that not everyone knows. It's like you have a secret superpower. Maybe we should come up with some kind of name for you besides Polaroid. Only Mom and Dad are old enough to even know what that is anyway. Let me think."

"That's not what I'm talking about, Tanner." I turned to look at him. "I'm talking about Mom. I know you know something that you aren't telling me."

"What do you mean?" He stopped playing with his keychain but didn't meet my gaze.

"You know what I mean. How can you lie to me like that?"

"I'm not lying to you, Lexie. I'm not."

"I know there's something going on. I heard . . . I mean I was coming to your room last week, and I heard Mom talking . . ."

Tanner gripped the steering wheel, the veins in his hands pulsing against his skin.

"Did Dad do something?" I persisted. "Did Mom do something? Just tell me now. Are they getting a divorce or something? I have to know." I grabbed his arm.

Tanner's shoulders relaxed and he finally looked at me. "No, no. They are still too lovey-dovey for their own good."

"Is it cancer? Please don't tell me Mom's sick." I squeezed my brother's arm tighter.

"Lexie, everything with them is fine. Really. No divorce. No life-threatening illness. Okay?"

"Okay." I let go of his arm. "Then what was that about?"

"I can't tell you. You just have to trust me and Mom."

"I do trust you—at least I thought I did—but I can see it's eating at you. Why can't you just tell me?"

"I can't." He swallowed and set his jaw.

"'Before a secret is told, one can feel the weight of it in the atmosphere.'"

"Let me guess, you're quoting someone again. What is that supposed to mean, anyway?" He let go of the steering wheel and picked up the car keys.

"I've seen you this past week, Tanner. Secrets are like scars. The cut *may no longer be there, but the scar's white line tells a story. Unless you share it, it's like you're hiding a part of yourself the whole world can already see. They may not know the how or the why, but they see it just the same."*

Tanner let out a long, slow breath and started the car.

"You know I'm eventually going to find out," I said.

He shook his head.

"Come on, you know everything about me."

"Yeah, and I'm still regretting some of it." He gave a weak laugh. "I do not want to know anything more about feminine hygiene." He made a disgusted face and I knew the conversation was over. I wouldn't get anything more out of him. Yet.

MY DORM ROOM WAS DARK, but it was already nearly seven in the morning. I sat up in bed. It had been over a month since a dream memory had played during my sleep. The last one had been of the crash—the car crash that took Tanner and my mom away from me. It had been nearly eight months since the accident, eight months that should have allowed a normal person to begin to forget the minute details of that night. Not me. My one consolation in all of this was that I could still see my brother and mom so clearly in my head that it was almost like having them with me. The good memories eased the ache I didn't believe would ever go away.

William couldn't fulfill his plans of taking me on a "real date" until Monday, since he had a Spanish teaching conference over the weekend. So, I finally had a few days to relax, as Golkov had told me to do. Or I could have some fun with my roommate.

"Casey," I whispered across the room. "Casey!" I said a little louder and tossed one of my pillows at her bed. "Are you awake?"

She frantically threw off her covers and jumped onto the area rug, then glanced around with her large, dark eyes. "What? What's going on? Did I miss class? Wait, was it the fire alarm again? Quick, where's my robe?"

I laughed and pointed to her desk chair. She was wearing only a long, spaghetti-strap tank top and boy shorts. She threw her fluffy purple robe over her pajamas. "Why aren't you moving?"

"Because it's more fun to watch you."

"Wait." She put her hands on her tiny hips. "It's Saturday. And there's no emergency, is there?"

"Not unless you count needing a distraction this weekend. Got any pranks in the works?"

Something sparked in Casey's eyes until they fixed themselves on the window and the nonexistent sun. She fell back onto her bed with her robe still on and pulled her covers over her head. "Can it wait until morning?" She groaned.

"It is morning."

"Not for any normal human. I'll see you around noon."

It only took about two minutes before her breathing settled into a steady rhythm. "Fine," I said to myself. "But when I get back from my run, I'm putting my cold hands on your face."

It took me nearly ten minutes to pull on my winter running clothes. January weather in Providence necessitated wearing two pairs of running tights, a jacket over my long-sleeved shirt, and a fleece-lined ear band. I considered wearing gloves too, but tossed them on my bed at the last minute. I would probably shed them after a mile or two anyway.

The sun brimmed over the campus buildings as I left Wayland House. Light shimmered off the snow that covered campus, reminding me of how the Columbia River water glimmered in the summer time. Watching the scene in my head from my Washington State home didn't make me feel as homesick as it used to. Providence had become a place I could call home.

I ran past a couple walking shoulder to shoulder while drinking from Coffee Exchange cups. The boy's wide smile reminded me of Tanner's goofy grin. An ache filled my throat. I might not miss Wenatchee as much as I used to, but I missed my only sibling. Losing Tanner was more than just losing a brother—he had been my best friend too.

My foot hit a patch of ice on the sidewalk and I started to slide. I compensated by throwing out my other leg to catch myself. Though I didn't fall, realizing it could happen slowed me to a jog until I reached Brooke Street. My scarred leg still wasn't as strong as it used to be.

At two stories high, Marston Hall was one of the smaller buildings on campus. I had been inside more times than I could count, yet passing near the steps yanked me back to my other life—the life where I helped Golkov solve puzzles and search for truth. The life where I was a spy. Saying it in my mind still made the logical realist side of me shake my head.

Suddenly I didn't want to be out running in the cold. I wanted to find Daly and start another sparring match. I knew the front doors would be locked this early in the morning, so I walked around to the back of the building, glancing behind me several times to make sure no one was watching. The single doorknob on the back door looked like any other bronze handle. It wasn't. Millard had made sure of that. Having a tech guy who could turn a cell phone into a taser came in pretty handy. I reached for the knob and held it for a few seconds before something clicked inside the door. I didn't even have to turn the knob—the door opened for me. I wished my dorm room opened so easily. I'd already had to have the RA unlock my room twice in the last month.

My shoes squeaked on the tile floor as I made my way through a narrow hallway, down the stairs into a large storage room, and to the hidden entrance of The Company. When I reached it, Daly was standing in front of the closed door, breathing hard. The bloodshot eyes and absent smile looked foreign on his face.

"What are you doing here on a Saturday morning?" I asked.

"What are you doing here?" He crossed his arms and blocked the retinal scanner with his back.

"I just thought I'd run on the treadmill or something until you came in."

"On a Saturday?"

"We both know you practically live here. I would have called if you hadn't shown up."

"Huh." He nodded his head.

"So are we going in or not?" I took a step forward.

He held his ground. There was something off in his expression, and it wasn't just that he looked like he hadn't slept the night before. He widened his stance. "Golkov told you to take a break this weekend. Why don't you head home and study for that test of his?"

"I will, but I wanted to finish my run and maybe spar. If you aren't free, I'm sure I can find someone else. If you'll just move over, I can—"

"You can't go in, Alexandra."

"What?"

"You just can't come in today."

"Wait. You knew I was coming when the doorknob upstairs read my fingerprints, didn't you? That's why you were out of breath. You came to stop me before I stepped through the door. What are you hiding?" I didn't have to grasp Daly's wrists to know he was keeping something from me—something big from the way he held his head, with his chin slightly raised and his eyes staring over my shoulder instead of at my face. It was his tell. Now I understood why Golkov preferred Daly as a handler and not an operative like me. He was fairly good at pretending while he trained me in different scenarios, but in real-life stressful situations, Daly was a terrible actor.

"Don't force this, Alexandra. Believe me."

"Why shouldn't I?" I stepped back a foot.

"You're not ready for this one. Just give it a few weeks, maybe a few months." He rubbed one of his eyes. "Maybe never."

That was it. I wasn't going to wait forever to find out what was going on. I plunged forward, kneed Daly in the gut, and let the light from the scanner run over my eye. I felt for the handle and pulled the door open. He reached for my shoulders and I lunged as he caught me, causing both of us to fall through the doorway and onto the hard marble floor.

I hopped up and glanced around at the empty offices. *Where is everyone?* Even on weekends, this place was a bustle of organized chaos, with operatives running from office to office, talking on phones or working away at their desks.

I ran through the glass corridor until I got to the gym door.

Daly followed me. "Alexandra, wait. At least let me prepare you . . ."

I pulled open the door. The gym was empty.

"What's going on, James?" I rarely used his first name. I knew he liked it and for that reason alone, I usually called him Daly. But the stillness of the gym had taken me by surprise and I'd let it slip.

He joined me at the top of the gym stairs. His eyes fell on the door that led to the interrogation room. "You have to understand. We wouldn't have brought him here unless it was absolutely necessary. I know how hard this whole thing has been on you. I even told Golkov to give it a few more weeks—a little more time for you to recover from Moscow. But now he thinks . . ." Daly ran his fingers over his cropped hair.

"I am recovered. Now tell me what's going on."

He blinked several times before he spoke. "We found him and brought him here."

My hands started to shake and my vision blurred. "Who . . . who did you bring here?"

"We found Elijah," Daly said solemnly.

I gripped the stair railing as my bad leg started to give way.

3

FILL IN THE BLANK

The scenes moved so quickly through my mind that I hardly had a grasp of one before the next memory came. A man stood in the alleyway, the barrel of a gun pointed in my direction through the smoke of the burning warehouse. *Flash.* The same man chased me through the damp night and to the rooftop of a factory. *Flash.* Elijah's hands flew at me, the force propelling me backward. The scene paused in my head. His dark stare pierced through me as my body floated in midair on the verge of falling off the ten-story building. It had taken me nearly three weeks of meditation with Sensei Itosu to keep those eyes from making my hands shake every time they appeared in my mind.

"Alexandra?" Daly's voice shook the memories from my head. He had his hands on my shoulders, his face only inches from mine. I pushed back from him and wavered on the step until he came to my side and lowered me down with him, only releasing me when I sat securely on the top step next to him.

"How? How did you find him?" I tried in vain to stop the tremble in my voice.

"Millard created an algorithm using facial-recognition software he borrowed from the CIA. There was a hit in Omsk two days ago, and our agents found Elijah breaking into a private hospital there. I just returned with him last night."

"He's here? Right now?" My lightheadedness was starting to fade. I reached for the handrail above me.

Daly gripped my shoulder. "Alexandra, don't."

"You can't stop me."

"I know." He let go of my shoulder and hung his head so it rested on his knees, then turned a resigned gaze to me. I had never seen him this exhausted. I held back the snide remark sitting on the tip of my tongue. I wouldn't fight him, not like this, but he wouldn't stop me from seeing Elijah, either. "He's not who we thought he was." Daly reached out and touched my arm. "Be careful."

"I will."

I stepped down the stairs and moved slowly across the gym floor. Daly was right. I wasn't ready to face Elijah. I wasn't sure I'd ever feel ready. Moscow and that acrid timbre of his voice would always haunt me. Unless . . . unless I filled in all the blanks. I had to know why he'd saved me from the waters of the Kryukov Canal only to try to take my life away a month later. It made no sense. How could he be working for Red Eye and The Company at the same time? And why? Why did he give me all those Shakespeare clues and warn me before the Moscow mission about being a double agent? What did it all have to do with my mother and her involvement as an art-recovery specialist for The Company?

There was only one way to get those answers. I had to meet him face to face.

My throat started to burn. I took in a deep breath. *You can do this, Alex. You saved yourself from him before.* Tanner's words from my first day at the community college gave me strength once again. *You are strong.* I was strong. I could do this.

I unzipped the pocket of my running jacket and felt for my Millard-enhanced cell phone. If things went south, I could always use the taser on Elijah again.

My security code let me into the hall that led to the interrogation room. Two guards flanked the door. I didn't recognize either of them, and I never forgot a face. They didn't move or meet my eyes when I approached. I should have known it wouldn't be easy.

"Excuse me," I said to the guard who stood directly in front of the keypad. "Can I get by?"

He continued to stare past me, just like the Royal Guards at Buckingham Palace. His hand rested on a holster at his hip. I didn't want to make these guys angry.

"They are there for a reason, Alexandra," Golkov said behind me. "I need to see him." I stared at the door.

Golkov exhaled and came to stand near me. "I am not going to stop you," he said.

"You're not?" Both he and Daly hadn't wanted me to find out about Elijah, but they weren't trying very hard to keep me away. My code had even worked in the hallway. What was going on? Why have Daly there to stop me if they were just going to let me see him anyway?

"Elijah has not been as cooperative as we had hoped," Golkov explained. "In fact, the only words we have been able to get from him have been a request."

"Request?" I tightened my hands in fists at my sides. "He doesn't deserve anything."

Golkov put a hand on my shoulder. "I agree with that assessment, which is why you weren't told earlier that he'd been apprehended. If I could have kept him from you, I would have."

"Why bring him here now? What does it have to do with me?"

"Since we found him in Omsk last week, he has insisted that he speak with no one but you."

"Me?" My voice caught in my throat. Golkov dropped his hand as I stepped back.

"Now that you know he's here, I realize keeping you from him is no longer a possibility. Maybe now we'll get some answers."

I cleared my throat. "Okay."

"Before I open that door, Alexandra, I just want to make sure this is really what you want."

"It is." I straightened my posture.

"He's not the man you met in St. Petersburg," Golkov said.

I flashed back to the first time we met when Elijah was just my chauffeur. Those kind eyes had just been a ploy—one I had easily fallen for. I wouldn't make that mistake again.

"I know what he is," I said.

Golkov nodded to the guards and they moved away from the door. As he pressed the numbers on the keypad, I thought I saw his worn fingers quiver for just a moment before the door beeped. He cracked it open and took a step forward.

"No." I put a hand on his arm. "Just me."

His pale lips closed in a thin line. I knew he wanted to protect me from Elijah, but I had to do this on my own.

Golkov stepped back and motioned for me to enter the room. I could tell from the look in his eyes that he wanted to trade places with me. But if Elijah would only talk to me, we both knew this was the only way. "We'll all be waiting right here," Golkov said loudly enough for anyone in the vicinity to hear.

Daly now stood beside Golkov. He didn't say anything, but I could feel his eyes on me as I pulled the door all the way open.

A burst of heat and the stench of sweat hit me as I crossed the threshold into the room. The door closed behind me. Everything looked just as it had during my interrogation with Daly—the metal chairs and table, the gray walls and concrete floor. It was all the same except for the man that sat at the table. I didn't want to look at him. But I had to.

I lifted my head and finally focused on Elijah's face. I drew in a sharp breath.

His bottom lip was split and swollen on one side. A dark shadow encircled one of his eyes, while the other had a deep gash running from his temple through his eyebrow. I would have barely recognized him if it wasn't for his shaven head and that piercing gaze. Even with one of his eyes partially swollen, their icy blue shade looked almost inhuman. I stared straight at him.

"Welcome, Dana, Ms. Stewart, Alexandra—what name are you going by these days?" His deep accent, not quite Russian but not anything I recognized, somehow made my name sound filthy. He raised his hands from his lap, and his cuffs clanged as he rested them in front of him on the table. "Oh, don't worry about these. They'll be off soon enough."

Elijah turned his hand in the cuff until the light caught on the silver ring on his finger. I touched a copy of the ring on my own finger and traced the face of The Company's emblem—the bittersweet nightshade—the flower, a symbol of truth. I clenched my jaw.

"Ah, yes. The ring. A nice touch, isn't it?" He stroked it with his thumb. "They tried to take it off, but apparently it was meant for my finger."

"You're a liar and fake. You don't deserve to have that ring on your hand." My voice cracked on the last word.

He moved his face from side to side, showing off his wounds. Do you think 'The Company' is all truth and goodness? Maybe you should ask that Mr. Daly of yours how his fist feels right now."

Daly did that? Normally I would have been horrified that he could hurt someone so badly, but this time I wasn't. All I wanted to do was pat Daly on the back for saving me the trouble.

"Come, take a seat," Elijah invited. "I'm so glad they finally sent for you. We have a lot to discuss."

I crossed my arms and remained standing. "They didn't send for me. I came on my own."

"Well—" he shrugged "—no matter. You're here now. So let's get down to business."

"I'm not saying anything else until you answer my questions," I growled.

He leaned back in his chair and dropped his hands into his lap. "Okay. I'll humor you. You can ask me any three questions and I'll answer them truthfully. If I answer them to your satisfaction, then I would like you to consider my proposition."

"Proposition?"

"Is that one of your questions? Three of them for one proposition. That is my offer."

"Fine." As long as I got some kind of answers from him, I didn't care what I had to listen to after that. It didn't mean I had to do something for him. "How long have you been a part of Red Eye?"

He laughed. "If you are referring to the Russian terrorist organization that is still stuck in the Cold War, my answer is never." Elijah winced and touched the side of his head with the back of one of his hands.

"But you were with them, in Moscow."

"You people here really have no idea what you're up against. I'm not your enemy."

"If you're not a part of Red Eye, who is?"

"Is that one of your questions?"

"No, I just . . . fine." There was a question I wanted answered more. "How did you know my mother?"

"Iolanta," he said her name with almost a kind of reverence.

"Working with her was like driving an M6, so smooth and effortless." He stared past me and smiled as much as he could with his swollen lip. The darkness that had shadowed his face seemed to disappear. "She was the first one I drove, you know. Had to be what, ten years ago?" I waited for him to continue. "She had this knack for finding things that were lost or stolen. She recovered that Rembrandt, you know. The one lost in the heist of 1990."

The Rembrandt painting jumped into my mind. Though I saw it hanging in the Rejnikof Museum of Art in Moscow over a month before, the movement of oil paint on the canvas was fresh to my mental eyes. In the duplicate of *The Storm on the Sea of Galilee* hanging in Golkov's university office, my mom had painted herself into the scene as a clue. The clue led me to confirm what Elijah had told me on that roof—that my mom had been a spy too, for the CIA and then The Company. At least Elijah hadn't lied about that.

"She probably found at least fifteen other missing pieces of art those nine years we worked together. It really is too bad about the accident. She had so much more potential." Elijah looked down at the ring on his finger, and if I hadn't known better I would have thought he almost looked sad.

I waited, hoping he would give me more—tell me something else about my mother that I didn't know, a piece of information that would somehow make me miss her less. When he didn't continue, I asked my last question, the one eating away at me more than the others.

"Why did you jump in the canal to save me? You could have just left me if you wanted me gone. Why did you save me then, but later . . ." I couldn't say the last part out loud because the memory of Elijah nearly killing me on the factory roof was still playing on a loop in my head.

His face softened and I saw a glimpse of the man I once knew. "I never meant to hurt you, Alexandra. There was so much at stake. I may not have been a part of Red Eye, but they had eyes and ears on me at all times. They may not know where I am right now, but they will find me." He rubbed at the side of his head, behind his ear. Something in his eyes changed and it was like he was fighting a battle within himself.

I pulled out the chair across from him and took a seat. The cold metal seeped through my running pants. "You didn't try to push me off the roof?" The hope in my voice betrayed my thoughts. *Elijah is not the man you thought he was. He hurt you. He'd do it again.*

His callous expression returned. "I believe I have answered your three questions and more. Now it is my turn."

"What is it you want?" I asked.

"I need your help." The way he said it, I wasn't sure if he was being sincere or mocking me. He used his thumb to roll The Company ring around his finger, taunting me. *Mocking, definitely mocking.* I started to stand.

"It's not really a question of whether or not you're going to help me."

"Then what is it?" I sat again. Elijah had a way of making me hear him out, even if deep down I didn't want to listen.

"It's a matter of what you're willing to do to get what you want most."

"What do you know about what I want?"

"All in due time, *opasno tsvetok.*"

Did he just call me a flower? A dangerous flower?

"But first, my proposal."

I leaned back in my chair and concentrated on the gaping cut above his eye. It probably needed stitches. I hoped he wouldn't get any.

"As I said before, your mother was a phenomenon in the art world. I believe some of that talent was passed on to her daughter." Elijah paused and studied my face. I knew what he saw—my mother and I could have been twins. Except for her darker shade of blond hair, our gray eyes, full lips, and high cheekbones were almost a perfect match.

"What does she have to do with anything?"

"Everything." He gave a twisted smile. "You see, I'm in the market for a rather rare painting. And you're going to get it for me."

4

FAITH

"Over my dead body," I said, and then wished I could take back the words. My mind flashed again to the roof and what could have happened. Something in Elijah's gaze changed, and I wondered if he was seeing what I saw in the movie playing in my mind.

"I don't want you dead, Alexandra. What I want is Van Gogh."

"Van Gogh?"

"Better yet, what I want is the painting *View of the Sea at Scheveningen* by Vincent Van Gogh." Elijah leaned forward in his chair. "It is a scene as viewed from the beach with a—"

"I know the painting." I saw it in my head, along with the description below it from an art book I'd leafed through nearly five years before. It depicted a scene from the beach resort where Van Gogh apparently painted it. The wind from the day not only influenced how the artist painted the blowing flag of the ship on the sea, but it also blew grains of sand into the thick, oil-based paint, leaving some permanently embedded in the layers. "He painted it outdoors, which was nearly unheard of at the time," I went on. "Most impressionists sketched on-site and painted at home to avoid . . ." I stopped myself from nearly reading all the words below the painting in my head.

Elijah cocked his head to one side. "I knew you were your mother's daughter. Art is in your blood."

Or in my mind. Elijah didn't know about my eidetic memory and how, at that moment, it was flashing to every book, article, or website I had ever seen on Van Gogh or his paintings.

"*Sea at Scheveningen* was stolen in 2002 and hasn't been recovered by any of the agencies searching for it," I said. "Why would you think it still exists?"

"I have my reasons."

"Even if it does exist and I actually wanted to help you, what makes you think I could find it?"

"You are forgetting how well I know The Company."

I cringed at his tone when he said "The Company." Plus, it was an insider's right to refer to the organization that way, and Elijah no longer had the right. In fact, it turned out he never had it to begin with.

"If you and that team of yours can stop a Russian terrorist organization from poisoning a water supply, you can find a minor painting.

"If it's so minor, why do you want it? It's not like you can hang it up in your jail cell."

A boisterous laugh rumbled from Elijah's chest. A silver filling in one of his back molars caught the light. "'There's no art, to find a mind's construction in the face.'" Then he winked. I knew what that quote meant, and it had nothing to do with art. Shakespeare was referring to the fact that you can't tell what a person is thinking by looking at his or her face.

My mind recalled the last time Elijah had quoted Shakespeare to me. It had been a clue to lead me to discover that Elijah was a double agent. If he really had something he wanted to tell me, he should just come straight out and say it. I'd had enough of his games.

"You can quote MacBeth all you want" —my voice began to rise— "but it's not going to convince me to do anything for you, let alone find a painting. You have no leverage here, Elijah. I can't believe I've listened to you for this long." I jumped up, nearly knocking over my chair, and headed for the door.

"You'll change your mind." Elijah sounded so sure of himself that my grip on the door handle tightened until I felt my blood pulsing against the metal. I took a deep breath to keep myself from losing it completely, then gave up. I no longer cared about the camera in the interrogation room. I marched back to the table and bent over it until my face was just a foot from Elijah's. The only way to keep the memories of him from haunting me was to prove to myself that I didn't need to be afraid of him.

"No, I won't." I glared at him.

He returned with an icy stare that didn't scare me this time. He leaned forward a few more inches and whispered in my ear. "Talk with your father first before you make a promise you can't keep. Ask him what really happened after the accident."

It took everything I had to not punch Elijah in the nose. He was just taunting me again, trying to rile me up so he could see me break. I wouldn't give him the pleasure. I pushed myself back from the table and left the room, slamming the door behind me.

Golkov and Daly stood against the wall in the hallway, sharing an electronic tablet. From their sympathetic expressions, it was clear they had been watching the conversation between Elijah and me on the other side of the door.

"What did he say to you at the end there?" Daly asked. "Audio didn't pick it up."

"Nothing. He was just trying to get a reaction out of me," I replied, not wanting the only family I had left involved in any of this. "I need some time to think."

Daly touched my arm. "Why don't you take a break?"

I looked between him and Golkov. I wanted to stay and figure out our next move. This was supposed to be my mission—to uncover everything about Red Eye and bring them down. But talking with Elijah had ripped away every ounce of energy in my body. "Do you guys mind if I just go home?"

"Yes, yes," Golkov answered. "There's no rush on any of this. We can pick this up on Monday and discuss our next action."

Daly started to say something, then stopped and nodded at me.

I walked back through The Company in a haze of irritation and confusion. Elijah wasn't a member of Red Eye. I don't know why I believed it, but I did. He also didn't want me dead, or at least he didn't right then. He wanted a painting. That was the strangest part about the whole conversation. Elijah, Van Gogh, and Macbeth. I shook my head. It was all too much for a Saturday morning.

I LEANED against the iron railing at Waterfront Park and watched the moonlight flit about the tiny ripples of the river. I loved how everything about the water reminded me of the Columbia River back in Washington. The calming sound of water soothed my emotions.

An older couple, bundled up in thick coats and stocking hats, walked hand in hand along the bridge on the other side of the water. Besides them, the park was empty, which made perfect sense on a freezing Sunday night. After a day and a half cooped up in my dorm since talking with Elijah, I needed fresh air, even if it meant braving the cold alone in the dark.

I buttoned the top button on my coat and let my mind wander through memories. Tanner and I had once borrowed inner tubes and glided down the Wenatchee River. Despite the sunburn on the top of my thighs that stung for days afterward, my brother and I had loved that trip. I promised myself I would go back there someday and ride the water, just for him. I smiled at the thought.

"It's not exactly the nicest night for a park-side stroll, but I can see the appeal," Daly said, coming up beside me. His presence didn't startle me as much as it should have. He looked out over the water. "You know, they light the water, or at least those braziers in the water, every summer."

"Really?"

He pointed to a metal bowl a few feet in diameter that rested on a pole rising about a foot above the river's surface. From where I stood I could count several dozen bowls. "It's amazing to see over a hundred braziers burning across the water, like the flames are floating."

"I'd love to see that."

"Yeah. I'm surprised that boyfriend of yours didn't bring you here before the season ended last fall. It's supposed to be pretty romantic." Daly elbowed me in the side.

"I guess I was a little too busy traversing the globe to Russia, finding out my mom was a spy, and saving your rear end."

He smiled. "I thought I saved you."

"Yeah, it's still debatable."

"So what are you doing out here all by yourself?" He leaned his side against the wrought-iron railing.

"Studying."

"Huh?" He looked at me questioningly. "Oh wait, yeah. I guess you could be doing that, couldn't you?"

"Not really. I'm done with school, at least for today." I rested my forearms on the railing and set my chin on top of them. Imagining the strategically placed braziers bursting into flame, I wished one would light right then, like a sign of hope.

"Listen, about Elijah . . ." Daly paused and I felt his gaze upon me. I looked up at him, at the moonlit shadows playing across the angles of his face. If he wasn't so annoying sometimes, I would have thought him good-looking. Okay, I did think he was handsome, but after that "loathsome" kiss, as he had called it, last November, we were more like brother and sister. We taunted and teased and fought, but we would always have each other's backs.

"Do you think he's right?" I broke in. "Does he have something on us? On me? Something worth finding that painting for?"

"I don't know." Daly leaned forward on the railing too, and now our elbows touched. I was glad he'd come. Somehow having him there helped me settle my thoughts. "What I do know is that he will only talk to you. No amount of convincing is going to get him to say anything more."

I pondered that. Why wouldn't Elijah talk to anyone else? He could have asked any operative to do his bidding, as long as he had something of value in return. I thought of what he had said about my father. I had tossed it aside, convinced it was a final ploy to get me to do what he wanted. Now, staring out at the calming ripples in the water, my mind focused on Elijah's words. *"It's a matter of what you're willing to do to get what you want most."* What did finding a painting have to do with my father or the accident?

"Daly?" I said.

"You can call me James, you know."

"I know. There's something . . ." I turned my head until my cheek rested on my forearms. My hair cascaded over the railing. Did I dare share what Elijah whispered to me? Did I really believe there was some foundation to his words? "I don't want to help Elijah in any way. I don't want to do his bidding, but what if I don't listen to him? What if it backfires?"

"You know why they say we don't negotiate with terrorists?"

I thought I knew, but I still asked, "Why?"

"Because if you give a mouse a cookie, he'll ask for a glass of milk."

I laughed and nudged his elbow with mine. "And then he'll want a straw and a napkin. Yeah, yeah. I know the story." Pages from the classic children's book turned in my head, the words and pictures a familiar rhythm in my brain. My mom had only read that story to me on a few occasions during my childhood, but my mind had played it many times since.

"So you get it then?" Daly watched my face, his expression a mixture of amusement and something else. Concern?

"What if he's not a terrorist? What if he's telling the truth? What if he *had* to do what he did?"

Suddenly, Daly straightened. "He tried to push you off a ten-story building, Alexandra. He can't explain his way out of that." Daly pulled me from the railing to face him. His large hand easily wrapped around my bicep, even with the bulk of my jacket. "Do you seriously believe him? You can't be considering doing what he says."

"I don't know what I believe anymore. I've got to go." I shook myself from Daly's grasp and started back to campus. After a few steps, I began to run. I don't know why I did it. My feet just started to move, almost at their own accord, and I raced down the sidewalk in my jeans and leather boots. I wasn't running from Daly—I was running from myself. Elijah's words turned over in my head. I didn't want to admit it to Daly or even myself.

I believed Elijah.

I knew it was irrational. He'd tried to kill me and was asking me to be a thief. I had no factual reason for trusting anything he said, but my gut told me there was more to all of this than anyone could see.

Knowing I believed Elijah sent me faster down the sidewalk, ignoring the hammering footsteps behind me. If what Elijah said was true, it meant my father might be hiding something from me.

Daly caught up just as I reached the steps of Wayland House. He grabbed my arm. "What are you doing?" He leaned over and placed his free hand on his knee, heaving a few breaths.

"There's something I have to do."

"Let me help. We're partners, you and me. We work together."

I squeezed his hand and lifted it from my arm. "Don't worry," I said, meeting his eyes. "I'm not going to go blow up a building."

"Then where are you going?"

"To see my father." I turned from Daly and hurried up to my dorm room to get my car keys.

"DAD?" I dropped my keys in the ceramic bowl on the entryway table, below a portrait of George Washington atop a stallion. When I didn't hear an answer, my pulse picked up. "Dad, where are you?"

"In my office," he finally yelled from the back of the apartment. I'd been there nearly every Sunday since coming to Brown University with him over four months before, but each time I came I noticed something new. Today it was a gold-framed copy of the Emancipation Proclamation hanging in the hallway. Without my mom tempering his passion for history, my father's obsession had exploded. I was just glad he had something to focus on now that I wasn't living at home.

I found him bent over his large desk with a magnifying glass in one hand. His blond hair was nearly as long as Golkov's, and Dad held it out of his eyes with his free hand. Since the accident, my mom wasn't there to trim his hair anymore. A pang of sadness pulled at me.

Organized stacks of papers barricaded one side of his desk, and a large map was spread on the remaining surface. He looked up briefly and grinned. His smile was just like Tanner's, warm and goofy at the same time. That and Dad's large brown eyes always made me feel relaxed, at home.

"Alexandra, what are you doing here tonight? I thought you had a big test in the morning." He returned to his map, running the magnifying glass from the top to the bottom. "Did you know that if you mark each successful Northern battle from the Civil War, the pattern creates the letter *E*?" He drew a line from one dot to another on his map. "Oh wait, no, that one ended in a stalemate." He turned his pencil over and erased vigorously. "It's more like an *F*."

"I didn't know that, Dad. Sounds like some kind of secret code our forefathers created to keep history professors from talking to their daughters on Sunday nights."

His eyes lit up. "Do you really think they left . . ." He trailed off. "You're joking, aren't you?" He gave me a wry grin.

I was joking, at least mostly. My dad's mind could interpret any number of historical facts, but social cues were often lost on him. He was like a living textbook—or, more accurately, a whole *stack* of textbooks. Wikipedia had nothing on him. My mom once said I inherited his mind, but I didn't believe it. Where my dad knew information and words, I saw pictures. Where my dad had columns of dates and historical facts, I had movies in my head. Conversations with him often led to something in the past. I couldn't forget anything from my past. We were an awkward pair.

My father set the magnifying glass on the desk and slid his pencil into the drawer. "Sorry, you said you had to study tonight. Or did I miss something?" He came around his desk and we walked out of his office together. His dress pants and shirt hung more loosely than I remembered. No more of Tanner's brownies or Mom's Sunday dinners to pad his waistline.

"Can I ask you something?" I sat on the worn loveseat, a remnant of our Washington home. It still smelled of pine and cinnamon.

"Sure." Dad crossed the living room from the kitchen with a bag crinkling in his hand. "Licorice?" He offered me the bag of his favorite candy, a mixture of red and black licorice. Most of the black pieces were gone—he never ate the red. He only bought the mix because red licorice was my favorite.

"Is everything okay with you?"

"What do you mean?" He chewed on a piece of licorice.

"I don't know. Just worried about you, I guess. We never really talk about . . . well, I just wanted to make sure you liked your new apartment and living here and all." I cringed at how easy it had become for me to lie to him.

"Honestly, I think I was always meant to live close to where it all began. There's so much history here on the East Coast. I can almost feel it in my bones." He held out his arms like he was waiting for more knowledge to sink into his very being. "What about for you, Alexandra? You're not having second thoughts about coming here, are you?"

"No, no. I like it here. It's just . . ." I couldn't figure out how to form the words into the question I wanted to ask.

Dad stopped chewing on his licorice and faced me. "Is there something you wanted to talk about?"

Yes. Everything, I thought. *The basement of Brown University is really an organization that solves puzzles and crimes, finds out truth, and stops terrorist organizations. There's a man named Elijah who once saved my life and then tried to take it away, but now wants me to find him a stolen painting or . . . or.* "I don't know." I grabbed another stick of red licorice and bit off a piece. "Do you ever just trust your gut and do something based on a feeling, without a lot of supporting facts?"

"Like having faith in something?" Dad sank into the fluffy couch cushions and propped up his feet on the coffee table.

"Yeah, I guess."

"History isn't all about facts, you know. Most of what we know about our past is evidence based, but the further back we go, there's some supposition. So, yes, I guess I trust some things I can't prove."

I pulled my knees up to my chest and rested my chin on them. "Dad, I know this is going to sound really weird, but is there something I don't know about . . . when, you know . . . the accident happened? Maybe something I should know?"

He started to cough and pound on his chest with one hand. "Sorry, licorice in the wrong pipe." He took a deep breath and pulled a loose string on one of the couch pillows.

"Dad, what is it?"

"I've never thought it was wrong to lie." He lifted his feet from the coffee table and placed them back on the area rug.

"What?"

"I've always believed if the truth could hurt worse than a lie, then lying was justified—that the lie was really a sign of love. Does that make sense?"

"Strangely, yes. I get it." I knew more than he realized about that sign of love. My mom had shown it, and now I was the one doing the same thing to many people in my life.

Dad took a deep breath. "Alexandra, do you remember the day of the accident?"

My head shot up and I stared at him.

He shook his head vigorously. "No, no, of course you remember it. I mean, you know how you were in the hospital for a few weeks?"

"Yes." Blue hospital gowns and the smell of hospital antiseptic came alive in my mind.

"When you were in the hospital recovering . . ." He paused and set the licorice bag on the scuffed surface of the coffee table and leaned his elbows on his knees. His eyes moved from the table to the wall across from us, where a single picture hung on the wall. This was the only frame in the house that didn't hold something from before the twentieth century. The family photo, taken only weeks before the crash, was one of my favorites.

I didn't have to stand to clearly envision the faces in the picture. The scene opened up and a wave of gratefulness rushed over me. I often used my eidetic memory to recall information or help me with school and, most recently, missions. Only rarely did I replay a scene just for the fun of it—just to enjoy the moment and feel the emotions again. I sat back on the couch and let the scene play in my mind.

"I NEARLY HAD YOU," Tanner stuffed a stack of chips into his mouth and crunched them loudly. We still wore our running shorts and T-shirts from the 5K race that morning. Large oak trees dominated the park, the green leaves shading us as we ate a picnic lunch of sandwiches and chips.

"You'd think someone with such long legs could run faster," I teased.

"You'd think someone with such a small body wouldn't have such a big ego."

"Me? Big ego? Who's the one wearing a T-shirt that says 'Awesomeness isn't a crime'?" I pulled on his sleeve.

"Okay, you two," Mom broke in. She and Dad sat next to us eating their sandwiches. "How about we just call it a tie and you save your energy for the carnival tonight." Her face lit up with a smile. The Apple Blossom Festival was her favorite time of year, and we had an event every day for over a week to prove it. That morning's race and parade were only the start of this last day, which would end with the family tradition of eating Dad's homemade ice cream.

"If your mom had run, she could have beaten both of you." Dad put his arm around her shoulder and squeezed. His forgotten sandwich flipped off the paper plate on his lap, sending lettuce, tomato, and bacon onto the blanket. A mayonnaise-drenched tomato landed on my bare leg.

"Hey!" I said.

"Here, let me help you with that." Tanner tossed a handful of chips at my head.

"Oh no, you don't." I grabbed the uneaten crust of my sandwich and threw it at his face.

"You asked for it."

"Alex and Tanner, stop it," Mom said in a serious voice. We both glanced at her and then at Dad. They both looked guilty. I didn't notice their hands

behind their backs until it was too late. A spray of liquid rained over us. Mom had a can of pop in her hand. Dad jumped up and pulled slightly on his tab. More liquid flew through the air onto Tanner and me. I wiped some of the sticky pop from my face and armed myself with baby carrots before hiding behind a tree. We spent the next few minutes in an all-out food fight until all our ammunition littered the grass around us. We made our way back to the picnic blanket, laughing at the mess.

"I've got to get a photo of this." Mom reached for her camera and asked a passerby to take a picture. I looked around our ragged group. The front of Tanner's hair stuck to his forehead in a wet clump, mayonnaise dripped from the collar of Dad's shirt, and Mom had a chip in her hair. We all smiled at the camera. Just before the photographer snapped the shot, Tanner burped loudly. We burst out laughing as the camera clicked.

I LOOKED OVER AT DAD. His eyes were red and watery. I wished he could have viewed what I'd just seen in my mind. Maybe, in his own way, he did.

A tear slipped down his cheek. Sometimes I forgot I wasn't the only person who had lost someone.

"Dad." I reached for his arm. He pulled away. "Dad?"

"I can't do this anymore." He heaved himself from the couch and ran his fingers through his light blond hair, one feature we shared.

"What is it? What can't you do?" I asked. *Does he know about Mom's work for The Company?* It relieved me to think that was what was bothering him so much. *That has to be it.*

"I can't lie to you anymore, Alexandra. You deserve to know the truth." He paced in front of the coffee table a few times before he stopped and met my eyes. Something in his gaze caused me to hold my breath. "The accident. I didn't tell you all that happened after." Dad took a deep breath. "Tanner didn't die on impact. He was taken to the hospital just as you were."

My throat felt dry. My dad had never talked about the day of the accident or the weeks that followed. I only knew that my mom and

Tanner had been killed instantly, and that paramedics had rushed me to the hospital in an ambulance. After that, I'd been in and out of consciousness, so the days were a blur until the morning of the funeral a few weeks later when I was released from the hospital. The smell of fresh-cut flowers and sounds of organ music pressed to the front of my mind. The image of closed caskets containing the remains of two of the people I loved the most would always put an ache into my heart.

Dad sat on the coffee table in front of me and took my hands, his expression serious. I looked away.

"That whole first day at the hospital was . . ." He shook his head. "They had moved you to surgery so they could set your shoulder. Tanner was still in the ICU in bad shape. I wanted to be there, but they wouldn't let me. They made me sit in the waiting room."

"Dad, I'm so . . . I didn't know . . ."

He shook his head. "Just let me get this out, please." He took a deep breath. "While I was in the waiting room, a man walked in. He said he knew your mother, and he gave his condolences. I was so messed up from losing your mom that I couldn't think straight. I just thanked him and waited for him to leave. Instead, he sat down next to me. I kept staring at his silver cufflinks, hoping he would leave me alone. Tanner" —Dad's voice cracked— "Tanner was in a coma, and the doctors were saying all these things about brain activity and life support. I was falling apart. I'd just lost my wife, and that man . . . he just sat there."

I squeezed Dad's hands. We'd had so many conversations in the last eight months, but we'd avoided the one thing we needed to talk about—losing Mom and Tanner.

"At first, I wanted to be mad at the man. I wanted to yell at him, but there was something calming in having him there. Eventually he told me that he understood what I was going through, that he had someone he couldn't be with either. Right before he left, he said something I'll never forget. He said that no matter how hard it got, I should continue to hope, because no matter how dark the night became, how bleak the blackness that fell, the dawn would come. Sometimes early, sometimes late, but it would always come."

I'd never heard my father talk like this or quote anything that wasn't in a book. I reached over to squeeze his knee. Instead of pulling away, he put a hand on mine. "Two hours later a doctor came in and told me Tanner was gone, that his heart had stopped and they'd done everything possible to bring him back, but it wasn't enough."

"Dad, I'm so sorry. I didn't know you had to go through that too." The ache moved from my heart to my throat, making my eyes burn. "I'm so sorry I couldn't stop it—that I couldn't save them."

"Alexandra, no. This wasn't your fault." My dad slid from the coffee table to the spot right next to me on the couch. "No one could have stopped this. It was an accident."

Now the tears fell freely down my face. "I just wish . . . You and Mom always talked about my memory being special, that I could use it to do something extraordinary. I can see everything in the past with perfect detail. Why couldn't I see the future? Why couldn't I see that car? Why couldn't I save them?" My body began to shake and the sobs overtook me. My father wrapped his arm around my shoulders and pulled me into him until my head rested on his chest. He held me close like he had done so many times when I was a child.

After some time, I lifted my head and sat up. Dad held my hand for a second and squeezed it tight before letting go.

Suddenly he tensed. "How long have you had that?"

"What?" I asked.

"That ring."

I put my fingers around The Company ring I wore. "A few months. Why?"

"I just . . . I swear I've seen it before."

I waited for him to tell me he had seen the one my mom had worn on the chain around her neck.

"Yes. It was that man. I think he must have had the same brand or something."

"What man?" My back stiffened.

"The man from the hospital waiting room, with the cuff links and shaved head. He had a ring just like yours."

My head felt light and my extremities began to tingle. I leaned forward on the couch to calm my breathing. There was only one man I knew that had a shaved head and wore silver cufflinks and The Company ring.

Elijah.

5

ALIVE

I made it to the interrogation room in record time. The guards stepped aside while I input the code and let myself in.

Elijah lifted his head from the table when I walked through the door. "I knew you'd be back, though I thought it would be sooner."

"Why did you visit my dad after the crash?"

"I knew you couldn't resist asking him."

My insides churned, yet I couldn't rely on my feelings. My mind kept flashing between Elijah's once-kind smile and the dark, sinister grin that haunted my flashbacks. Golkov and Daly were right. I couldn't trust this guy.

"What right did you have being there when he was at his worst? Do you even have an ounce of sympathy in you?"

"Of course." Elijah frowned. "I cared about your mother, too."

"No." I rushed to the table. "You don't get to talk about her." I slammed my fist against the tabletop, and my mind flashed to the scene on the roof. "You wanted her to join you on some sick crusade before she died, and now you think you can talk about her like you were family? She was my mother, and Tanner was my brother. They were my family, not yours."

"I know."

"My dad had just lost my mom." I was yelling now. "Then you give him some stupid advice about hope. There was no hope." The ache in my throat returned. "He was my brother." The words came out so low and hoarse I hardly recognized my own voice. I slumped into the chair across the table from Elijah.

A flicker of compassion passed over his face. "And I may be the only one that can save him." Elijah reached his cuffed hands across the table and latched onto mine. I immediately pulled away and he dropped his hands back into his lap.

"It's too late." I dropped my head. All the raw emotions rushed to the surface. I couldn't even muster the strength to push myself away from the table.

"Your mother may be gone, but your brother isn't," Elijah said.

I raised my tear-stained face. "What kind of sick joke is this?" I said through clenched teeth.

"Tanner is alive," he said.

"Why would you say that? You're a liar!" I stood.

"He didn't die that day. I was there in the hospital room."

My heart began to hammer so rapidly I felt the pounding pressure in my ears. I hated myself for even considering what Elijah was saying, yet the serious look in his fierce blue eyes tore through my disbelief. "My dad said there was no brain activity."

"The doctors were wrong." A shadow passed over Elijah's eyes. "Medicine has never been an exact science."

"But my dad said Tanner's heart stopped."

"They revived him."

"If that is true, where is he? Is he okay?" I couldn't hide the pleading in my voice. Just the tiny glimmer of possibility had my pulse racing faster and faster.

Wait, no, this has to be a trick—some sick game to get the best of me. I sat up straight and wiped my face with my jacket sleeve. "I don't believe you."

Hurt flashed over Elijah's face before he jutted out his chin. "I was there."

"The doctors told my father that Tanner was dead. Why would they say that if it wasn't true?"

"Some things even I don't understand."

"You've been lying to The Company and to me since the moment we met. Why should I believe you now?"

Matching his stoic composure with his voice, Elijah said, "I can prove it to you."

"The only proof I'd ever accept is seeing him in person." I couldn't believe I was even considering what this guy was saying. My brother was gone. I'd gone to the funeral where his casket sat next to my mom's. I'd stood right in front of his closed casket and cried and ached over losing the only person who ever understood and accepted everything about me.

But what if it was true? If there was even a remote chance my brother was alive, I would take it. "Where's Tanner?"

The darkness returned to Elijah's face. "I want your word first."

"What word?"

"Your promise to do what I asked." He pushed himself back from the table. The cuffs at his hands and his feet clanged loudly. "That you'll recover the Van Gogh."

I couldn't believe he would want a useless painting worth only a small fraction of the Rembrandt my mom had discovered. Then again, neither painting was worth a life.

I let out a breath, stood up, and pushed in my chair. "I'll do it. I'll get your stupid painting. Now tell me where Tanner is."

A cruel smile crept from Elijah's lips to his eyes. "I knew you'd come to your senses."

THE TINY PIECE of paper crinkled in my fist. I didn't need to see the address I'd written down, but I held onto it just the same.

It only took fifteen minutes to drive from campus to downtown Providence, yet it felt like an eternity. I parked my Miata along a street lined with tall, narrow apartment buildings. Light from a few vintage-style street lamps cast shadows along the deserted sidewalk.

I looked down at the ring on my finger. *Solanum dulcamara,* the bittersweet nightshade, a symbol of truth. The five-petaled star-shaped flower etched into the face of the ring stared back at me hauntingly. It might have been a symbol for truth, but I wondered if Golkov had understood another side to the flower—the dangerous one. Though the bittersweet nightshade was a beautiful flower, ingesting it was often lethal. Could truth be a poison as well?

The sound of a slamming door echoed down the street. I didn't see anyone, but just in case, I held my keys with one of them jutting out between two of my fingers to use as a self-defense weapon, a move Tanner had taught me before . . .

I stopped in front of the address—455 Hattery Road. A yellow light glowed through one of the windows. I came up the concrete stairs, my stomach lurching like it did on a plane takeoff. Sweat prickled under my arms. Was Elijah telling the truth?

I knocked on the paint-chipped door and waited. No answer. I knocked harder this time. After a few seconds, the door cracked open. A woman in a pale blue turtleneck and navy slacks answered the door. She tossed her bobbed hair back. She couldn't have been older than thirty.

"Yes?"

"Elijah sent me," I said simply.

The woman's hazel eyes went wide and she scrambled to hold her composure as she opened the door wider. "Yes, of course. Sorry. I just wasn't expecting . . ." She led me down a hall lit only by a lamp on the side table. "He told me someone would come. It's just been so long." She looked over her shoulder at me. "I didn't expect such a young person."

She stopped at a door and opened it partway. "There's an armchair by the bed that can lean back if you are going to stay a while. Coma patients may not be responsive, but I believe they know we are there."

Coma?

"Are you going to stay long?" she asked.

"I . . . I'm not sure. I'll let you know."

She gave me a stiff smile and stepped around me. My feet wouldn't move. I'd spent so much time in the last eight months accepting that Tanner was gone and that I could survive without him. Now it might all be different.

"It's okay," the woman said. "You can go in."

I gazed back at her, still unsure.

"Believe me, there's nothing . . ." She looked at me more closely and stepped back. She gasped and brought her hand to her mouth. "You . . . you look so much like him. It's like you could be siblings."

My heart nearly exploded in my chest, I burst through the doorway, rushed to the twin-size bed, and collapsed to my knees beside it.

Tanner's face was just as I remembered—angular jawline, high cheekbones, same wide nose as mine. I reached out and touched his cheek. It was real. *He* was real. Tanner was there in front of me, and all I could do was sob uncontrollably.

His blond hair, though cut shorter than the pictures in my head, was combed back from his face with a side part he never would have worn. A blue-and-green-plaid comforter covered most of his body. The gray T-shirt was something he might have worn with a pair of jeans. His once-muscular arms were thin and rested on either side of his body. A blood-pressure cuff encircled one of his upper arms. A large rectangular machine beeped slowly next to him. His heartbeat. Tanner had a heartbeat. I buried my face next to his shoulder and cried.

My brother was alive.

6

———

HOPE

I shut the door to Tanner's room quietly behind me, even though I assumed he couldn't hear anything.

The woman—the nurse, I now realized—met me in the foyer.

"Will he wake up?" I'm not sure why I asked. I knew enough from all my studies of medical journals from the mission last semester. Still, I braced myself for the answer.

"All I know is that the swelling is gone," she said. "His brain activity is normal. His lungs are good, too."

A breath of relief escaped me.

"As for waking up." She shrugged her shoulders. "I'm not a doctor. Maybe someday. Right now I just make sure he is nourished and moved every day. I wish I could give you more information."

"I understand." Tanner was alive, but he might never wake up. The thought that I might have to lose him all over again pressed hard on my throat.

The drive back to Brown passed with a blur of memories. Flashes of moments with Tanner before the accident overtook my thoughts. By the time I reached campus, the emotional exhaustion of the weekend had taken its toll on my body. I staggered to the front of

Wayland House and sat on the cold, concrete steps. I was tired and numb.

"Nice evening for a stroll, wouldn't you say?" Daly said, coming down the sidewalk.

"Not really." I searched the dark sky and felt the frost on my face. "What are you doing out here, and so late?" If I hadn't known better, I would've sworn he had followed me.

"Do you really believe your handler wouldn't have a handle on what is going on in your life? It's my job to keep track of you, you know." Daly made his way to the stairs and took a seat. "Golkov put me in charge of Elijah. Didn't you think it was strange that you could just walk into the interrogation room? I told the guards to let you in if you came back and to let me know when you did."

I couldn't believe it hadn't even occurred to me how easy it had been to just walk in and speak with Elijah. Everything my father had told me about the accident was messing with my head.

"As soon as I saw the video from the interrogation room, I had to find you. Why didn't you come to me? I should've been with you."

"He's alive, James, really alive! I saw him . . . I touched him!"

"I know." Daly scooted closer to me.

"He's been in Providence all this time and I had no idea. How did he get here?" I folded my arms to cover my freezing hands.

"All I know is what I heard Elijah say to you." Daly pulled off his leather gloves and gave them to me. I put them on and in seconds the warmth from his hands defrosted the chill in my fingers.

"He's been in a coma for nearly eight months, James. What if he never wakes up?"

"He might not."

I wanted to hit Daly for saying that, except I knew it was the truth. That was one thing I could always expect from him.

"I confronted Elijah, you know," he said. "I really let him have it. I know they say you shouldn't let your emotions get in the way of a mission. I didn't care. What he did to you . . . what could have happened . . . he deserved everything I gave him."

"Yeah, I saw his injuries. I know I shouldn't be happy about someone else's pain, but I was."

"I deleted the video surveillance. Well, actually Millard did it."

"What?" I looked at Daly's tired face.

"The last time you were there. I had Millard replace the feed that showed you visiting him. Somehow he was able to extend or loop my own visit with Elijah. The guards saw you, but I doubt they will say anything. Even if they did, there is no footage to back them up."

"Why would you do that?" I asked.

"Golkov isn't going to go for it. Don't get me wrong, Alexandra. I think he would do almost anything to make you happy, but there's no way he will let you help Elijah. Besides Millard and me, no one but you and Elijah has a clue what was said in that room. No one knows about your brother."

"Would it matter if they did? He's in a coma. The chances of him waking up are miniscule." I shook my head. "It doesn't matter."

"Actually it does." Daly paused. "When I said I replaced your video with one of my visits with Elijah, it wasn't an old video. I went to see him again." Daly ran his hands up and down against his thighs to warm them. "I think your suspicions are correct. I think Elijah is telling the truth. I believe he can help Tanner."

"What does he know that doctors don't?"

"Well, that's the thing. He used to be a doctor. Before he joined The Company, he worked for a prestigious Russian Hospital near the Kremlin, known for treating political leaders, business moguls, and the culturally elite."

"Elijah was a doctor?"

"Apparently one of the best. They don't let just any doctor treat the Russian prime minister. I tried to find out more about Elijah's work there, but all I came up with was that he did side work for The Company for several years and continued to do so when he worked at the hospital. I'm not sure when he started working for Red Eye."

Letting that information sink in, I watched Daly's breath and mine crystallize in the air in front of us. Elijah claimed he wasn't a double agent—that he wasn't part of Red Eye. I flashed to the roof scene again. He had told me he wanted my mother to join him. Had he asked her to do the same thing he was asking me to do now? Either way, she had told him no.

"How can he help Tanner? From what I've read about comas, it doesn't seem like much can be done, without traumatizing his brain all over again."

"Alexandra, I don't know." Daly touched my knee. "But I'm willing to take the risk if you are."

I grabbed Daly's hand and held onto it tightly. "I am."

"Then let's get started." He jumped up, pulling me along with him. I wavered on the step before he caught me under the arms. "But I don't think either of us are any good tonight."

"You're right." I couldn't believe I was agreeing with him and that we hadn't gotten on each other's nerves for nearly two conversations. Maybe there was some hope after all.

7

FIRST DATE

I stared at the B on the computer screen. There had to be some mistake. I had never received anything less than an A in any class in my entire life. The best part about having an eidetic memory was the ability to retain information. My head was a library of countless facts, including everything there was to know about the Russian language. Except, there it was, the second letter in the alphabet glaring at me in disgust. I pressed "print" on the screen and waited for Casey's new printer to spit out my sub-par progress report. I'd always liked school. Now I was beginning to see why not everyone enjoyed being there.

"What's that?" Casey grabbed the paper.

I ripped it from her hand. "Nothing."

"Alexandra! Did you get a B on your Russian test? With all that time you spend working for your professor, I thought he'd give you an A on everything as payment." Casey lay down on our shaggy rug and stretched a leg in the air in some yoga pose.

"Yeah, you'd think so." I folded the paper and stuffed it into my bag. The words were already ingrained in my mind, but I wanted something to show Golkov when I talked to him later. "I guess he gives grades based on merit. Imagine that."

"You mean you actually deserve the grade?" Casey rolled over and put her other leg in the air.

"Well, I thought I pulled off something better, but I probably need to get back to the basics. Maybe it was my verbs-of-motion conjugations."

"Or maybe you had your head on more important things. Like baby-blue eyes and adorably cute curls."

"Seriously, Case, there's more to life than guys. Unlike you, I've got more on my mind besides handsome smiles and warm lips and . . ." I sighed.

"See. I told you."

"Speaking of William"—I laid on my side on the floor by Casey and began to stretch with her— "He wants to go on some fancy date."

"It's about time." She dropped her leg and sat up. "Where is he taking you? Do we need to go shopping? What about that blue dress with the lacy sleeves?"

"What is the big deal? It's not like we don't spend time together. I see William more than I see you."

"Oh, come on, let a guy be chivalrous. Sometimes you're too independent for your own good." Casey started to braid the front of her hair while sitting cross-legged beside me. "Maybe you wouldn't be so independent if your brother was still around to keep you . . ."

I stopped stretching and turned away. I stared up at the photos of my family taped to my wall. I'd only recently told my roommate about the accident after nightmare memories woke me in the middle of the night for the zillionth time and she wondered what was going on. I certainly couldn't explain why I'd really gone to Russia. Casey didn't know about The Company or what I really did for Golkov.

"Oh, Alex, I didn't mean it like that. I'm sorry." She reached around my neck and squeezed me in a hug.

"I know. It's okay." I couldn't just blurt out that my brother was still alive. I couldn't even muster the courage to share the news with my own father. He deserved to know, but it would only cause him pain, since Tanner would probably never wake up. If I could save my father from that agony, I would.

"So where are you going with William?" Casey asked.

"I don't know." I glanced at the alarm clock on the desk. "But I don't have to wait much longer. He should be here in about twenty minutes." I hopped up and tried to brush my tangled mess of hair out of my face.

"And you're wearing that?" She looked disapprovingly at my jeans and sweater.

"What?" At least the jeans were fitted.

"Have I taught you nothing?" She crawled to the closet and tossed me a pair of high heels. "Let's find something to go with those."

WILLIAM PULLED on the sleeve of his tweed overcoat as we waited to be seated. "You look great," he said.

"Thanks." Casey had convinced me to wear a royal-blue dress that flowed to just above my knees. I hadn't removed the formal coat I wore on top.

"So, have you been here before?" William asked.

"Nope. This place is really nice." White table clothes covered small round tables scattered throughout the restaurant. A tiny pendant light hung above each table from the low ceiling, sending a shimmery glow over each single-rose centerpiece.

Wearing a white suit jacket, the maître d' glided over to us. "May I take your coat, mademoiselle?" He extended a hand.

"Yes." I started to shrug out of my coat. William rushed behind me and lifted it from my shoulders. His thumb brushed the skin at my neck, making my insides tremble.

"I take that back," he whispered to me as he handed my coat to the maître d', who scurried away with it.

"Hmm?" I said.

"You look . . . wow."

Heat rushed to my cheeks. I looked down at my four-inch stilettos, wondering why I was self-conscious and nervous. William and I had jogged together many times and had eaten lunch at the Ratty on multiple occasions. We'd taken walks on campus and hung out at his house. He was right, though—we'd never been on a real, romantic date, just the two of us. Maybe that was what had my stomach in knots—I had no idea what to expect.

The maître d' led us to our table, where William pulled out my chair for me. Once we had sat down and ordered drinks, I stared at him over the top of my menu. He was biting down on his lip in intense concentration. After about thirty seconds, I started to laugh. He looked at me with a question in his eyes.

"You didn't know the menu would be in French, did you?"

"No." A guilty smile crossed his face.

"The restaurant is called La Petite."

"I know." He put down the menu and placed his hands on top. "Maybe we should just ask for the special or something."

"What are you in the mood for?" I scanned the menu. I'd never taken a French class, but my brother had studied the language in high school and I'd quizzed him a few times before a test. In my mind, I opened his book and looked up the words I didn't know.

"I'm craving something with chicken. Maybe some mashed potatoes too. Why?"

"Don't worry. I can order for us." I found a dish on the menu with chicken, along with a pasta dish that looked good. I set the menu down.

A crease formed between William's eyebrows. "I thought you had only taken Russian, Spanish, and Chinese. Don't tell me you added another class to your schedule."

"No, no. I think my load is full enough as it is."

"Then how did you . . ." His face relaxed and he shook his head at me. "You've read a French dictionary, haven't you?"

I shrugged my shoulders. "Not exactly a dictionary. It was a textbook. But the words I needed were all there."

"Yeah, I don't think I am ever going to get used to that. Where do you put all the information?"

"Sometimes I wonder that myself."

The waiter brought our drinks. I ordered our entrées, trying to re-create the words I'd heard before and not butcher the rest of the beautiful language.

After the waiter left, William reached across the table and clasped my hands. "I'm glad we're doing this."

All my nerves melted away. "Me too." I rubbed the top of his fingers with my thumbs.

"So how are things going with Professor Golkov? He sending you off on any secret missions in the near future?"

My fingers froze, along with the rest of my body. *How does William know?* "What?"

William shrugged his shoulders. "You never really talk about what you do for him. For all I know, he could be sending you off as a trapeze artist for the Russian circus or something. Which might explain why you always have bruises."

My body relaxed and I laughed, probably a little too loudly. "No circus for me."

"Really, what do you do?" William brushed a thumb over mine.

I bit the side of my lip. "Well, I sometimes help him correct papers and get organized." That much was true.

"What about when you travel for him?"

I tried to keep my breathing even. "Research, meeting with colleagues, bringing him back information." *Scaling warehouses, causing explosions, rescuing agents, exposing terrorists . . .*

"Kind of sounds boring."

"You have no idea."

"So have you thought about this summer? Do you think you want to do the study abroad in Mexico?"

I had thought about it and even brought it up to Golkov. The problem was, I'd just gotten back into the swing of things at The Company. Being in Mexico from June to August would be an amazing opportunity, and Golkov would definitely let me go. I just wasn't sure if it was the course I wanted to take in my life. There was so much I wanted to do at Brown, and being an agent was part of who I was now. I wasn't ready to give that up, even for a few months. The other cause for my hesitation was Tanner. I couldn't imagine leaving him, even though there was very little chance he would ever wake up. But I couldn't share either of these concerns with William.

The hardest part was that I didn't want him to leave. In the last month, we'd spent so much time together that I wasn't sure I could survive three months without him. "It sounds like a great experience," I said finally, looking down at my hands in his. The light above us reflected on the surface of my thick ring.

"But?"

"I really want to spend the summer with you, William. I do. I just . . . I just feel like I need to stay here."

"Oh."

The waiter came to the table with two steaming plates in his hands. William and I let go of each other, and our entrées were placed in front of us.

"Bon appétit," the waiter said before leaving our table.

William and I ate in silence for a few minutes. The food, though exquisite in every way, didn't have the appeal it should have had.

"Are you set on going?" I had to ask.

William put his fork down and concentrated on my face. "I've already made the commitment, Alex. I applied for this special program over a year ago, and if everything works out, then . . . well, then the students in my 301 class are counting on me. I can't disappoint them."

"I love that you're committed to your students."

"I'm committed to you too." His foot tapped mine under the table. I scooted mine forward until our ankles touched. "That's why I wanted you to come with me," he said.

"I know." I focused on the hem of my white napkin, unable to look at him. I didn't want this choice to come between us. Maybe there was a way I could work it out. "I need to think about it more, maybe talk with Golkov and my academic advisors and see what the possibilities are."

"Okay." William sounded relieved. "How's your dinner?"

I looked down and realized I'd only taken a few bites. I sliced off a piece of *foie gras*, put it in my mouth, and chewed. "It's really good, but not quite as yummy as your empanadas."

He dabbed his lopsided grin with a napkin. "You're just saying that because you want me to cook dinner for you again."

"Maybe I do." I smiled. "Or maybe I just want to eat with Dr. Red again. His Schwarzenegger impression was epic."

"Okay, now I know you're lying." William tossed a crouton onto my plate.

"Hey!" I peered around at the other tables. An older woman looked at us disapprovingly. "You're supposed to eat your food, not throw it," I told William quietly. I flicked a piece of my bread off my plate. My aim was off and it landed right on his head. I covered my mouth with my hand and tried desperately not to laugh.

My mind flashed to Tanner throwing chips into my hair at the park. Thinking of him brought the image of him lying unconscious in a bed in that apartment.

"Alex?" William's voice echoed on the edge of the memory.

I blinked my eyes and focused on his face. "Wait, what?"

"Were you watching a rerun in your head? Let me guess . . ."

A movement behind him caught my eye. I dropped my fork. "Daly?"

"No," William said. "Not *The Daily Show*. I was thinking more like *Grey's Anatomy* or *Law & Order* or something."

It took me a few seconds to confirm that Daly was in the restaurant—and heading toward our table. *What is he doing here? Breathe.*

"We need to talk, Alex," he said, not even looking at William.

Since when does he call me Alex? "Right now?" I peeked at William, who placed his napkin on the table beside his plate.

Daly nodded his head. "Yes."

William lowered an eyebrow and looked Daly up and down. Then Daly did the same thing to him.

"How do you guys know each other?" William asked me.

"Sorry, William, this is Dal . . . I mean this is James. He works for Golkov too."

"Wow, is Golkov some kind of celebrity I don't know about?" He eyed Daly's black suit and white shirt. He did kind of look like a Secret Service agent.

Daly ignored him. "Alex?" He pointed to a private corner of the restaurant.

"I'll be right back, William." I put my napkin next to my plate and gave him a weak smile.

Daly placed his hand on my back and ushered me away. I glanced over my shoulder at William. He sat with his arms crossed in front of him, his lips in a tight line.

"Do we have to do this now?" I whisper-yelled at Daly.

He grabbed my arms and guided me behind a column, almost blocking my view of William. I wriggled out of Daly's grasp. "What is wrong with you?"

"Do you want to give your brother a chance?"

I glared at him. "Of course I do. But did you have to interrupt my first real date with William?" I glanced over at William, who still peered in our direction.

"You've never been on a date together?" Daly's brown eyes lit up and a smug smile softened the edges of his chiseled jaw.

"Never mind." I shook my head. "What do you mean about giving Tanner a chance?"

"Elijah still won't say more, but I did some investigating. Well, actually Millard did some hacking. You know how I said Elijah was a doctor at the hospital near the Kremlin?"

"Yes."

"Well, that part was true. And after that, but before he started working at The Company, he worked at a hospital in Omsk. A very secretive hospital."

"Wait, Golkov said Elijah worked for the CIA, like Golkov did when he was younger. How could Elijah receive a medical degree and work in all these hospitals and still be a part of the CIA? It doesn't make any sense."

"We can't know for sure, but it looks like the CIA originally had him undercover. He used a different name then, but Millard found a picture." Daly pulled a phone from his suit jacket and pressed a few buttons, then held the screen up for me to see. The man in the photo, with a full head of blond hair, was probably thirty years old. Had it not been for his piercing blue eyes, I might have missed the resemblance. It was Elijah.

"How do you know what he was doing in Omsk if it was so secretive?"

"I'm good at what I do." Daly peered over his shoulder at William, who still watched us. I could only imagine the thoughts going through his head.

"Okay, I get it. So what did you learn?"

"That's where things get a little tricky. We can't find anything on the projects Elijah was involved in or what he actually did for the CIA or the hospital. We just located this photo from his hospital ID, along with several others putting him in Omsk over a period of fourteen months."

"So he worked at a secret hospital near the Kremlin, and then he was in Omsk at some underground hospital." I paused for a few seconds, attempting to curb my impatience. "What does that have to do with Tanner?"

Daly's shoulders relaxed and his expression became serious. "Because it wasn't just any hospital. It was a research hospital."

"Okay. A lot of hospitals do research."

"They were doing a study that lasted a little over a year. Millard and I couldn't dig up a description of exactly what they did, or any of the study materials, which kind of makes sense if a CIA operative was sent there. But we did locate the title of one of the studies when Millard hacked into old hospital emails." Daly took a step closer to me and placed his hand on my forearm. "'Brain Stimulation of Amnesiac and Comatose Patients.'"

I inhaled sharply. Daly tightened his grip on my arm.

"There's more, Alex."

"What?"

"The name of the hospital was Poslednyaya Nadezhda."

I leaned on the column behind me. "Last," I whispered, "Last Hope."

8

UNSANCTIONED

Daly escorted me to the table with his hand on the small of my back. William rose when we got there

"I'm sorry, William, but I have to go." I stepped away from Daly and next to him.

"Now?" He glared at Daly. "What in the Russian Department could possibly be so pressing that it can't wait until morning?" His narrowed eyes and flushed face told me that if we weren't in a fancy restaurant, he would be using stronger words or maybe even his fist to convey his feelings.

"It can't wait. I'm really so sorry." I reached for William's hand. He took it and pulled me close enough to whisper in my ear, "You owe me." Then he kissed me on the lips with a little more intensity than usual. Right in front of Daly.

"I'll call you," I said in a daze.

"Okay." William turned to Daly and gave a steely nod. Daly glowered at him but returned the nod.

Daly retrieved my coat and started to help me put it on. I pulled it away from him and put it on myself before we headed out front. A valet popped out of the front of a black BMW with chrome wheels and handed the keys to Daly. *Figures. With his flashy smile and plat-*

inum cufflinks, of course he owns an ostentatious car. I wondered how he could afford it.

I stepped in front of Daly and let myself in the passenger door before he could reach the handle. "Where are we headed?" I asked.

He got in the driver's side and revved the engine several times. I followed his gaze to where William stood on the sidewalk. A cloud of frosty air traveled from his nostrils down over his pursed lips. He stuffed his hands deep into his coat pockets. I brought my hand up to wave, but Daly released the brake and I flew back in my seat.

"Hey!"

"Sorry," he said. "We've got to get to headquarters."

"Why can't we wait until morning? Maybe Golkov or someone else at The Company can help us. With his CIA connections, he can probably find out more about the research hospital and what Elijah did there."

Daly coughed a few times and turned south on Washington Street.

"Wait, why aren't we headed to campus?" I asked. He increased the car's speed in the opposite direction from Brown. "I thought you said we were going to headquarters."

"We are." He loosened the tie at his neck. "My apartment will be our center of operations for the next week while we prepare for the mission."

"Your apartment? Wouldn't Golkov prefer us closer to him?"

Daly focused on the road ahead and tapped at the steering wheel with his fingers. "Not exactly."

"What's that supposed to mean?"

"Golkov may not know all the details of this new mission."

"Like which details?" I asked.

"All of them." Daly lifted his shoulders and relaxed them again.

"Pull over."

"Why? We still have a block to go."

"I said pull over!"

"Fine." He pulled to the side of the road and turned off the car. I punched him in the shoulder. He threw up his hands. "What?"

"You want me to go on an unsanctioned mission?" My voice resonated through the small space of the car. "I can't lie to Golkov. I've had to keep my memory hidden my entire life, and now there is one place where I can be truthful and be myself, and you're asking me to give that up too—to keep something from one of the people I trust the most. Do you know how hard that is?"

"It's not like you don't do it every day anyway." Daly dropped his keys in the center console.

"What's that supposed to mean?" I released my seatbelt and shrugged out of my coat. I was suffocating in the warm car.

"It's not like William knows who you really are, yet you don't seem to have a problem being with him every day."

I turned my body to face Daly. "William knows about my memory and he knows me better than anyone except for . . . well, he knows me better than anyone." I was about to say that he knew me better than anyone except Tanner. But I didn't know if Tanner would recognize me even if he did wake up. He wasn't aware of my new secret life at Brown, either.

Daly's eyes burned into mine. "Oh really? Does he know how you hesitate right before your left jab or how you chew on your tongue when you're nervous? Does he know you can speak nearly four languages like a native and tread water for over an hour with only one hand?" Daly's face was flushed and the intensity of his voice increased. "I'll bet he has no idea that you have nearly every book in the Brown University library in your catalog of memories and that you hum Disney musicals when you think no one is listening. I know you haven't told him about The Company, for good reason, but have you ever told him about the accident or what happened to your mom? What about Tanner? Does William even know you had a brother?"

"Stop!" I jerked open the car door and jumped out.

I huffed down the sidewalk in my four-inch heels, wishing desperately I could trade them in for a pair of running shoes. After less than a block, I realized my coat was still in Daly's car, along with my phone and wallet. My arms and hands started to shake from the brisk January air. I sensed Daly's car behind me, but there was no way I was getting back in, no matter how cold I was. My best bet was to find the nearest phone and see if Casey could pick me up.

Lights from the lobby of a high-rise building enticed me up the stairs in front. A doorman opened the door of the building and motioned for me to come inside. If I wouldn't have been so cold, I might have continued down the street to find a gas station or something, but the old man seemed harmless enough.

"Good Evening, Ms. Laxer," the doorman said. We entered a grand lobby with gray marble floors and dark woodwork.

I furrowed my brow. "Do I know you?" I studied his white hair and kind eyes. I'd never seen him before. Not only that, but he was using the name I reserved for missions.

"Mr. Jesly said to expect you, though I thought he would be accompanying you tonight." The man adjusted his black suit jacket with red piping along the edges.

I wracked my brain, trying to figure out who would be expecting me. I'd never met anyone by that name. The only person I knew that lived on this side of Providence was Daly. James Daly. *Wait.*

"Do you mean Adam Jesly?" I asked.

"Of course." The man smiled.

Now I understood why Daly had pulled over his car where he had, just a block from his apartment building. Adam Jesly was an anagram for James Daly. I should have known Daly wouldn't use his real name.

"Should I expect Mr. Jesly shortly?" The doorman peered through the front doors.

"I'm sure he's on his way," I said, not hiding my annoyance.

The skin at the man's eyes crinkled as his smile widened. "A little quarrel, I see."

"No," I sighed. "Yes." He nodded as if he understood, and I found myself wanting to share my life story with a doorman I didn't even know. Instead, I said, "Why do people feel they have to interfere in others' lives without even thinking of the repercussions? It's so exasperating."

"I've found that people want to hurt us less than we think they do, and often interference is misinterpreted from something else."

"Like what?"

"Protection or" —he removed a leather glove and rubbed the back of his neck— "affection." He winked at me.

"Yeah. I think in this instance, 'overprotection' might be the right word."

The man chuckled. "It is the greatest sign of love."

Not liking where this conversation was going, I thought about asking the guy if I could use his phone to call a taxi.

"Mr. Jesly speaks highly of you, you know. You're the only woman I've ever heard him talk about and the first one he's ever invited to see his place. He's been talking about it for days."

"Oh." I looked down at the floor, realizing I couldn't escape now without seeing Daly's apartment. Besides, suddenly I was more curious than annoyed. "Well, I guess I should check it out."

"It was good to meet you, Ms. Laxer. The elevator is past the front desk to the right. Floor 26, number 2610. "

After thanking him, I found the elevator and pressed the button for floor 26. The bell dinged as the number on the vintage-style button lit up for the top floor. I hadn't realized Providence had a building so tall. The gold doors parted to reveal a travertine-tiled hallway. Miniature chandeliers hung from the ten-foot ceiling, casting a glistening light on the beige walls.

I walked down the hallway until I stood directly in front of the door marked 2610. I knocked twice. No answer. After the third attempt, I put my hand on the knob and turned, but it was locked. A short beep sounded. I tried the knob again and it turned easily. Daly must have had Millard install a fingerprint identifier there, just like at headquarters' back entrance at Brown. But why was my fingerprint programmed at Daly's apartment?

I stepped inside and shut the door. The room's white walls and coffered ceiling contrasted with the black-slate tile. Surrounding a wall of windows, gray drapes drifted from long curtain rods to puddle on the floor. Two contemporary sofas flanked a plush white rug in the center of the living area.

"Alex?" Millard stood at the entrance to a hallway off the main room. He wore plaid boxers, a stained T-shirt, and socks pulled halfway up to his knees. One hand held a carton of ice cream, while the other balanced a motherboard with wires hanging out of it. "Oh no, I totally forgot he said you were coming by." Millard, his face flushing red, looked down at his boxers. "Just a second." He set the ice cream and motherboard on a granite countertop in the kitchen and raced from the room. A minute later he returned in a pair of sweats. His brown hair, which he usually had combed over with a perfect part on the side, poked out like uneven quills all over his head.

"What are you doing here?" I asked.

"I have work off tonight. Don't you?" He adjusted his glasses before picking up the ice cream and digging in with a fork.

"Yes, I do, but why are you at Daly's apartment?"

"Oh, he offered me a room when I got evicted from my place last month." Millard stared down at the cookies-and-cream carton.

"You got evicted?" I asked. Millard was one of the last people I would have expected to get kicked out of an apartment.

"Yeah, I guess there were one too many power surges. I accidentally took electricity out of the whole building in December, and they figured out I was the source."

"I'm so sorry. You weren't creating something for The Company, were you?"

"Maybe." He scratched his head, making a few clumps of hair stick up in the other direction. "But don't worry. It was well worth it. When you see your new gadgets at work, you are going to thank me." He shoved another scoop of ice cream into his mouth and then held up his fork to me. "Want some?"

"Uh . . . maybe next time."

Millard's face brightened. "So do you want to see it?"

"See what?"

"The new headquarters for our secret-secret operation." He tossed his fork into the sink and placed the ice cream in the freezer.

"Ha! That makes it secret squared. We should totally call it that. I could even do T-shirts with the superscript 2 above the—"

"What secret operation?" I interrupted.

Millard lowered his voice. "He calls it Operation Nodanesay."

"*Nadeyat'sya*?" The Russian word for "hope" wavered as it left my lips.

"Yeah, something like that."

"What do you know about Operation Nadeyat'sya?" I asked quietly. Millard and I had become close over the last few months and I felt I could trust him. For some reason, though, it worried me that he was getting involved with Elijah.

"All I know is I have to have your new temperature-masking suit ready by this weekend, along with a few other things I'm not ready to reveal just yet." Millard scratched his head. "Well. Let's go." He turned around and started down a hallway. He peered back over his shoulder at me. "You coming?"

"Where?" It felt strange being in Daly's apartment, like I was intruding on a party where I didn't have an invitation.

"Don't you want to see our new lair?"

"Um, sure." I followed him. At the end of the hallway, he opened a door. Four large flat-screen monitors sat back to back at an oval cherrywood table in the center of the room. Long counters held boxes of computer and electrical equipment, along with several piles of wires and plastic. My mind flashed to Millard's desk at The Company, a similar scene of ordered chaos.

"Sorry about the lighting in here. I've gotten so used to working in the basement that having too much light throws me off. I unscrewed a few of the bulbs."

"That makes sense," I said, stepping into the room.

"I'll be back in a sec. I need caffeine if I'm going to get these earrings ready by Friday." Millard's footsteps disappeared down the hallway.

I walked to the far end of the space to a small window covered with wooden blinds. I parted them and couldn't help my sharp intake of breath. The building overlooked a large portion of the city.

Random windows glowed yellow in nearby structures, showing who was still awake. From this height, the vehicles moving through the streets resembled a maze.

"It is quite a view," rumbled a deep voice.

"You know, Daly, you'd make an excellent spy." I smiled and folded my arms in front of me. I hadn't completely forgiven him for what he said in the car, but learning he had taken Millard in after his eviction had softened my anger a little. "How do you sneak up on me so often?"

Daly reached around me and pulled on the string to open the blinds. "It's all in the footfalls. Have you ever watched Itosu walk? Only on the pads of his feet."

"Yeah, you try doing that in heels." I held up one foot in Casey's four-inch red heels.

Daly laughed. "I'd say I never really understood why women wear heels, but, well, they look beautiful on you."

I sighed. "Whatever that was back there in your car, I'm ignoring it right now." Daly looked down, his jaw tense, but I continued, "What we need to do is figure out how we can help Tanner."

"I thought we already established that. Why do you think we are meeting here and not at The Company? There's no way Golkov would give in to what Elijah wants."

"Are you certain about that?"

"I already asked him to."

I gasped. "You talked to Golkov about it? What did you say to him? Does he know about—"

Daly broke in, "No, no. We can't tell him about Tanner." My handler stared out the window to the office building across the street below us. A few lights flickered off.

"Why not?" I moved until we stood side by side. For days I had wrestled with telling Golkov.

"Remember how I told you I took care of the video footage of your last visit to Elijah? Well, it wasn't entirely my idea."

Speechless, I stared at Daly's reflection in the window.

"Elijah said if Golkov was involved in any way, there would be no chance to save Tanner."

"And you believe him?"

"I don't know for sure. It seems as though the ball is in Elijah's court right now. He could be lying to us."

I nodded. "But if there's a chance he isn't lying—"

"—then what harm is there in doing what he asks? We just have to come up with our own play."

I couldn't help smiling at the word "we." I wasn't alone in this.

"We don't have to hand anything over to Elijah until he gives us what we want." Daly turned to look at me. "Now, let's make our plans. There's no time to lose."

"Wait, are you really thinking what I think you're thinking?"

"If you are thinking we are going to discover the whereabouts of a stolen Van Gogh painting and get it for Elijah, you are only partially correct." Daly smoothed one of his eyebrows with a finger.

"Partially?"

"We are going to get the painting, but we don't need to search the world for it."

"Why not?"

"Because I'm pretty sure I've already found it."

9

____

ZOMBIE APOCALYPSE

"How? The Van Gogh has been missing for over thirteen years." I sat on a swivel chair at the center table and touched the computer screen. It lit up and letters scrolled across—"W-e-l-c-o-m-e A-l-e-x." Another one of Millard's fingerprint-recognition technologies.

"The first rule of a thief is to never get caught," Daly replied. "But even the smartest villain has to earn a living, and eventually the thief is going to try to sell the Van Gogh. No matter how well-known a painting is, someone will pay the price."

"And why haven't any authorities found it?"

"Maybe they haven't been scouring the internet and all the CIA and FBI resources I have access to. Maybe they go home every night instead of sleeping a couple of hours on the couch in their boss's office. And maybe that's why *their* research hasn't paid off yet."

A few days ago I'd noticed the worn look on Daly's face, so I flashed to that picture in my head. Gazing at him now gave me a side-by-side comparison, and he definitely looked worse. The dark circles under his eyes demanded better sleeping habits. His disheveled hair and clothes told me his focus had been outside of himself. My last bit of anger at him faded away. He was doing all of this for me. I wanted to thank him, but all I could do was ask, "What did you find out?"

"A Spanish philanthropist named Alberto Valdez hosted a party about six months ago. A few photos from the event were posted on the web." Daly leaned forward and started typing away on the thin plastic keyboard in front of me. His breath blew into my hair and warmed my cheek. After a few seconds, he pointed to the screen. "Here. Look behind the stocky man in the gray suit to what's hanging on the wall." I rolled my chair a few inches forward.

There was no mistaking it. *View of the Sea at Scheveningen* hung on the wall directly behind an obese man. His shadow obscured the lower half of the painting, but it was either Vincent Van Gogh's original or a very good imitation.

"How did you find it?" I said to Daly.

"Millard set the computer to filter using image recognition software, similar to how you would search for the source of a photo online, except it scoured every database and internet resource we could gain access to."

"How can we be sure it's the real thing?"

"Once the computer found all the images, Millard used some crazy algorithm to match textures and other factors—I honestly got lost halfway through his explanation. Anyway, the algorithm weeded out most of the prints and reproductions. When GPS revealed the location and we did a little more research on the mansion, with all its security measures, we were sure we had the original."

"I sure do love Millard." I shook my head. "I still can't believe you found it." I touched the screen to enlarge the image, but the resolution was poor. I turned to Daly. "Do you really think Elijah can help Tanner?"

"I can't believe Elijah would go to all this trouble with you if there wasn't some basis of truth. And knowing he was once a doctor and worked in that Russian hospital . . . well, too many facts are lining up. Don't get me wrong—I will never trust that man fully, but with this, even if there is only a small chance he could do something for your brother, I'm willing to help."

"I'll do anything for Tanner." And I would.

"How do you feel about theft?" Daly asked me.

"I think it's about time I channeled my inner sticky-fingers."

"Then let's steal ourselves a painting."

"Should I be worried?" William scooted closer to me on the cozy couch in the Wayland House lounge.

"About what?" I stuffed a handful of popcorn in my mouth. A movie was playing on the large TV screen on the wall, but neither of us had been paying much attention to it. It didn't really matter to me —I'd seen the film before. It played in my head while the music to the opening scene sounded in my ears. If I'd seen the movie once, I'd really seen it a thousand times.

"About that guy, James. You know, the cocky one who interrupted our date."

"Cocky, yeah, that about sums him up in one word." I laid my head in William's lap and closed my eyes. Daly and I had been up until after midnight the past two nights in preparation for our upcoming mission. That, along with classes and my normal operative training at The Company, was wearing me thin.

"So should I?" William ran a hand over my forehead and into my hair. I nearly sighed out loud. "Be worried, I mean. He seemed a little possessive of you or something. Do you guys always work together?" I didn't have to open my eyes to recall how William looked when he was worried, one eyebrow lowered as he chewed on the inside of his cheek.

"Daly is like a brother to me. Except I was way nicer to my real brother." I stopped. I never talked about Tanner or my mom. William knew about my dad being an American History professor at Brown and that we had come there together at the end of last summer. He had seen the pictures on the wall of Tanner and my mom. He knew there had been an accident. That was about the extent of the information I'd shared. The only people at Brown who knew the details of the car accident were Daly, Golkov, and Casey. Now that I knew Tanner was still alive, it made things even more complicated. I wouldn't even know where to start.

Daly had been right. I hadn't told William anything more about my family. It's not that I didn't trust William, or that I worried he wouldn't understand. He knew about my eidetic memory and probably understood me better than anyone else. There just hadn't really been a good time for me to blurt out that I had been in the accident that had killed my mother and brother. Or that I just found out my brother really was alive but in a coma, and the only chance I knew at saving him involved a stolen painting. It sounded like a soap opera. How do you bring that up in everyday conversation?

"Just so you know, I don't like the guy," William said.

"Noted." I opened my eyes and pretended to write on an imaginary pad of paper.

"Well, this is kind of nice. I'm surprised no one else is in your lobby right now."

"Casey said there was some dance party at the Granoff Center. That's probably where everyone is."

"Then this can be how our dinner date would've ended."

"I'd prefer sitting on a couch with you any day over a fancy restaurant."

We were silent for a while. I looked over my Chinese notes while my eyes faced the TV. I should've told William I had to study, but I didn't want to hurt his feelings again. Plus, the only time we'd spent together since "the real date" was our morning run at the park.

"Can you believe that?" He threw up a hand at the screen.

I stopped tracing a Chinese character on my palm with my finger. "Hmm?"

"Why do people make choices they know are wrong like that? Anyone could see if he wouldn't have opened the door, the zombies wouldn't have known he was there. Stupid people."

"You realize this is a movie, right?" I smiled up at him.

"Yeah, the zombies kind of gave it away, but it's kind of true. You know, unlike when you were in my class—"

I elbowed William in the ribs but he went on, "It's rare to find a student who actually has read the book and practiced speaking in Spanish. And yet they still expect to do well in the course." He shook his head. "It just makes no sense. Choices have consequences."

I rewound the film in my mind to find the part William was talking about, then said, "Open the door—zombie apocalypse. Walk past the door—you can't save the world. Sometimes choices aren't as easy as that."

"Hey, I thought you weren't even watching."

I sat up and faced him, my face burning. "You knew?"

"Yeah, but I thought it was cute that you were staying here anyway." He pushed his hair off his forehead, but two curls fell back in their usual position. "Speaking of choices. Would you want to try real date round two?"

"What did you have in mind?" I scooted closer to him on the couch until our legs touched.

"I have this awards dinner thing Friday night. I'd love it if you could be my date."

"Do you mean this Friday night?"

"Yes." William adjusted his polyester vest.

I turned so we faced each other. "You know I would love to be there, but I already have a flight booked for tomorrow night."

William paused, disappointment showing on his face. "Where are you going this time?"

"Barcelona."

"Without me?" Now he sounded truly hurt. I'd forgotten he had spent a year in Granada as part of his undergraduate work. "Why does your Russian professor need you to go to Spain?"

"Research. I wish I was going with you to the awards dinner." *Instead of going to Spain with Daly.*

"And there's no way you can change it?"

"No, it has to be this weekend." I thought about Tanner. Mission Hope had to happen this weekend or we might lose out on the opportunity to get that painting.

"Oh, okay. I understand." William's shoulders relaxed, though he still had that crestfallen expression.

"Wait. Is the award for you?"

"Don't worry about it. It's not that big of a deal. Just some teaching thing." He picked up a decorative pillow from the side of the couch and placed it in his lap.

"I still want to know about it."

"I'll tell you all about it when you return, okay?"

"Okay." I didn't want to push him. I put my legs on the couch and crossed them in front of me.

William stared intently at the screen for several minutes, then said, "I still think he was stupid."

"What?" I had been studying Chinese again in my mind.

"He could have saved the world without opening the door."

"Really?" I was now very interested in the plot of the movie, or maybe more so in the plot twist William had created.

"TNT." He grabbed the pillow in his lap with both hands and threw it in the air. I looked up just as it landed on my face. I caught it before it fell to the floor.

He grinned. "TNT could have solved everything."

I jumped off the couch with my pillow weapon in hand. "Yes, but will it save you from the power of my pillow?" I swung the pillow at his shoulder.

"Hey!" He rolled off the couch and found another pillow.

I held up a pillow shield and we started our own war, no zombies allowed.

"ALEXANDRA, how are you this lovely Friday morning?" Golkov said in Russian. We only spoke his native tongue at his university office.

"Fine." Being there made me nervous, especially since I was hiding a secret mission from him. I handed him the extra-credit essay I'd done to make up for my B on his test.

"Thank you." He set the essay to the side. "Now, I have a surprise for you."

"A surprise?" I looked around his office. Usually a surprise involved another crazy puzzle he wanted me to solve. He called it training by problem-solving. I called it fun.

"You don't think I would make it that easy, do you?" He motioned with his head to the antique cupboard hanging above his side counter. Wooden manipulatives, puzzles, and small contraptions overflowed on the surface of the counter. More mind puzzles decorated the space above the cupboard.

I walked over and turned the cube letters set in the wood until I spelled the words *Quid est veritas—ver qui adest*. My head translated the anagrammed Latin phrases. *What is truth? It is the man who is here.*

A heaviness pushed on my chest. I was leaving that night on a mission Golkov wouldn't have supported. I was standing there in front of a cupboard gifted to him by my mom because he stood for truth. And I was lying to him.

The cupboard doors clicked. The sound pulsed adrenalin through my veins. When I had first come to Golkov's office, the puzzles were his way of training me before I knew about The Company. Now, even in my somber mood, the idea of solving one made my breath quicken.

"This is probably one of the hardest puzzles yet," he said.

"And that's supposed to be a good surprise?" I looked at him over my shoulder. His grin and hair reminded me of Santa Claus.

"For you, yes, it is a good surprise."

He knew me too well. I peered inside the open cupboard doors. A shiny metal manipulative sat on the shelf. I gathered the puzzle into the palm of my hand. It looked to be made of three separate pieces of metal. Two inner metal rings moved around each other like a gyroscope in the center of a shape.

"It's called a Hanayama equa cast."

"What am I supposed to do with it?" I spun the center pieces again, but somehow they remained stuck in the center of the large circular one.

"That, Alexandra, is what you have to figure out." Golkov sat at his mahogany desk and picked up a pen. "I do have to leave in about an hour," he taunted.

"Don't worry, I've got this." I tossed my school bag on the floor and took a seat on the other side of his desk. I spun the inner circle a few more times and then did it again in my head, concentrating on the differences in the circles. One of the centerpieces had the word "Hanayama" etched into the side, along with a pin-sized protrusion on the outer edge. The other circle was plain with two notches just big enough for the edge of the outer sphere to pass through. All I had to do was get the inner circles out of the center to separate the three pieces.

For about ten minutes I turned and twisted the pieces, but nothing seemed to change. At one point, I thought I had one of the circles loose. When I tried to pull it out, the other piece wouldn't let it go. I let out a huff of air.

"I told you this would be a hard one. You can take it home if you would like." Golkov didn't look up from his paperwork.

"I'll get it." I bit the side of my lip and looked up in thought. The dome light in the center of the ceiling cast a warm glow down on the office space. Two thin bronze pieces crossed over the glass of the dome in an "X" pattern. The metal narrowed from the place where it crossed until it met with the large base of the dome attached to the ceiling. *Hmm.*

I continued to stare at the light and concentrated on the picture in my head of the metal puzzle in my hand. I turned it around in my mind until I saw the similarity. The larger sphere of the Hanayama narrowed on some of the sides. It had to be a clue to getting the notches of the inner rings to come through.

I turned back to the puzzle in my hands and started on each side until I found one where two of the metal pieces thinned out.

I twisted the inner rings until I pulled one of them through. It didn't come off of the outer sphere, but at least it moved from the center. Now the two smaller pieces reminded me of the cuff part of handcuffs without the chain attaching them. A small groove in each of them made them appear less like a ring and more like the letter *C* if laid flat.

Ten minutes later, my manipulations finally paid off. The rings fell away from the sphere and onto the floor. At the noise, Golkov looked up, and then his gaze dropped to the two rings on the floor. A broad smile broke through his gray beard and he laughed out loud.

"Nicely done. I have to admit you had me worried there. To be honest, I've never actually seen anyone solve that puzzle. Even Daly couldn't get it." Golkov winked at me. He understood my competition with my handler because he saw it every day in our meetings and training. "I'm glad I was right about you, Alexandra. I am certain we will see great things from you in the future."

"Thanks." I rubbed at my warm cheeks and bent down to pick up the rings. "Should I just leave them apart like this?" I held up the pieces in one hand. They looked so different now that they no longer worked together. It almost seemed wrong in a way to keep them separate. Guilt seeped through me. Golkov didn't know Daly and I had pulled away from him too.

"Yes, yes, that is fine." The professor pointed to his crowded countertop and got back to work at his desk.

I squeezed the pieces in next to a few wooden puzzles I'd completed. I flashed to some of the more difficult ones and watched the movies in my head of me completing them. None of the puzzles had taken me this long. Golkov had progressively given me harder and harder ones, no doubt preparing my mind for future missions.

The weight returned to my chest. I couldn't do it. I couldn't lie to him like this and go on a mission behind his back. I had to tell him. "Golkov?"

"Yes?" He still had his head hunched over his desk.

"I need to tell you something."

He set down his pen and swiveled around in his chair to face me.

Be strong, Alex. I swallowed and closed my eyes. All I could see was Tanner's pale face and thin arms. If there was even one chance in a million Elijah could save him . . .

"Alexandra?" I opened my eyes to find Golkov standing in front of me. "Are you all right?"

"Yes. I'm good." I picked up my bag from the floor and fastened the top button of my jacket. I didn't want to do it, but I had to trust Elijah and keep Golkov out of it. Not just for Golkov's sake—for Tanner's, too.

"I know these past few weeks have been hard on you, Alexandra. You seem to be taking all of this rather well, but it's okay if you're not. We're all only human."

"What's going to happen to him? To Elijah?" Why I chose that moment to ask about him, I didn't know. "I mean, where will he go now that he's been questioned?"

"He will be turned over to the proper authorities and given a fair but private trial."

"And then?" For some reason, the idea of Elijah being locked away didn't sit right with me. He'd tried to kill me, yet something inside me wanted to reach out and help him.

"A man like that is dangerous," Golkov said. "His involvement with Red Eye is probably just the tip of the iceberg."

I sighed inwardly. Maybe I was being naïve. "I know."

"Once we release him, he will be held in a high-security prison."

"Okay." I pulled my bag higher on my shoulder. "I guess I'm still getting used to the fact that not all missions are like ours. We find truth, we keep people safe, we help. Why would anyone want to do harm? I don't think I'll ever understand it."

"Honestly, Alexandra, I hope you never do."

10

MEMORY LANE

Daly's hand gripped the armrests of the plane, his white knuckles standing out against his tan skin. I looked out the small window to my right. All I could see were clouds floating around us. Millard "knew a guy" who had a private jet and asked no questions. I couldn't argue with that. It wasn't like we could get on a commercial flight without someone at The Company finding out.

"I can't believe you don't like flying. Don't you do it all the time?" I turned back to Daly, who sat in a large reclining seat to my left. Millard was across from us with his laptop on a table in front of him.

"Commercial flights aren't too bad. You don't hear about them going down as often as you hear about private jets and smaller airplanes." Daly closed his eyes and started breathing in through his nose, out through his mouth, the meditative breathing we often used with Itosu.

Millard and I looked at each other and then at Daly, whose hands hadn't left his armrests. We started laughing.

"What?" He opened his eyes.

"Nothing," we both said at the same time and burst out in another fit of laughter. When our giggles subsided, Millard lifted a set of large headphones to his ears and started typing away at his computer.

"Go ahead and laugh, but when . . ." Daly started. The plane lurched, causing my stomach to flip. "See, I'm just being cautious."

"How does being scared help you be cautious?" I asked.

"I'm not scared." He loosened his grip on the armrest. "I'm just preparing myself."

"For what? What would you do if we were going to crash? Jump out in a parachute or something?"

"Exactly. They're next to the cockpit. I checked before takeoff." Daly peered past Millard's seat as if making sure the parachutes were still there.

"Yeah. Well, there aren't always chutes on airplanes. Or in life, for that matter. There's always risk."

"And if I can steer clear of it I will."

"Why did you become a part of this spy business anyway, Daly? It's all about taking risks and facing danger."

"If you remember correctly, my job isn't the same as yours. I do some of the same training, just in case, but I like being behind the scenes. There's so much that goes on before you read a mission file—research, logistics, taking into account every possible scenario of what could go wrong. As a handler, my job is to consider all the risks an operative could encounter, and minimize them if possible."

I tightened my seatbelt. "I guess I never realized or understood everything that goes into mission preparations."

Daly leaned forward and some of the tension left his face. He focused on me with his dark brown eyes. "You know in Moscow, when you broke protocol and took out your earpiece so we couldn't communicate? That had never happened to me with an agent. I have to be a part of every decision you make. It's my job to keep you informed, but also to keep you safe. When you weren't responding, I could only think the worst. That's why I rushed to your location. If you wouldn't have had on GPS, I don't know what I would've—" He turned his head to his window, which had the shade pulled down.

"I'm sorry." In my head I watched a synopsis of the Moscow

mission in fast-forward speed. I hadn't thought through most of my decisions, and the mission could have been disastrous. Yes, I had recovered the missing agent, but it was Daly who had been there in the end. "That will never happen again," I said. "I promise to always keep our line of communication open."

"Do I have to use my super-lie-detector skills on you again?"

"If I remember correctly, and I always do" —*take that, Mr. Cocky*— "I beat your skills."

Daly's arrogant smile vanished. "You know, you never told me how you beat the lie-detection test. I'm actually quite good."

"I bit my tongue."

"What?"

"Every time you asked a question I could answer truthfully, I bit my tongue."

A soft rumbling sounded from across the plane. Millard was slumped over in his seat, his mouth slightly open and his eyes closed in a slumber deep enough to make him snore.

"Hmm. I see how that could ruin my baseline." Daly frowned. "But what about the stuff about Hermia and Oberon? Those were obvious lies, but I didn't notice any difference in your pulse between those and the baseline. You weren't sweating. There were no facial or body cues. How did you do it?"

"You really expect me to give you all my secrets?" I turned to the window and saw the clouds had parted. City lights glowed thousands of feet below.

"Whatever happened to open communication?"

I felt Daly's breath on the nape of my neck as I watched the city below. I froze in my seat. After a few seconds, I heard him lean back into his chair.

If I was really going to trust him, now would be the perfect time to tell him the rest of what my brain could do. I turned to him. "Do you want to know the full truth about how I controlled my breathing, pulse, and body language so you couldn't figure out when I was lying?"

"Yes."

"I watched memories in my head."

"I don't follow."

"It isn't just books or photos I can recall." I looked down at my leather boots. "My mind can also recall any event in my life."

"Can't anyone do that?"

I let out my breath. "Most people walk down memory lane. I live on it."

Daly still stared at me in confusion.

"Do you remember the first time we met?" I asked.

"How could I forget St. Petersburg?"

"Now I want you to think back to the Mariinsky Theater. Do you remember what I wore?"

"Yes, it was a long, black dress. Very flattering, I might add."

I ignored the compliment. "What about the opera itself? Do you remember any songs or specific actors?"

"Um, well, there was that one girl who played a guy. I'm not sure of the name."

"Cherubino."

"Yes, that's right."

"Anything else?"

"I remember feeling a pressure at my chest and then passing out. That's about all I recall until I woke up in a private hospital."

I closed my eyes and watched the night unfold. "You had on a black tux with shiny detailing on the edge of the collar. Your cuff links were gold with" —I paused the movie in my mind— "your initials engraved in them. J. D. Your shoes were glossy, except for a small scrape right along the outside of the left shoe."

"That was when I arrived at the theater. I scraped it on the curb. You remember that?"

"*Non so piu cosa son, cosa faccio, Or di foco, ora sono di ghiaccio, Ogni donna cangiar di colore, Ogni donna mi fa palpitar.* Do I need to go on?"

"I am assuming that was one of the songs."

"Yes, and if we had time, I could tell you all the words of the opera. If I was a singer, I could probably sing them as well."

"I'd love to hear that." Daly grinned.

I hit his upper arm with my hand. Millard opened his eyes for a second, shook his head, and then resumed his nap.

"This is serious," I said.

"Sorry. I'm just having a hard time believing you have everything you've ever seen in your brain. How can all that fit without making you crazy?"

"You think I'm lying? You were at the opera with me." Now I was the one gripping my armrests tightly. *It was hard enough deciding to tell him about my eidetic memory, and now he doesn't believe me?*

"Yeah, well, the rest of that night is still foggy." Daly rubbed at his shoulder, the spot where he had been shot that night.

"Okay, then test me. Think of an event or place we've both been to —something you know better than I would."

"That's easy. My bedroom. You've been in my apartment several times in the past week, but you've only seen my bedroom once."

Heat rose to my cheeks at the memory of my glimpse into his personal space. I had stood in the doorway that day, waiting for Daly to find a pair of black gloves for one of our Mission practice scenarios. "Black comforter, silver pillows, white fur-like rug." I started to describe the furniture and artwork on his wall.

"Okay, okay. I get that you can remember furniture and décor."

"I was just getting started. Can I go on?" The images from his room continued to stream through my mind. "There was a book on your desk—*The Art of War* by Sun Tzu. The bookmark sticking out of the side showed you were about three-quarters of the way through."

"Okay." He massaged the back of his neck.

"The garbage by your door had a takeout box from The China Hut and clear packaging from a new dress shirt, I think." I couldn't see under anything else in the can.

"That's right, I did buy a new shirt last week." Daly rubbed his chin. A shadow of stubble covered his lower face and neck.

"And it smelled like . . . lavender?" I wasn't sure why I hadn't thought about the smell before, but the strength of the aroma reached from my thoughts to my nose, almost like I was there again.

"My room did not smell like—wait, last week, right? The maid used a flowery-smelling fabric softener in my wash. I had to tell her to try something different. It could have been lavender."

"The black bookshelf next to the bathroom has five shelves and each is organized by genre." I hesitated until Daly nodded, and then I began to say the titles on the first two shelves. I threw in a few authors of the obscure books I'd never heard of, for added flare.

"I forgot I had that one," he said when I got to the third shelf and mentioned *How to Win Friends and Influence People* by Dale Carnegie. If I hadn't already read the book myself, I might have made a joke about it.

"Should I keep going?" I said.

"No, no, I think I'm starting to get it. You really can see the whole scene in your head like a movie?"

"Yes."

"What about stuff from when you were younger?"

"Mostly. I don't have full memories of when I was a baby—just colors, lights, and feelings. It was when I was about three that my mind began to record things I could recall in perfect detail."

"I don't remember anything from that age. I think my first memory is from kindergarten." Daly gave a wry grin and I wondered what kind of kid he was.

"That's how most people are," I said. He nodded and I continued, "A lot of my memories used to play in succession. Since Moscow and all that meditation with Itosu, my memories jump out at me in my sleep from different times and places. Sometimes I wake up in the morning and realize I have gone to a football game with my parents, visited the Space Needle, and raced down the streets of St. Petersburg, all in one night. I call them dream memories. They are dreams like you probably have, except they are always real things that have happened to me and so vivid that when I am in them, it's like I am actually there, experiencing it."

"But during the day, you can recall anything whenever you want?"

"Yes, except sometimes the memories push themselves to the surface when I don't want them to."

Daly sat back in his seat. His eyes scanned the ceiling of the plane until they rested on me again. "That must be tough, but you realize how amazing it is, right? I always thought your thing with books was phenomenal. Now that I know about the movie thing, we can start having you observe more missions and watch more videos. It could change what we do for your training. You could be a kind of secret weapon for The Company. You'd never have to carry anything with you on missions. Everything would be here." He touched my temple. His touch sent a shiver through me.

"Let's just get through this mission, okay?" I faced my window again. The lights from the city below were closer. I yawned. "Then we can talk about new training techniques. I just need to close my eyes for a minute."

"Now?" Daly sounded disappointed.

I couldn't pull my eyes open. "So tired . . ."

THE COLD OF *the metal bleachers seeped through my jeans and penetrated my body. I pulled at the collar of my puffy coat, trying to keep in some of the heat. Mom wrapped a furry blanket with Eastmont's Wildcat logo on it around our shoulders.*

"I'm glad this is one of Tanner's last football games. It's too cold to sit outside for over three hours." Mom squished closer to me on the bench.

"Hey, where's my blanket?" Dad pressed into Mom, who wrapped the blanket around his shoulders as well. We sat on the front row of the bleachers, as close as possible to the action of the game.

"Tanner sure is playing his heart out tonight." Mom shivered.

"Because of the scout," I said.

"What?" my parents exclaimed at the same time.

"The one from WSU came down after seeing him on the news. Tanner didn't want to say anything that would jinx it."

"Well, he's been showing some good stuff," Dad replied. "What's the thing he did earlier when he pretended to hand the ball to the one guy and then ran to make the touchdown?"

"It's called a bootleg, and he faked to the running back." I said. "How

many games have you been to and how many times have we all listened to Tanner talk about his plays? I think by now you'd have them memorized."

"We all aren't as talented as you when it comes to remembering, sweetie." Dad nudged Mom's shoulder and she pressed into mine.

Tanner had the ball in his stronger left hand and was about to pass it down the field, where one of his teammates was open. At the last second, a Davis High School player jumped into his path. Left with no other choice, Tanner pocketed the ball under his arm and started to run.

"Go, Tanner, go," Mom chanted quietly next to me.

My brother's strides reminded me of a ballet dancer's leaps across the stage, though I would never tell him that. He flew down the field faster than I could ever run. Players rushed in his direction, but he was too fast. Two Davis defensive lines were about five yards from the goal, each one ready to rush Tanner, depending on the direction he moved. He hesitated and then ran straight at the larger player. I jumped to my feet and threw up my hands. What was he thinking? I would have yelled to him, but the audience on both sides of the field now stood screaming at the top of their lungs. This play could make or break the game for Tanner's team.

When he was only about three or four feet from colliding with the Goliath-size player, Tanner sprang into the air. The linebacker threw his hands up a second too late. Instead of slowing down or tackling him, the player pushed upward at Tanner's hips. The move propelled Tanner even higher into the air just over the opposing player's head. For a fraction of a second, Tanner looked like he was flying with the football under one arm and the other arm extended into a fist toward the end zone. I wished a photographer would catch the moment like my mind could.

Then Tanner was falling and tucking his head as he flew forward. A blur of orange-and-black jerseys scrambled in his direction. Tanner flipped once and landed on his stomach. The opposing team piled on top of him just as he hit the ground. The football was nowhere in sight. Did he drop it? There were several players at the end zone now, and no one was cheering. The Davis players moved off Tanner when the whistle blew.

My brother wasn't moving. His arms were tucked under his chest, and his football pads blocked any view underneath him. The lower half of his body lay on the interior of the field, while his upper body stretched into the end zone. The crowd seemed to pause in their cheering. The referees just stood there. I held my breath and waited with the spectators. After what seemed like an hour, Tanner's red helmet moved. He lifted his head just enough to see his position on the field. I knew now that he was seeing what everyone else saw and probably understood the silence. He didn't stand up, but instead slowly rolled over until his arms were visible—with the football tucked safely in his grasp. The blaring whistle of the referees sounded in our ears. Tanner had made the touchdown.

But he still wasn't getting off the ground. I hopped from my seat, ignoring the calls of Mom and Dad as I flew onto the field while cheers filled the air. When I reached Tanner, I fell to my knees. The trainer was already there, along with half of the team. I ignored them and shook his shoulder. "Tanner, Tanner?" He blinked his eyes several times. "Are you okay?"

"Ow." He nodded his head and sat up, despite the protests of the trainer. Now Tanner's entire body was out of the end zone. The trainer started asking him questions about his vision and pain level.

Tanner waved him off. "I'm okay. Just give me a minute." He handed the ball to a teammate, who tossed it in the air while the rest of the team whooped and hollered.

"Here." I grabbed my brother's arm and pulled him up. He wavered to one side until he found his footing.

"That was amazing," he said as he started to stagger to the sidelines. "Did you see that? Tell me you saw that."

"I did." We stopped near a bench, where his coach patted him on the back. The coach eyed me disapprovingly and then went back to work prepping defense for the remaining minute of the game. Tanner motioned to Mom and Dad, who had moved in our direction. He reassured them he was fine and they returned to their seats. I sat on the bench with my brother. I knew I wasn't supposed to be there, but no one tried to stop me.

Tanner took a swig of water from a bottle next to him. "I've never felt anything so exhilarating in my life. I thought for sure I was a goner and that WSU scout was going to leave without an offer. I thought my life was over."

I knocked my knuckles on his helmet. "Drama queen."

"Goody two-shoes."

"Empty-headed jock."

"Polaroid."

"Too bad that mouth of yours wasn't damaged," I said.

"Hey." He swatted me with his hand.

"How's your back?"

Tanner undid his chin strap and lifted his helmet from his head. "Okay,I think." He rolled his head and stretched out his arms.

"Seriously, hotshot, what were you thinking? You could have broken your neck."

"I was thinking the goal was in my view and there was only one thing in my way. Sometimes it takes a leap of faith." He took another drink of water.

"And you thought trying to fly right over him was the best move, instead of, I don't know, going around him?"

"I wouldn't have made it to the end zone before getting tackled." Tanner shrugged his shoulders. "A playa's gotta do what a playa's gotta do."

"I'll leave you here with your ego. I'm going back to the stands and my warm blanket."

Tanner looked over his shoulder to Mom and Dad. They both smiled and waved in our direction.

"Hey, Lexie?" Tanner said.

I turned back and saw a line of worry on his forehead.

"Will you apply to WSU next year?" he asked.

"What? Why?" He knew my desire to attend school on the East Coast. We'd talked about Ivy leagues since I was twelve.

"Just promise me you'll consider it."

"Okay," I said. "I'll think about it."

He smiled. "Good. Oh, and Lexie?"

"What?" I folded my arms across my chest.

"I totally looked like Superman, didn't I?"

I shook my head and found my way back to my seat.

I JERKED AWAKE. Outside the window, red-blinking tarmac lights illuminated the way for landing planes. I'd almost forgotten about Tanner asking me to join him at WSU. After the accident, all I'd cared about was getting far away from anything that would spark a memory of him. Brown University had been the perfect choice when my father had received the offer to work there too.

"Don't forget to use your *theta*," Daly said next to me. He was standing and gathering his things.

"I speak Spanish better than you," I said in Spanish.

"We'll see about that." Daly tapped Millard on the shoulder to wake him. How he had slept that long on the plane was beyond me.

After customs, Daly drove us through town in a car he'd rented as Adam Jesley. To annoy him, I sat in the back with Millard. Listening to Millard's excitement over seeing the city made the back seat worth it. I'd never been to Barcelona either, but his eyes nearly bugged out as we passed by the Sagrada Família with its eight ornate towers rising into the city's morning sky.

"Is that a castle?" he asked.

"It's actually a church," Daly replied.

"It looks almost like it was built by aliens," Millard said.

"Yeah, well, they've been building it since 1882, so it has passed through many generations of builders and architects," I explained. My mind began to recall a book in the library on Spanish architecture. "It's not even completed yet. Once it's done it will have sixteen towers and be the tallest church in the world. When Gaudí died in 1926—he was one of the original architects—it was evident the building had a long way to go. See those cranes at the back?" I pointed over Millard's shoulder. "They're constantly at work. The planned completion date is 2028. You should see the facades. It is all etched in stone in intricate detail . . ." I continued sharing the information I'd read until Daly cleared his throat loudly and the towers of the Sagrada Família were well behind us.

Millard was now staring at me, instead of the city. "You act like you've visited it before. I thought you'd never been to Barcelona."

"I haven't."

"Alex just has an obvious interest in Spanish architecture." Daly looked over his shoulder and gave me a warning look. I'd nearly forgotten Millard didn't know about my eidetic memory. Now that Daly knew, I kind of wanted to tell Millard too.

"I've just seen several pictures and documentaries on the building and its . . ." A buzzing in my pocket stopped my words. I pulled out my cell phone. William was calling.

"Sorry guys, I need to answer this." I pressed the button and put the phone to my ear.

"William?"

"Were you expecting someone else?" he asked on the other end.

"No, I just . . . what are you doing up? Isn't it like 5:00 am there?" I got as far as possible from Millard, then leaned my head close to the window. Barcelona's buildings passed by quickly, the light colors brightening as the morning sun rose over La Pedrera. I almost asked Daly to stop so I could really take in the moving lines of the beautiful buildings that reminded me of gentle ocean waves.

"I'm just headed out for my morning run." The cadence of William's feet on the pavement reached through the receiver. "I have classes all day and wasn't sure if I would be able to talk to you until after the Fulbright ceremony tonight."

"Fulbright?" I shouted into the phone. "Wait, that's the award ceremony you were talking about? You're getting a Fulbright?" I lowered my voice when I saw Daly glance over his shoulder at me.

William cleared his throat. "Yes."

"Why didn't you tell me? Maybe I could have stayed one more day. I can't believe you're getting one of the most prestigious awards a professor can receive and I'm not even going to be there."

"It's okay. This trip sounded important to you. I don't ever want to hold you back."

"You don't." I glanced up at the rearview mirror. A somber Daly still had his eyes on me. I looked away and said quietly into my phone, "William, I wish I could be there for you."

"I know. Honestly, the whole thing is kind of embarrassing. I wish they weren't making such a big deal out of it. I'm just happy to accept the grant and get to work in . . . whoa, uh . . ." A loud bang followed by a few crunching noises vibrated through my phone's speaker and I had to pull the phone away for a second.

"William?" I whispered into the phone when I returned it to my ear. "Are you okay?"

I recognized his laugh in the distance. "Sorry. Dropped my phone on the sidewalk."

"Did it break?"

"No, just a few more battle wounds to add to the scratches. Serves me right for running in the dark on an icy sidewalk while talking on the phone. Wish the sun rose earlier in the winter."

"So you were saying?"

"Oh, just that Brown doing this reception thing seems a little much. I'd rather just celebrate with you."

"Yeah." My mind pulled up information I'd seen on Fulbright scholars and grants. A pit began to form in my stomach. I had a feeling I knew why William hadn't mentioned the Fulbright earlier, and it wasn't just because of my trip to Barcelona. "So when you say you are getting the Fulbright, you mean a Fulbright grant, right?" I concentrated on the Spanish architecture passing by through the car window, but even the great designs of the famous architect Gaudi couldn't distract me from what I knew was coming.

"Yes," William said. I could hear the uncertainty in his voice.

"Which means to use that grant, you have to live aboard, right?" I knew the answer; I just wanted to hear him say it.

"Yes."

"So that study-abroad opportunity you told me you were doing in Mexico, it's not just a group of your students going to study Spanish for a few months, is it?"

William didn't answer right away, but I could hear his breathing on the other end of the line.

I closed my eyes and pinched the bridge of my nose. "Why didn't you tell me it was for a Fulbright?"

A door opened and closed on his side of the line. "I . . . listen,

Alex. It wasn't at first, and then when I found out, I didn't want to put any more pressure on you to come with me. I knew I couldn't turn this opportunity down. Maybe if I'd met you before I applied . . . I don't know. This is really my dream—to teach Spanish and to study Mexican literature with some of the brightest minds on the subject. I have to do this. I want to do this. It's just—"

"When do you leave?" My voice sounded hollow, just like my body felt at that moment. William was leaving Brown as a Fulbright scholar, and I should have been so happy for him. I was proud of him. I just didn't like the ramifications of what it could do to us.

"I'll leave the day after final exams. May 10th."

I didn't like the "I'll" part of his answer, like it was already decided without me knowing anything about it. "How long?"

"Eight months."

"That's a . . . long time."

"I know." William sounded as conflicted as I felt.

I stared out the window at the blurring buildings of Spain, wishing I could see his face and know exactly what he was thinking. My mind could record every moment we'd been together, but I would still never have the luxury of seeing into his mind.

He let out a long breath into the phone. "Listen, Alex. It's only February. There's still plenty of time for us to work things out."

"Yeah," I swallowed. *But you seem to already have made your own decision.* "I have to go, William."

"All right." He paused. "But we're okay, right?"

I straightened in my seat and did what every good spy would have done—I pretended everything was just fine. "Yes. Good luck tonight. You really do deserve it."

"Thanks."

Daly turned the car into an underground parking lot of what I assumed was our residence for the next few days. He pulled into a stall. Both he and Millard stared at me sympathetically. My quiet talking had apparently not been quiet enough.

"I've gotta go, William. I'll see you when I get back."

"Okay. Call you later?"

"Sure. Adios."

"Adios."

I turned off my phone, opened the car door, and vowed silently to make this one heck of a mission.

"So you'll wear the bodysuit underneath your dress." Millard adjusted the fabric at my shoulder. The black skin-tight suit was actually pretty comfortable. The Spandex-like fabric covered my whole body from my ankles to my wrists. Except for the thin zipper on the front of the suit, it appeared to have no seams.

"And this will make me undetectable to heat sensors?" I slid my hands over my stomach and down my legs. "Where are the wires?"

"Everything is interwoven into the fabric."

"And it really works?" I spun around in the full-length mirror of the hotel room. The fabric clung to my body so tightly, every ounce of me was exposed for the world to see. I resisted the urge to cover myself with my arms. It was just Millard.

"Check it out. This is like a camera, except it reads body temperature." He showed me what looked like a small cell phone with a video screen. He held it in front of him. "See? You can tell I'm here because of the red-and-orange light." He moved his body and the screen reflected his movements in colors. "Now look at you." He stepped back a few feet and held the temperature reader screen to face me. "You can only see your hands and face." It was true. The screen only showed the parts of my body not covered with fabric.

"So how am I supposed to hide them?" I tried to pull one of the sleeves over my hands. It barely made it if I put my hand in a fist.

"Don't worry. I've got you covered." He reached over onto the couch and held up more black fabric. "Ha! Do you get it? Covered!"

I laughed for his sake. "Yep."

"Gloves, socks, and a head covering. I thinned the fabric by the eyes so you can see through."

I imagined what I would look like in the full suit. At least it was black. Tanner had worn a blue morph suit one year for Halloween. He looked like he'd stepped off the stage of the Blue Man Group.

"This is really great, Millard. There's just one problem. How am I supposed to attend a formal event wearing it?"

"Don't worry, Alex." Daly stepped into the living area from one of the bedrooms. "Your dress is hanging in the bathroom. In fact" —he glanced at his watch— "you should probably start getting ready. We only have a few hours until showtime."

Mortified in my body-hugging attire, I hurried into the main bathroom and shut the door behind me. On a hook hung a garment bag, which I opened carefully. Thanks to Casey my fashion sense was improving, and the idea of wearing a formal gown wasn't as repulsive as it used to be.

An emerald-green dress sparkled in the bright bathroom lights. I lifted it from the hook and removed the bag. Beautiful, intricate beading made the gown heavy. The green beadwork began at the high neckline, moved down the bodice, and continued through the mermaid-style skirt.

I unzipped the back of the dress and stepped into it with Millard's suit still on. I slipped my hands into the arms. Each sleeve ended in a V about halfway down my hands. I zipped up the dress as far as I could from the bottom. Then I stretched my arm over my shoulder and pulled up the zipper the rest of the way.

I turned to look in the mirror and gasped. The gown embraced my body from my neck to my knee. Though it was definitely snug, the fact that it covered most of my skin gave it a classic, elegant feel. I turned back and forth in the mirror. The skirt flowed out like a bell and draped gracefully onto the floor. I knew Daly had taste, but this gown was exquisite. After briefly examining the swirly patterns of tiny beads that must have been sewn on by hand, I readied myself for the benefit event.

A light knock sounded on the door just as I added some gloss to my lips. "Are you ready, Alex? Daly left a few minutes ago and I told him I'd make sure you made it to the gala in time."

"Yes, yes." I bent over to slide on the sling-back heels Daly had managed to find in my size. Maybe he did know everything about me. I took one last look in the mirror, adjusted a bobby pin in my hair, and opened the door.

"Whoa!" Millard took a few steps back. "That is so cool."

"Um, thanks." I tucked a loose piece of hair back in my high ponytail.

"No, I mean, it's so cool you can't even see my suit." He walked around and looked me up and down. If it had been anyone else, I might have found it creepy or objectifying. Not with Millard. I could really tell he was impressed with his own handiwork.

"Oh, here's your earpiece." He handed me a sparkly pair of sunburst-shaped earrings. "Don't worry, they aren't real emeralds, but I would suggest keeping them on all the time anyway."

"Don't worry. I plan to." I put the earrings on and slid the small, skin-colored wire attached to one of them into my ear.

"Okay, well I guess I'm off." I smiled at Millard.

"Aren't you forgetting something?"

I never forget. I patted the small purse at my side. "Nope."

He raised an eyebrow and motioned to a side table. "Daly made me promise you would take it."

"I'm not taking it." I walked around him to the front door of the hotel room.

"Alex, come on. It's not like he's asked you to bring a gun, which most of the other agents carry."

I frowned. "I know."

"Come on, you have your taser-laser phone. What harm is a little mace that looks like lipstick? This may be one of my best inventions yet." Millard handed me the so-called tube of lipstick.

"Fine. I'll bring it. But this is totally unnecessary." I dropped the tube into my purse. "I know karate, you realize." Actually I was thankful for any kind of protection—I just didn't want to admit that to Millard or Daly. Eventually I would carry a gun, so I had to get used to the idea that my fighting skills wouldn't always be enough.

"Have a good time." Millard held the door open for me. "Remember. In and out. Find the room, get the painting, come back here."

"I remember."

11

A CHANGED MEMORY

Four columns rose from the large porch at the front of the house. *Porch* and *house* might have been the wrong words. *Mansion* and *expansive veranda* were more fitting for the edifice before me. A tall man in a tuxedo waited for me at the door.

"*Su nombre?*" he asked.

"Dana Laxer."

He scrolled through a list on an electronic tablet. "Ah, yes. *Bienvenido* to the Valdez estate. Your companion would like you to meet him at the bar," the man said and opened the door. "You may leave your coat." He held out a hand.

I shrugged off the coat and handed it to him. I had a feeling it was the last time I would see it. Several other guests moved slowly down the gray-and-white marble hallway. I followed them until we reached a large ballroom. Soft violin music drifted from a small orchestra in the corner of the room. Paintings hung on the walls about every five feet. Several more canvases dotted the outskirts of the room on easels covered with black silk. Dancing couples swayed to the music in the center of the room.

I navigated my way through the crowd and around several paintings until I saw the long bar on the far side of the room. A section of small windows framed the liquor-filled counter. My eyes scanned the group until I found Daly. Seeing him in a tux brought back memories of the first time we met, in the Mariinsky Theater in St. Petersburg. So much had changed since then. I was no longer the lost girl searching for a place to fit. Daly had changed too. Some of his cockiness had worn off, and having him there in that moment made any lingering jitters about the mission subside.

His broad smile sent a wave of self-consciousness through me. "I do love a good piece of art," he said, looking directly at me.

"Y–yes," I stammered, then stood up straighter and composed myself. "The Picasso is one in a million."

Daly set down his drink. "Wait, there's a Picasso here?" He peered over me and around the room several times.

"He was Spanish after all." When Daly didn't respond, I said, "And we're in Spain . . ." I peaked an eyebrow.

"Ha ha ha." He smiled. "So, where is it?"

I pointed to a painting about twenty feet away. "It's called *Maisons à Horta.*"

"That's Picasso? I thought he was more of an impressionistic painter."

"That's probably Monet you're thinking of. They lived around the same time period, but Picasso was a cubist."

"Ah, yes, cubist." Daly straightened his bowtie.

"You don't know what that is, do you?'

"Of course I do, it's when . . . well, it's . . . You know if it was anyone else, I could easily make something up, but since you've read that somewhere, why don't you just tell me?"

"In cubism, objects are analyzed, broken up, and reassembled in an abstract form. Instead of depicting a subject from one viewpoint, the artist shows it from a multitude of viewpoints to represent it in a greater context," I quoted from an online encyclopedia.

"Well, that does make sense. I may be well-versed in the theatrical arts, but painting has never really been my forte." Daly took a sip from his glass.

"And you didn't think to study, say, some art, since that's what our mission is all about?"

"I've been preparing for this mission for weeks." He pressed his lips together. "I worked seven days last week while you were at university classes and hanging with your roommate and boyfriend." He turned to face the windows behind the counter.

"Sorry, I know you and Millard have been working hard." I touched Daly's arm.

He relaxed his shoulders a bit. "I just wanted to minimize risk."

"No, I get it. Really, I'm sorry. My mouth always runs away with me when I'm talking to you. I should just carry duct tape."

Daly turned to me with a slight smile. "Pink duct tape?"

I hit him playfully with the back of my hand. I'd nearly forgotten he knew about the first prank Casey and I pulled at Brown. My mind replayed my traverse across campus in the middle of the night and how I'd added that duct-tape prosthetic arm to the missing one on the Caesar Augustus statue. That adventurous night calmed my memories and helped my mind go still. It was the first time I realized that risks and thrills were part of who I wanted to be.

Daly's eyes were fixed on me when the memory faded. Something seemed different about him tonight—a softness in his features. I liked him better this way.

"So when does the mission commence?" I asked. He handed me a glass of clear, bubbly liquid. I stared at it for a few seconds. "Um, I'm seventeen, remember?"

"Right now, you definitely are not seventeen." His eyes never left mine, but all I could think was how my dress hugged my body. "And it's just sparkling juice."

I accepted the wine glass and downed the whole thing. The liquid bit at the inside of my mouth, but I would have done anything to avoid his eyes. I cleared my throat. "But really, when do we start?"

Daly scanned the room and said in a low voice. "Not quite yet. We have to wait for the distraction, remember?"

"I read the mission details. I know Millard is supposed to create a distraction so I can get past the security guards. You just never specified what."

"Don't worry, you'll know." Daly finished the last of the liquid in his glass. "But now, we dance." He took my glass from my hand, set both of them on the counter, and extended his hand.

The beadwork on my sleeve glittered as I reached my hand out to his. He escorted me to the back of the ballroom, only about ten feet from a dark hallway. A red velvet rope hung across the entrance, and two men in black suits stood on either side of the opening.

"I may not know about all artists, but I know about Van Gogh." Daly placed his hand at the small of my back and led me in a waltz. "In fact, I think I learned a little too much. His art may be impressive, but imagine what he could've done if he had lived longer."

"I know. Many artists' lives are cut short." I turned my head away from Daly. "My mom was an artist too." Though her life hadn't ended like Van Gogh's, they had both died so young.

"I'm sorry it wasn't both of them," Daly said.

"What?" I stopped dancing.

"No, no. What I mean is I'm sorry your mom is gone, sorry that we can't save her like Tanner." My handler didn't say the words, but I knew what he left out—that we *might* be able to save Tanner. Daly pressed his hand to my back, and we began to move again with the music.

"I see her, the accident, in my head." I concentrated on Daly's pocket handkerchief. "It was different with Tanner. I didn't see him during the crash, but I saw her. I knew she wasn't coming back even before I saw her lifeless eyes." The movie memory of that night started to play. *No. No. Think of something else. Anything else.*

"Breathe." Daly squeezed my hand. "Look at me, Alex."

I lifted my eyes to his. Standing this close, his eyes weren't really brown like I thought. They were a marble mixture of blues and oranges, like the sunrise reflecting in a stormy sea. The ocean. I pushed my mind from the trauma of the accident to another direction and concentrated on the ocean like Sensei Itosu had taught. A memory rushed to the surface of my mind and I let it engulf me.

"WHY DO you think Mom and Dad make us come to the beach every year?" Tanner asked. He rubbed the skin of his scalp, which was visible from a head shaving—some male-bonding experiment after the championship game, one I thought went completely wrong.

"I don't know. It's not like it's warm enough to suntan or even really get in the water," I said.

"At least we have this." He held up a white plastic tower mold. It had once been blue, but we used it every year to make our sandcastle. This year we'd gone the medieval route and added a moat.

"I can't believe I still like making sandcastles." I pressed moist sand into one of the molds and turned it over to add another tower. When I pulled the mold off, the sand crumbled around it.

"You'd think with your memory, you would get better at it every year."

"Hey!" I fell back onto the sand and pretended to pout.

"You've got to make your eyes show the hurt too if you want that expression to be believable."

"Come on, I thought I was good at this one. It always works on Dad."

"That's because he'd give you whatever you want even if he knew you were faking it. Me, on the other hand, I'm not so easily swayed."

"Yeah." I sat up and smoothed the spot I'd ruined on the castle. "Then I must be a pushover, because I always give you what you want."

"Ha!" Tanner reached across the castle and replaced my tower with a perfect one using the same mold I had. He sat back, his face more serious now. "Well, I think we both know I would do anything for you."

"Me too." It was true. I would sacrifice anything for my brother.

"Where'd Mom go?" I asked. Dad reclined in his beach chair in his flannel shirt, his hat pulled over his face. I chuckled to myself. The sun rarely broke through clouds in April in Oceanside, and yet Dad had applied SPF 70 sunscreen an hour before we came to the beach. Mom's chair was empty.

"I don't know. She probably forgot something. Oh wait, there she is on that rock." Tanner pointed to an area several hundred feet away, closer to the parking lot. Her back faced us and she had her cell phone at her ear.

"Work stuff," I groaned and hopped up. "I'm telling her to throw that thing in the ocean."

I waded through the sand toward her. As I drew near, I heard her voice.

"By next week?" Mom asked the caller. Pause. "Yes. That's fine." Pause. "Just let me know when it comes through. You are such a lifesaver." She put the phone back in her pocket and turned to face me. She gasped. "Oh, Alexandra, you scared me."

"Sorry." I looked down at her pocket with the phone inside. "Who was that?"

"Oh, just work." She jumped down from the rock and landed lightly on her feet.

"You never talk about people from the museum." We started back in Dad and Tanner's direction.

"Oh, he's not from the museum. Just a company that helps me with work every now and then."

I nodded my head. We moved slowly across the sand. Every time we took a step, water would gather around our feet and disappear instantly as we lifted them from the sand.

"Mom." I kicked at a broken clamshell in the sand. "How would you feel if I didn't apply to Brown or Harvard?"

She threw a hand out to stop me. "What? Why? Please don't tell me there's a boy."

"Well, actually there is." I paused long enough to scare her. "It's Tanner. I don't want to leave him when I go to college. Of course he'll already be at WSU when I'm a senior, but I could transfer my community college credit and do satellite courses from there while at Eastmont. Or" —I played in the sand with my toes— "I could graduate a year early and go with him this fall. I know, I know we talked about this already." I felt my mom's gaze on me. "But the closer it gets, the more I realize I don't care what school I go to. It's the people that make a place. It's the people that make life worth living."

Mom let out a long breath. "You know, I didn't really learn that until I married your father and had you two. I want you to be able to shine, Alexandra, but I'd never take you away from your brother. I wish I would have had someone like that growing up."

"And then you and Dad would only be a few hours away. We could come home on the weekends that Tanner doesn't have games."

"I do like the sound of that," Mom said as we continued walking. "But I still want you to apply to the other universities just in case you change your mind. I wouldn't be disappointed if you considered Brown, at least in the future. That was where I found myself, you know."

"I'm not going to give up on my dreams, Mom, just because I want to be near Tanner. I'm just willing to change my course a little so we can live our dreams together."

"How did I luck out to get such a level-headed daughter?" She wrapped an arm around my shoulders.

"I don't know. I didn't get it from Dad." We stopped beside him. A muffled snore came from under his hat. Mom and I laughed. The sound woke him and he sprang from his chair, knocking it and his hat into the sand.

"The Redcoats are coming, the Redcoats are coming!" He searched the nearly empty beach and then relaxed his stance when he saw us. "What?" He rubbed his face. "What's going on?"

Mom picked up his hat, wiped off the sand, and placed it on his head. Tanner joined us with our sandcastle kit in tow. "Well, apparently the Redcoats are coming so maybe we should head back inside," she said.

"Fine by me. I think I might be getting sunburned anyway." Dad picked up the chairs and moved like the British really were on his tail. Tanner ran to catch up to him.

Mom's phone buzzed in her pocket and she reached in to grab it. "Sorry, Alexandra, he's calling back. I have to take this."

"It's okay. See you in a few." I started toward Tanner and Dad.

Behind me, Mom answered the phone. "Did it work?" Pause. "Oh, good." Pause. "You're always swooping in to save the day. Thanks, Elijah."

"ELIJAH!" I gasped into Daly's chest. He let go of my hand and pulled me into him.

"Don't worry. We'll get Tanner back and beat Elijah." Daly stroked my back while we swayed to the music on the edge of the dance floor.

"No, no." I put my palms on Daly's lapels and pushed myself back so I could see his face. "I thought there had to be more to it." I flashed to the ocean scene and watched my mother's face again as she spoke on the phone. "She counted on Elijah. She trusted him."

"How do you know?"

"I saw it. In my head. It was a memory. I saw it in her face and heard it in her voice when she talked about him."

Daly placed his hands over mine on his jacket and carefully pulled them free. "Maybe he just turned bad. It happens." He led me to the side of the dance floor, only a few feet from the security guards protecting the hallway.

"No. My mom was so good at reading people. There has to be another reason for Elijah being the way he is."

Daly found my arm and turned me to him. "He tried to kill you, Alex," he said in a low voice. "Either way, it doesn't change the mission." He scrutinized the room. "We still have to get that painting."

"It changes everything," I said. "We need to go back and tell Golkov so he doesn't . . ."

Near the center of the dance floor, the crowd parted. Everyone stopped dancing and talking.

A man with a white tux jacket and slicked-back hair stood facing away from us, holding a wine glass in each hand. He staggered a little and said something I couldn't make out over the music. As if on cue, the violinist stopped playing.

"Cheers to all you filthy-rich pigs!" the man slurred. It was the first time I had heard anyone speak English at the mansion. He held his wine glasses high above his head. Some of the red liquid sloshed out and splattered his sleeve and the floor. He spun around. I nearly fell off my four-inch heels as Millard gave me an inebriated grin.

"Congratulations on your ostentatious and high-faluting society." He wobbled to the side. "You deserve a night to feel good about yourselves by bidding on paintings that will hang in your mansions and second homes while half the world lives in poverty."

A half-empty glass flew from his hand and shattered on the floor. The guards beside us rushed from their post toward Millard.

"Daly, what should we do?" I asked.

"*We* shouldn't do anything. *You* should hop over that velvet rope and get to the painting."

"What about Millard? He's drunk and off his rocker and . . ." Daly put a finger to my lips.

"He's the distraction."

I looked back at Millard, who peered around the guards and gave a wink. Then his step faltered and the other glass toppled from his grasp right onto a woman in a pale pink gown. He started to fall and grabbed at the guards on his way down.

Daly pushed me with both hands to the hallway. "Go! I'll be here." He motioned to my earpiece earring.

I glanced around. No one was looking in my direction. *It's now or never.* I hopped over the rope and sprinted down the hall, my heel clicks only drowned out by Millard's yells of "Save the orphans! Save the whales! Bring back Elvis!"

At the fork, I turned right into an even darker hallway. I unzipped my dress and shimmied it to the floor, exposing my black bodysuit. I tossed the heels on top and emptied the contents of my purse into a pile next to it. I grabbed my phone and the lipstick tube of mace and tucked them into the pocket at my lower back. Then I put on the gloves, socks, and head covering.

The schematics of the mansion came into view in my mind. Instead of racing toward the private collection room like I had planned, I grabbed my dress, shoes, and purse and moved to a hallway at the back of the mansion. I pulled open the small window and tossed my belongings into some bushes, then closed the window and backtracked until I found the right hallway.

The space I needed to find wasn't on the schematics, but according to Millard and Daly's research, the owner of the mansion had hired a crew a decade ago to renovate a section of the second floor. All I had to do was find how to get into that space.

I moved down three more hallways until I realized I was moving in a square. That meant there had to be something inside the square. I pulled out my phone and turned on the flashlight app. I ran through the same hallways again, visually scanning the walls. After one trip, I stopped and turned off my light—no need to draw attention to myself if someone looked down a hallway. My mind re-created its own map of the square halls. Each wall had a few small paintings and tapestries. I didn't have time to search behind every one. I fast-forwarded along each wall until I saw it. A seam just under one of the tapestries. I hurried to the correct hallway.

The tapestry hanging over the seam depicted Joan of Arc holding a sword. Her regal air and determined eyes gave me a boost of strength. I yanked back the tapestry to reveal a rectangular metal door with no handle. I thought of the Red Eye warehouse in Moscow. *Why do shady people always have doors without handles?*

"Adam." I whispered Daly's code name. "You there?"

"Yes." His voice sounded in my earpiece. "I just got Millard to the car. You okay?"

"You guys were right about the hidden room. It's obviously pressure sealed to control the temperature. And Millard was smart to make the bodysuit. It's a metal door—no handle—which probably means it is high security like we thought."

"Is there a keypad or anything?" Daly asked.

I used my fingers to feel around the rectangular indentation in the wall. I put my hand on the door itself, trying to feel for anything other than metal. *Wait.* The door was warmer in one area, right around where a knob or handle would have been.

"There's a hotspot on the door."

"Tell her to hold her hand to it for ten seconds," Millard's voice carried through Daly's intercom.

"Okay." I removed my glove, pressed the palm of my hand over the hotspot, and held it there while I counted in my head. When I reached eight, a red light started to glow under my hand. I pulled it away quickly. "It's glowing."

"Seriously?" Millard said. "It must be a Marlow1000. I've always wanted to get my hands on one of those. Its biometric authentication system is based on palm-vein-pattern recognition technology. The authentication accuracy has extremely low false rates. Its non-intrusive and contactless reader has—"

"Get to the point, Millard," Daly cut him off. "She needs help, not a technological tutorial."

"Sorry. It must be embedded in the door. The only way to open the door is with the palm of the person who is programmed into it."

"So how do I get past it?"

"You don't," Millard said.

"What?" Daly and I said one right after another.

"You don't understand. This isn't some code you can crack. It reads the veins in your hand. Unless you are in the system, there's no way to trick it. At least not within our timeframe."

"What about the laser in my phone? Couldn't I just cut around the Marlow1000 or something?"

"Doubtful. Even if you could do it in time, it still wouldn't release the locks in place. You'd have to make a pretty large hole to get yourself through it, along with the painting on the way out."

"Wait," Daly said. "I have an idea. Dana, are you still in your dress?"

"Uh, I kind of threw it out the window."

"Why would you do that?" Daly asked.

"I didn't want to leave it . . . because of evidence . . . you know, can't leave any behind." Though that was also true, I didn't want to admit I really loved the dress and hoped to somehow get to it after I grabbed the painting.

"Okay, well, that spandexy number might just work. You'll want to take off the mask and gloves. Try to keep in low lighting so he can't see your face."

"Who?" I asked.

"Alberto Valdez. Your new date."

12

LEAP OF FAITH

I leaned back against the tapestry wall, bent one knee, and set that foot on the wall. *I can't believe I'm doing this.* I put one hand behind my head, then thought better of it and rested it on my hip. *I have a hard enough time flirting in my real life.*

"Are you ready?" Daly asked in my earpiece.

No. "Yes." I gave up on the knee pose and just rested my side against the wall. I undid my ponytail and tossed my hair a few times to get the matted locks to flow over my shoulder. I was as ready as I would ever be.

"Wish I could see you in action, though I think hearing it will be somewhat of a consolation," Daly said. If I hadn't promised to always wear my earpiece, I would have removed it and tossed it out the window with my dress.

I didn't need to look to know my "date" was approaching. Alberto Valdez's feet slapped against the marble floor like he wore flippers. He moved at an uneven pace—*slow, quick, quick. Slow, quick, quick.*

"Remind me again why I'm doing this," I whispered through gritted teeth.

"It's the only way in," Daly answered in my ear. "Remember who you're doing this for."

Memories of Tanner flooded through me. The last image was of him lying in that bed in a coma. *I can do this. I can do this for him.*

"Good luck, Al . . . Dana," Daly said.

The hefty Valdez paused when he saw me and then proceeded in my direction, moving in a snake-like pattern. The darkness of the hallway made it hard to make out his face, but I could have sworn a bit of light bounced off a gold tooth in his grin.

This is worse than having a gun pointed in my direction.

"Buenos noches, señorita. So you're the one that sent me the text?" His words came out in a stream of barely distinguishable syllables, making his Spanish hard to interpret. He stopped a few feet in front of me. I couldn't help staring at his receding hairline and bushy goatee. His eyes traveled from my head to my toes. I resisted the urge to wrap my arms around my middle to hide.

"Si, Alberto." My attempt at an alluring tone made me sound like a man.

"So you saw me across the ballroom tonight and wanted to meet privately? I don't normally allow strangers in this part of my home, but for you" —he reached out and touched my hair— "for you, I will make an exception."

I flipped my hair and let out a bubbly laugh. "Gracias." I stepped back a few feet until my back brushed the edge of the tapestry. "So this is your home?"

He threw his hands out wide. "Of course. Do you like what you see?" A wide smile broke out on his face, right above his double chin. He did have a gold tooth.

"I would love to see more . . . of your home." My earpiece vibrated with the muffled laughs of Daly and Millard.

Alberto stepped in front of me and rested his hand on the wall, inclining his head toward mine. "I think I can arrange that. We could start on the third floor. I have a hot tub off my bedroom balcony." The smell of onion and garlic almost overpowered the fermentation drifting off his breath. All I wanted to do at that moment, besides puke, was use a choke-hold on that chubby neck of his and knee him in the gut. In fact, if Daly hadn't already warned me that any harm to the man might call attention to my location and lead to a lockdown of the mansion, I would have used my strong right roundhouse kick to the side of his balding head.

I held my breath and smiled as flirtatiously as I knew how.

"Let me show you the way." Alberto's hot, sweaty hand found mine near the wall. It took everything I had within me not to pull away.

"That would be perfecto. But first . . ." I used my pointer finger to tell him to come closer.

His face was only inches from mine. I squeezed his hand and interlaced my fingers with his. Though he was obviously drunk, I had to make sure the man didn't realize my true intentions. I swallowed back the bile rising in my throat and whispered in his ear, "I've never seen a man " —I moved his hand until it was behind me and pressed his palm against the wall, my hand holding his in place for several seconds— "who makes me feel quite like you do." I let my lips brush against his earlobe before I released his hand.

Alberto's breath quickened against my cheek. I froze as he pulled me into him and wrapped both his arms around my back. His leg brushed against mine as he lifted it to close all the space between us. I slid one of my hands behind me until I felt the lipstick mace in my pocket. There was no way his lips were going to touch mine.

Just as I had it in my grasp, the mace slipped from my fingers and bounced onto the marble floor. The man stepped back and looked down at the tube of lipstick as it rolled between his legs. He bent over to pick it up. *Oh no.* I prepped myself, ready to run. A rip sounded from behind the man. "*Mis pantalones!*" He jerked to a standing position with the lipstick in his hand. "I . . . they must have ordered me the wrong size. I wish I had—"

"Shhh." I silenced my "date" with a finger to his slimy lips. "Why don't you slip into something more comfortable and I'll meet you on the third floor in a few minutes?" I traced my finger down his chin and neck and played with the collar of his shirt. My other hand found his and I slowly slipped the lipstick from his sweaty grasp. "I should probably freshen up too."

"Yes, yes." His eyes went bright. "Let me get one of my men to escort you to the—"

I yanked on his lapels and pulled his face toward mine until our noses nearly touched. "The only man I want tonight is you." I pushed him away playfully and giggled.

"*Te veré en un minuto.*" Alberto toddled down the hallway with one hand covering his rear end.

I waited about thirty seconds, all the while listening to the roaring laughter of Millard and Daly in my earpiece, before I turned around and lifted the tapestry. A crack of light seeped through the edge of the door, which was now partially open. I found my mask and gloves on the floor near the tapestry and slipped them on before I used my fingers to pry open the door.

The tiny, dimly lit space was lined in gray metal. If I extended my arms, I could've touched both sides of the room at the same time. My fingers grazed the ceiling when I reached up. *What is this place?* I left the door behind me open a crack.

A red light glowed from a keypad directly in front of me. Another door took up almost the whole wall. "Daly, there's another door blocking the entrance with a number keypad."

"Can you take a picture of it?" he asked.

"Just a sec." I pulled out my phone from my back pocket and used the camera to take a picture. I was about to send it to him when Millard said, "Why would they use something so old-school?"

"I haven't even sent the picture to you yet."

"I have an autofeed on your phone," Millard said. "Anything that happens on your phone is linked to my computer."

"Oh." I thought about that for a minute. Did that mean he heard all of my calls and saw all of my texts to William and Casey? I made a mental note to get a separate phone for personal use.

"Millard's in tech-mode now," Daly said. "Just give him a minute. You won't need to guess any codes today."

"That's a relief," I replied. The buttons lit up on the keypad for a few seconds before the door beeped and opened. "I'm not even going to ask how he did that." Having a team was so much better than working on my own.

"I've got to cut communications while you're inside the room," Daly said. "They may have the place bugged for wireless receivers, and if it's protected like Millard thinks, our devices probably wouldn't work inside anyway."

"Okay."

"We'll be at the pickup point," Daly said, and I could tell he was trying to hide how worried he was.

"I'll be there."

"Be safe."

Light flickered and then burst into my eyes when I opened the door. I blinked until my eyes adjusted to the brightness. The private collection room had to be at least five hundred square feet, with a ceiling over ten feet tall. A bright white paint covered the walls, and the white marble floor shone with silver veins of stone.

The Van Gogh caught my eye in the far corner of the room. I sprinted across the floor and slid in my socks to a stop in front of it. The gold-gilded frame accented the gold brush strokes in the waves of the sea. I reached out but stopped myself before lifting the painting from the wall. It couldn't be that easy.

I peered around the back. Sure enough, it wasn't just a screw or nail holding the painting in place. A long wire attached to the back of the frame ran horizontally from one end to the other. One side of the wire hung on a small hook, while the other hung on a hook with a thin white housing around it.

I turned pages in my head of everything I'd read about museum security. When that came up empty, I scrolled through my memories until I found one that might help. Tanner was ten and I was almost nine, Dad had dropped us off at Mom's museum while he went to a meeting. Tanner, a little terror before he discovered football, had sprinted down a hallway in the museum. He hopped onto a bench and bet me that he could jump from there to the next bench about six feet away. He flew through the air and his shoulder hit the frame of a painting. Before the painting struck the floor, an alarm rang out.

Security guards came running, followed by Mom. She pulled a thin white disk from her pocket and placed it over where the painting had hung. Immediately the alarm went silent. When Tanner asked her how she had stopped the alarm, she had mentioned something about a magnet.

A magnet. Why didn't I think to bring one with me? So much for Daly planning ahead on this one. I tried to come up with another way to trick the alarm system. I pulled out my phone and silently thanked Millard that my fabric gloves could somehow still work on my phone's touch screen. *Wait, I don't need the software on my phone. It's the hardware I need.*

I banged the corner of my phone into the marble floor. Nothing happened. I tried again, with more force. Still nothing. I recalled Millard's words when he gave me the phone. "It can be submerged in water or run over by a car with little or no damage." *Darn!*

I needed the magnet in the speaker or microphone hardware. Maybe I could use my phone without breaking it open. Holding the phone as flat as possible, I reached behind the painting. I placed my other hand on the frame of the Van Gogh. One . . . two . . . three . . . I lifted the painting and held my phone over the sensor at the same time. The frame was so heavy I couldn't keep it upright with just one hand. It swung from the wall and hit into my hip and knee. I bit my lip to keep from screaming.

No alarm went off, so I gently set the painting on the floor. I had a problem. My phone might have prevented the alarm from sounding, but what should I do with the phone after I got the painting? Would the alarm sound if I moved my phone from the sensor?

In the interest of time, I decided to take a chance. Soon the mansion owner would realize I wasn't going to show up for our hot-tub rendezvous. Eventually, he would know I had tricked him, and I didn't want to be there to see what he might do.

I slowly pulled the phone away from the sensor and waited. Nothing happened. I let out a quiet sigh of relief. Now all I had to do was get out of the room and find the getaway car.

I tucked my trusty phone in my pocket next to my mace. With

both gloved hands holding the painting, I raced from the room. I closed that door and the next one before I stepped into the hallway. It seemed darker now, and I could barely make out the walls. I used the pictures in my mind to navigate.

After sliding into two walls, I pulled off the socks and tucked them inside my sleeve, along with the face mask. Three hallways later, I found the window where I'd tossed my dress. I pulled it open. Cold air rushed at my face as I peered down at a pile of green sparkles on a bush about ten feet below. I could jump it. I squeezed the painting through the window. Did I dare drop a piece of art worth hundreds of thousands of dollars?

An army of shuffling feet filled the hallway. I had to go now. I held the painting down as far as I could and let it fall into the bushes. I climbed onto the windowsill, found what looked like the softest landing spot, and hopped out the window.

"Ow," I said under my breath.

"Are you okay?" Daly asked in my earpiece.

"Just tell Millard this suit is not branch resistant." I checked my legs where the bush had ripped through and scraped my skin. "And it might be able to trick temperature sensors, but it doesn't keep you warm." I shivered in the winter air. *At least it's not Moscow.*

"Where are you?" Daly asked.

I searched through the darkness. "On the southeast side. There's a pathway through the backyard. It leads to a forested area behind the mansion."

"Can you make it out that way?"

"There's a tall concrete wall on the other side of the trees. Carrying the painting will be tricky, but I think I can make it." I inspected the painting. No permanent damage was visible, just some dirt and debris on the frame.

"Did you hear that?" someone whispered around the corner of the patio.

I didn't wait to see who the voice belonged to. I hoisted the painting over my head and sprinted down the pathway in my bare feet, leaving the dress and shoes behind. I made it to the wall in under a minute. It rose at least fifteen feet above me and enclosed the forested backyard, which appeared to extend at least a quarter mile in either direction. Streetlights on the other side of the wall gave me just enough visibility to realize there was no place to wedge in a hand or foot.

There has to be another way. I rested the painting against a wide tree beside me. The stormy sea of Van Gogh's scene taunted me, as if it accepted its fate by allowing the outside wind to joust its waves. Despite the tempest, the mast of the small ship remained strong and true like it was rooted to the floor of the sea.

Rooted. My eyes followed the tree trunk to the top. Branches interrupted the vertical line of the tree as it extended into the starry sky. I could climb a tree. Tanner and I had done it plenty of times when we were kids. The problem was the painting. How was I supposed to get up a tree with a large priceless painting in my hands?

"Dana?" Daly said.

"Sorry. I just got to the wall. Where are you?"

"We've run into a little problem. They're checking all the guests before they leave. I don't think they know about the painting. It's probably just—"

"Actually, I think they might," I cut him off. "Someone heard me at the back of the mansion. I can't be sure they saw me, but I've got to get out of here."

"It will probably be five or ten minutes until we can go."

Muffled voices traveled through the trees. "That might not be soon enough. I'll stay online, but I may be unable to talk for a bit."

"We'll find you. Just keep moving northwest in the direction of our hotel. If anything happens, meet there."

"Got it." A beam of light hit the wall in front of me. The security guards were near. I had to go.

I lifted the painting from the ground. Something on the back of the painting caught one of the tears in the leg of my bodysuit and ripped it farther up my thigh. I turned the painting over and saw the wire attached to the back of the frame. *Yes!* I slid the wire over my arm and positioned the painting onto my back like a backpack. The wire dug into my bodysuit at my shoulder and under my arms, but the painting stayed in place.

The first branch was about two feet above my head. I squatted and jumped and managed to wrap my gloved hands around the branch like a gymnast on the uneven bars. My muscles burned as I pulled myself up until my waist rested on the branch. Using the trunk as a stabilizer, I found my footing on the branch. I reached for the limb above me and continued to climb, careful to keep the painting clear of any branches behind me.

"There he is!" a guard bellowed from the base of the tree. He shone a flashlight through the branches. "There's a painting on his back. Wait, is that a girl?"

I wasn't about to let them find out. I hoisted my body onto a branch that protruded from the tree in the direction of the wall. Once I found my footing on top, I knew what I had to do. I hesitated for a moment until Tanner's words sprang to my mind. "... The goal was in my view and there was only one thing in my way. Sometimes it takes a leap of faith." Concentrating on the words, I channeled my inner gymnast and ran across the balance beam of the branch, then thrust myself from the tree.

As I flew through the air in a skin-tight bodysuit with a rare painting on my back, the only thing that flashed through my mind was the beautiful green dress I'd left back at the mansion.

13

—————

WHITE-HAIRED MAN

My feet hit the ground on the other side of the wall a second sooner than anticipated. I pitched forward and slammed into some shrubs, knocking the air out of my lungs. I turned my head to the side and wheezed in air, then coughed a few times.

I pulled myself to my knees just before a flash of headlights blinded me. Once the car passed, I blinked several times and made out a paved road about ten feet from my location. As I stood, the ache in my feet was overshadowed only by a sharp pain in my left wrist. I staggered from the trees and approached the street. Two more headlights burst out of the darkness, but this time the car slowed.

"Do you see me? I'm right here, Daly." I waved my uninjured hand. The car pulled along the curb and stopped a few feet from me. "I made it. I got the painting. Everything is—"

"Dana, we are still about two minutes from your location," Daly said in my ear.

"You mean, you're not . . ." All four car doors opened at the same time and several men stepped out of the vehicle. The headlights of the car backlit their large frames.

I turned to run.

A tall man stepped in my path. "I wouldn't do that if I were you," he said in Russian. In the beam of a headlight, his thick white hair looked like a halo around his shadowed features.

Another car sped from the other direction and came to a screeching halt only inches from my legs. Four more men filled in any gaps between the cars, boxing me in on all sides. Two guys gripped my shoulders, while another ripped the earrings from my ears, along with the earpiece attachment. "No!" I yelled just before the items were tossed onto the road and smashed under the heel of a boot.

"Search her for more bugs and tracers," ordered the white-haired man, obviously the group's leader. Strong hands patted me down.

The leader pointed to the frame on my back. "Thank you for retrieving my painting. Van Gogh holds a special place in my heart."

Someone lifted the painting off me. Other hands found my phone and mace in the pocket at my lower back. "Let me go." I elbowed the man behind me. He slammed his knee into my kidneys and I doubled over in agony. Two guys flanked me on either side and grabbed my arms. I wriggled and turned until one of them kicked me behind the knee, sending a shooting pain down my leg.

"He said you were feisty, but this—this is most enjoyable." The leader chuckled.

"What are you talking about? Who are you?" I struggled against the men holding me in place.

The leader pulled out a small flashlight, flicked it on, and illuminated his face. I searched through my memories. I had never seen the man before, but those silver eyes—there was something about those eyes. My stomach seized and my mind went gray, like a smoky haze diffused through my thoughts, and the only thing keeping me upright were the strong hands gripping my arms. The eyes stared through the fog in my mind until dizziness overtook me and vomit erupted from my mouth onto the pavement. Several more heaves wracked my frame until there was nothing more inside me.

"It's nice to finally meet the great Dana Laxer," the leader said, and I noticed he had stepped back. "Though from what Elijah told me about you, I would have expected someone with a stronger stomach." He motioned at one of the men to his left. "Clean her up. And, you two—" he spoke to my guards "—bring her over here."

They dragged me to the back of the first car. Another man opened the trunk and retrieved a white cloth. He brought it to my face, but I turned my head to the side. The leader stalked over and seized my chin in black-gloved fingers. He took the cloth with his other hand and wiped at my forehead and around my mouth. When he finished, I noticed the cloth was streaked with something dark. *I must've cut my head open.*

"Elijah told me so much about you, but he never mentioned what a beauty you are. Almost flawless, though I would say" —the leader forcefully lifted my chin— "you're a little young for my taste."

I ripped my face from his grasp. "What do you know about me?"

"Very little actually, but clearly you appreciate art and its value almost as much as I do." He stepped to the side and lifted the painting from another man's arms. "This one is really such a priceless treasure." He removed a glove and fingered the paint strokes.

I gasped, knowing that if he really appreciated art, he wouldn't let his hand oils touch the Van Gogh. "What would an animal like you know of art?" I blurted. If there had been anything left in my stomach, I would have forced it out in his face.

"You speak like I am the villain here. Yet it appears you don't even know who I am."

"Who are you?" I let the bitter taste in my mouth chafe my words.

He handed the painting back to the man, replaced his glove, and rubbed his hands together. "You can call me Ivan, but who I am isn't quite as important as what I represent."

"And what's that?"

"*Vlast' i svoboda.*" He buttoned a long coat over his dark suit.

I shook my head. What did freedom and world power have to do with this painting?

"Ah, yes, I forgot. You Americans have another name for us. *Krasnykh glaz.* How do you say—Red Eye? I would have never given such a name to my legacy."

I swallowed. "Your legacy? But I thought Elijah—"

"Yes, yes. Elijah. There is so much you need to learn, my dear."

My mind went a million directions at once. I stared up at Ivan—a stranger, except for those knifelike eyes and the fact he was somehow connected to Elijah.

A van pulled up next to the cars, its headlights brightening the space around us. Ivan nodded to the man on my right. As he faced the lights, Ivan's gaze captured me again. His eyes were so bloodshot that the whites couldn't be called white at all. They were red.

Memories of the Moscow mission and the burning warehouse flashed through my mind. I was staring up at the leader of Red Eye. He had me in the perfect place to take care of me, like Elijah had tried to do months before. The memory was so vivid this time that for a second, I felt like I was falling again.

Something hard hit the back of my head. The memories stopped.

I sat in a metal chair, unable to see. I didn't know if the room was dark or if it was the cloth tied over my pounding head. My injured wrist throbbed under the zip ties that bound my hands behind me. I twisted my body to alleviate the pain, but I could barely move. My legs had been crossed and lashed together at the ankles.

Footsteps sounded in front of me and stopped at my chair. The cloth was yanked off my head, and I blinked away the bright light.

"Good morning, Dana." Ivan tossed the cloth onto a desk in the corner of the room. "I hope you had a nice rest. Sorry about the restraints. We never know how our guests will respond to questioning." He smoothed a piece of his white hair. Seeing his face in good light, I decided he couldn't be older than about forty-five.

The room's pale blue walls and shiny linoleum floor reminded me of a hospital. The only thing missing was the smell of antiseptic. My stomach churned and growled.

"I apologize for not offering you breakfast," Ivan said. "After last night, we were leery about letting you eat anything."

I've only been here one night. Somehow that was reassuring.

"I notice we aren't as talkative this morning. Don't worry, I'm sure you will have a lot to say once our expert interrogator arrives." Ivan paced from one side of the room to the other. One stride fell short of the other, as if he had an old leg injury. "No harm will come to you as long as you cooperate."

"Cooperate?" My voice didn't sound like my own.

"I knew that would get you talking. Now I should warn you, Galina knows how to get to the truth."

"What do you want from me? You already got your precious painting." Suddenly I realized what losing the Van Gogh to Red Eye meant. Any leverage with Elijah was gone. I had blown my only hope for Tanner. Hot fury raced through my body.

"Thank you, by the way. Elijah was right about your talent." Ivan opened the door and motioned for someone to enter. "Don't mind the scowl. Galina's actually very pleasant once you get to know her."

The doorway revealed a short woman with a heavyset frame. She pushed a metal cart into the room and parked it beside me, then started pulling at wires attached to the computer on top. She wore a white lab coat, and her bobbed black hair was kept off her face by metal clips. She placed a pressure cuff around my upper arm and wrapped a wire around my chest. By the time she finished, at least five different wires ran from my body to the computer.

Just remember what The Manual said, and the interrogation test with Daly. Worry flitted inside me. Daly hadn't made me as nervous as Galina did, and her wires would reveal much more than a pulse or facial expressions. She could read my skin temperature, blood pressure, muscle tension, and heartbeat. Biting my tongue and picturing the ocean or William might not save me this time.

I turned to Ivan. "Is this really necessary? I will tell you what you want to know."

"My dear, you misunderstand how things work around here. Even our most trusted supporters are kept—how shall I say?—honest. I thought Elijah would have shared that with you. No matter." Ivan nodded to Galina. "Let's begin."

"State your name," the woman said in a voice like a lullaby, not at all what I expected from her scowling face.

Think of something pleasant, something calming. The first memory that came to mind was of Daly. We stood on the basement stairs of Marston Hall after my initial visit to The Company. He said, "You can have a normal life, graduate from Brown, have a career and a family. If you join us, things will become more complicated. You'll have to keep this, what we do, from everyone around you, even the people you care about. Yes, there will be intrigue and excitement, but you need to understand that in committing to this cause, the good may not outweigh the dangers placed in your path."

My reaction to the memory wasn't the same as when it actually occurred. Daly's words were less important than the expression of compassion behind them. For the first time since the accident, I felt someone was there to protect me. I could fight. I could defend myself. I could rescue paintings and break secret codes. I really did want that life. It was a part of who I was. I hadn't admitted it until now, but I also wanted someone to rely on. Daly had always been there, right from the beginning. Somehow, somewhere, I knew he was still looking out for me. And that gave me hope.

"Dana Laxer," I said so calmly I would have believed it myself.

"How old are you?" Galina asked.

Dancing with Daly on the dance floor. "Twenty-one," I said. I figured I might as well lie about my age. I'd always felt older anyway.

"What color is your hair?"

I pushed my injured wrist against my other bound one behind my back. The pain bit hard. "Blond."

"Are your eyes" —she squinted at my face— "gray?"

"Yes." The agony at my wrist made my eyes water. I blinked a few times.

Galina nodded to Ivan, who was leaning against the door. He strode forward. "Now we are ready." He cracked one knuckle at a time on his hand. "Did you steal the Van Gogh painting?"

I continued to press on my wrist. "Yes, though 'steal' might be the wrong word. I would say I retrieved it, since in essence it had already been stolen."

"Please keep your answers brief," Galina said. The permanent grimace on her face remained.

"Is this the first time you have stolen a painting?"

"Yes," I said. Ivan looked toward Galina, who gave a quick nod.

"So you've never stolen anything from a museum or bank?"

"No." *What is he getting at? Do I look like a thief? Okay, so maybe I am wearing a black bodysuit.*

"Did you come to Barcelona with anyone else?"

"No." Ocean waves washed over my toes. Galina nodded again. I had no idea if Red Eye knew anything about The Company, but they wouldn't find out about it from me. Since Ivan continued to call me Dana, maybe my cover wasn't compromised just yet.

"Do you love your family, Dana?"

My head shot up. "What does that have to do with anything?" I asked before I had a chance to calm myself.

"Do you know how long it would take me to find out more about you and, say, who your family is?" Ivan asked.

"Why do you care?" I narrowed my eyes at him. That was definitely not in The Manual. *Stay calm.* I took a deep breath and floated away on an inner tube down the Wenatchee River with Tanner.

"It would take me less than a day. No matter. I now know the importance of your family in your life. I just needed to make sure you would do what I ask."

"You already got the painting. Why would I do anything more for you?"

"In America, you have a little city called Las Vegas. I hear it is the place to go to play cards. But you know the problem with that city?" Ivan adjusted the cuffs of his crisp white shirt. "They make you trade in your cash for these little plastic coins—chips, you call them. Now I could hold these plastic chips in front of you, but their value wouldn't seem as great. People often waste away their money in your city of lights because the chips make it seem to be a game, as if they are only losing pieces of plastic." Ivan bent over and placed his hands on my knees, his face close to mine. I tensed my muscles but didn't flinch. "You seem like a smart girl. Do you understand the value of the bargaining chip? Or do I need to do my research and hold the real money in front of you?"

My hands itched to get this man in a chokehold. I could have totally taken him. "I'm listening," I said.

"Good." He let go of my knees and stood tall again. "Now, where were we? Ah, yes. I got to see firsthand your retrieval of the painting." He lifted a tablet computer from the top of Galina's cart and typed on the screen. "How you managed to get good ol' Valdez to meet you in the hallway was genius." Ivan held the screen up to my face. A bird's-eye view of my work in the hallway played on the screen in infrared. "And the acting skills. What talent. It was perfection. I don't know where Elijah found you, but you've passed the test."

"Test?"

"Yes. You don't think I would waste my precious time on a Van Gogh worth a mere few hundred thousand dollars, do you? Now that I know your skills are sufficient, I can give you the real job."

"What job?"

"I want the most valuable Van Gogh, and you're going to steal it for me."

I couldn't help but laugh. All the readings on Galina's machine had to be going crazy. "*Dr. Gachet*? You seriously think you are going to find it?"

"*Portrait of Dr. Gachet* was sold for $82.5 million in 1990," Ivan reported. "Can you imagine how much it would be worth today?"

"That painting is gone." An article I'd read years ago flashed into my mind. "It hasn't been seen in years. Ryoei Saito was the owner, and he died over ten years ago. If you have such an amazing team that can track people, why don't you just find the painting yourself."

"Oh, I've found the painting. It took me some time to be sure, but I know exactly where it is."

"Then go get it."

"Therein lies the problem, Dana. You see, when Saito died in 1996, the painting found its way into the hands of another private collector. Later, he sold it to another collector, and then he sold it, and so on, each collector selling the painting for more than the next. Finally the last owner, a Frenchman, bequeathed the painting on his deathbed to his favorite museum. The Louvre."

I burst out laughing harder than before. "You're telling me *Dr. Gatchet* is at the Louvre? Musée du Louvre? One of the largest museums in the world?"

"Yes." Ivan crossed his arms over his chest.

"You realize the place has higher security measures than any other museum on the planet?"

A broad smile lit up Ivan's beady, unnatural eyes. "That's why we need you."

"Even if I wanted to, I couldn't break into the Louvre."

"I think you are underestimating yourself, Dana." He scrolled through his tablet, probably watching every video he had on me during my "test," as he called it.

I did the same thing in my mind. *Wait, does he have the entire mission on video?* My heart picked up in my chest. Daly at the bar. Daly on the dance floor. Millard with his wine glasses. I had told Ivan I worked alone. I had fooled the lie detector, but if he watched anything from the ballroom, he would see my interaction with Daly. Would he believe Daly was just a stranger I made part of my plan to get into the hallway, or would Ivan figure out I had a team after all? I couldn't take that chance.

"Fine, I'll do it." I bit my lip. "I'll find the painting." Ivan looked over at Galina, who nodded. It wouldn't have mattered, since I didn't need to pretend to tell the truth on this one. I had to keep Ivan from looking too closely at any video of the mission. I believed his threats to find the people I cared about and hurt them. I also knew he would never let me go unless I promised to do what he wanted.

"Great, then it's settled," Ivan said.

"Wait, if it's at the Louvre, shouldn't there be something in the press about the lost painting and its recovery? I haven't heard anything about it."

"It's not yet on display. As far as my sources can tell, it's still with the curators, who must be trying to remove over a hundred years of grime from the frame and any damage caused by its previous owners. There has been talk of a special unveiling next month, but no information is available on what that will entail. Of course, we already know."

"You realize that even if you got the painting, you wouldn't be able to sell it, don't you? No one in their right mind would even consider buying it—it's too well known."

"Oh, how naïve you little Americans are. All those recent television dramas. A priceless painting doesn't have to be sold for money to have great value."

I wracked my brain, trying to figure out what Ivan was getting at. The words from an article on the famous Martin Cahill flashed through my mind. Cahill was an Irish mobster who stole eighteen paintings in the 1980s, including a Vermeer, a Goya, and a Gabriel Metsu. Unable to sell the paintings, he used them in an underground bartering system as part of a drug ring. Some of the paintings were used as collateral for a loan Cahill took out from a shady diamond dealer. The dealer eventually sold the paintings to an undercover Scotland Yard agent, but Cahill got away with the money. If Ivan was going to use the Van Gogh as collateral, maybe he was smarter than I thought. Or hopefully he'd be stupid and get caught anyway.

"When do I start?" I asked. The sooner I got out of this interrogation room the better.

"Any good heist requires weeks or months of study and planning before the actual job is carried out. During that time, I expect you to remember what could be at stake. Your plan must not fail." Ivan reached down to his black boots and pulled a knife from its sheath. The black blade shone like obsidian.

I cringed and held my breath as he moved toward me and then around to the back of my chair. He leaned forward with the blade in his hand until the stubble on his face scratched the back of my neck. The blade snapped the zip tie at my wrists. "You have three weeks. Then I come for you."

14

BLIND

"I don't understand," Daly said as he used a washcloth to remove the blood from my forehead. "Ivan just let you go?"

"He left me alone in that basement room. When I realized no one was returning, I broke off the door handle."

"You didn't see anyone?" Daly rinsed the washcloth in the hotel sink. Rust-colored liquid poured down the white ceramic bowl.

"It was as if they'd never been there. Everything, even Galina's cart, was missing." I scooted back on the bathroom counter and slouched against the mirror. "Ow!" I sat up straight again, touching the tender spot on my skull where I'd been hit.

Daly gently grasped my head and turned it to the side. "There's a lot of dried blood in your hair. What did you do?"

"Oh, it happened right after they took the Van Gogh, before I was interrogated."

Daly let out a sigh. "I should have been there. Well, I guess we'll have to put your head in the sink." He had me bend my knees and lie back until my neck rested on a towel on the edge of the sink.

"The painting was my task, not yours." I said. "And I made it out okay, didn't I?"

He turned on the water and guided my head under the faucet. I closed my eyes and let the warm water wash away the last twenty-four hours.

"I can't believe Red Eye let you go. From what I understand, they either convert you to their cause or make you disappear." Daly turned off the faucet and used a towel to pat my hair dry around my face. He supported my neck with his hand and helped me sit up.

"Maybe they had to get out fast." I stared at the rips in my black suit. I'd told Daly almost everything that happened after I jumped the wall at the mansion, including how Ivan tried to find out if I was working for someone. I just hadn't mentioned that Ivan wanted me to break into the Louvre and steal the painting he was really after. I only had three weeks or he would find a way to get to my family or other people I cared about. *Ivan might not know my real name yet, but Elijah does, and if Ivan finds a way to communicate with him, everyone I love will be at risk.* No, I couldn't involve Millard, Daly, Golkov, or anyone else in this mission.

"Here's your stuff, Alex." Millard came into the bathroom with my small suitcase.

"Thank you. I think it's about time I got out of this suit and into something more comfortable."

Millard's face flushed and he rushed from the bathroom, hitting his shoulder on the door jamb on his way out.

"What did I say?" I turned to Daly, who had one thick eyebrow raised. I flashed back to my last words and blushed. "Oh."

Daly laughed and lifted me from the counter to the floor. "Any other way I can be of assistance this afternoon, my lady?" His hands lingered on my waist before he released me.

"I . . . um . . . can . . . you . . ."

"Yes?"

I held up my wrist, but he stared at me blankly.

"The zipper on my back?"

"Oh, yes." Now he was blushing. "Uh, let me see if I can find a female staff member to help you." He rushed from the room almost as quickly as Millard had.

"He brushed your hair?" Casey fell back onto my pillow. "Wait, I thought you only sprained your left wrist."

"I did." I spun my desk chair in a circle while holding up my pencil in my right hand, then stopped at the desk and began writing Chinese characters on my paper.

"Then I don't understand why you couldn't do it yourself." Casey adjusted the bottom of her geometric-print leggings. "Wait, you wanted him to brush your hair, didn't you?"

"No, I didn't. He's like an older brother to me. I just couldn't put my hair in a ponytail and he offered. I wasn't going to turn him down."

"Uh-huh." She rolled to her side. "So how does William feel about you working with Professor Golkov's assistant? Does he even know he's a he?"

"He has met Daly." I erased a Chinese character and started over again.

"Hmm. So how can you fly all the way to Spain and spend a few days in the same hotel room with another guy—"

"Same suite. We had separate rooms and there was another guy there too."

Casey shot up from the bed. "There were two guys?" She stared at me in disbelief.

"We are colleagues, Case. That's it."

"Wow, how many people does Professor Golkov have working for him? I thought he just taught college Russian."

I nearly choked on my own saliva. "I don't know," I said truthfully. *Twenty-five or thirty, maybe more . . .*

She sighed dramatically and fell back onto my bed. "You have such an exotic life."

"Yeah, yeah. Now let me get back to my dreadfully non-exciting homework." I scratched out a few more words and checked them against the images in my head. They weren't half bad.

"Hey, this James Daly guy sounds kind of dreamy," Casey said all of a sudden. "Any chance you could set us up?"

"Um . . ." Something stirred inside me at the idea. "Wait, don't you have a boyfriend?"

She rolled off my bed. "Don't you?" She put her hands on her hips. "I'm just trying to keep up with my roommate." Her face remained serious for a moment before she broke into a grin. "You really sprained your wrist pretending to be a gymnast?"

I returned her grin. "Next time I'll work on my dismount."

"You sure you can run?" William asked. We had met on the university's indoor track that morning because the roads were icy.

"It's my wrist, not my foot. Besides, the swelling has gone down." I looked at the splint on my wrist. "It only hurts now if I bend it."

"I don't know what I'm going to do with you. It's a good thing you want to teach languages instead of going into acrobatics or race-car driving. Then we'd really be in trouble."

I giggled. "Hey, I think I'd make an excellent tightrope walker."

"Alex, with your luck and affinity to gravity, I'd be worried about you making it up the ladder."

"I'll try not to take offense to that." *Too bad I can't tell him that my real job does include a little acrobatics every now and again.*

"So how was your weekend, besides tumbling over a concrete barrier and hurting your wrist and head?"

I flashed to the events of the weekend. "Honestly, it started off great. I got to see some great works of art, wear an amazing dress, and dance."

"You danced?" William's voice sounded strained.

"It was only one dance."

"With a guy?"

"He was just a colleague." I wiped at some sweat running down my forehead.

"Oh."

We needed a change of subject. "Was your ceremony as bad as you thought it would be?"

"Worse. College students I can handle. Professors and alumni, not so much. They made me stand up in front of over a hundred people and explain what I would be doing for the Fulbright grant in Guadalajara."

"Oh." Now I was the one that didn't know how to respond. All I could think about was how William was really going to Mexico for eight months.

We lapped a few times around the track in silence. I wanted to tell him about the weekend, about finding the painting, the painting that gave me a chance to help my brother—a brother he didn't even know was still alive. I wanted to tell William how that hope was crushed when Red Eye took the painting away from me. I wanted to tell William that I was scared for him, Tanner, my father, Daly, and Golkov. I wanted to tell someone about the storm brewing inside me, threatening to burst. But I couldn't.

And that wasn't all. I felt guilty because Casey had been partly correct. Replaying scenes from the weekend, I realized I didn't think of Daly as a brother or even just a friend. Something had changed. It scared me—made me feel out of control. Seeing William that morning was so comfortable and seemed so right. He understood me. He treated me like I wanted to be treated. But Daly had been right. William didn't know everything about me.

"Penny for your thoughts?" William said beside me.

I pushed some loose hair off my face. "Do you really think you can know someone without knowing everything about them?"

"What do you mean?" He slowed a bit and I fell back with him.

"I just mean, do you think . . . oh, I don't know what I mean." I was talking about myself, and my mom, and Tanner. Most of all, I was talking about keeping a dark secret from everyone, even The Company. I wasn't going to tell anyone what Ivan had asked me to do.

I picked up my pace. If I pushed my body, my mind would have a blank screen—if for just a moment. Looping around the track a few more times, I thought I might lose William, but he kept in stride with me. Soon it became like a game—I would speed up for about a hundred yards and then he would push out in front of me and I would chase him for a hundred yards.

After about two miles of sprinting like that, I came off the track by the drinking fountain to catch my breath. Sweat poured from my face and I wiped it on my sleeve. My wrist throbbed inside the splint.

"I'm so glad" —William took a breath— "you stopped there." He pulled up the bottom of his shirt to wipe at his face. His nicely toned abs shone in sweat. "I was ready to stop the lap before. Don't you ever get tired?"

"Don't you ever slow down? I almost didn't catch you on that last straight stretch."

"I should probably hit the showers. I've got my 202 class at eight. You want to meet after your tutoring session for lunch?"

"Maybe. I'll text you from Golkov's office."

"Okay." William kissed my cheek, oblivious to the sweat on both of us. He looked at me seriously. "You know you can tell me anything, right?"

"I know."

My question wasn't whether I could tell him. The question was whether I *should* tell him.

"See you soon." He squeezed my good hand and ran to the locker room.

For a minute, I debated on whether to run home and shower first or just head straight to The Company. I was supposed to meet with Sensei Itosu before my nine o'clock class. Deciding I'd probably get sweaty there anyway, I threw on my running jacket and ran across campus to Marston Hall. I paused before rounding the corner to the back entrance. I hadn't come up with a good story yet. Millard and Daly knew what happened over the weekend, but no one else at The Company did. I looked down at my wrist. Casey and William might believe my clumsiness got the best of me again, but Golkov and Itosu knew better. I wasn't clumsy. In fact, over the past month, I had proven to myself and The Company how light I was on my feet.

I undid the Velcro straps of the splint and pulled it off. I bent my wrist about an inch in either direction before the pain was too much. I could do this. Hopefully Itosu would only ask me to do meditation exercises. I tossed the splint in a nearby garbage can before I entered the building through the private entrance out back.

Sensei Itosu was sparring with Daly when I reached the gym. I sat on a bench and stretched while I watched the entertaining scene. Daly was nearly a foot taller than Itosu, yet from what I'd seen so far, the sensei had the advantage. Whenever Daly tried to kick him, he ducked or stepped to the side at amazing speed. The force of Daly's last attempt at kicking Itosu threw Daly off balance. While he steadied himself, Itosu managed to get a hit in right at Daly's calf. Daly fell to the padded floor. I thought he might be angry, but he started laughing. "One of these days, old man, I'm going to see that coming." He rose to his feet. "I don't know how you get me there every time."

"If you continue to think as you have always thought, you continue to get what you have always got." Itosu straightened his karate uniform.

"Japanese proverb?" Daly said.

"You realize I'm from New York," Itosu replied.

"Yes, yes. I know the whole story about leaving Japan when you were a kid to come here with your parents."

"Then you must also know that my knowledge of Japanese proverbs is about as good as your knowledge of gardening."

"Hey, how do you know I don't have a garden at my apartment?" Daly joked.

"I've been there. He doesn't," I said, joining the two of them near the middle of the gym floor.

"You're not supposed to tell him that. Did you just arrive?" He eyed my wrist with no splint and shook his head. I had told him I would take a break for a few days and he said he would cover for me. But I didn't want to take a break. That would mean my mind wouldn't be occupied and then I would have to think about stuff I didn't want to think about.

"No, I've been watching you guys spar," I said. "Actually, I've been watching the sensei here totally kick your rear end."

Daly chuckled and shook his head.

"And now it is time for Alexandra's lesson." Itosu straightened and bowed to Daly, who returned the gesture.

I met my handler's gaze. "I did want to talk to you, Daly. When do you think I'll get a new phone?"

"Millard's working on it. Probably by tomorrow. Apparently he's got a few more tricks up his sleeve."

"I'll bet he does." I laughed a little and Daly smiled at me. Itosu cleared his throat.

"Sensei calls. See you later."

"I'll be in my office for a bit if you want to stop by when you're done." Daly touched my shoulder and headed up the stairs.

My mind flashed to Barcelona with his hand on my back as he guided me across the dance floor. The violin music in the memory should have slowed my heartbeat, but instead I found my pulse had picked up. I shook the images from my head and turned to Itosu. "So what do we have planned for today? Meditation? Some strengthening exercises?"

"I thought we'd work on kicks, since your leg is healed."

"Great," I said a little too enthusiastically. "My legs are already warmed up." *But my wrist is killing me.*

"Now close your eyes."

"Why?"

"It is part of the exercise. Just close your eyes. I have a blindfold, if that makes it easier."

I can't peek with a blindfold. "Okay."

"Now I want you to take a ready stance."

I put one foot in front of the other, then raised my hands and turned my good wrist out, leaving the injured one tucked near my body. I hoped Itosu didn't notice. I peeked at him with one eye.

"Clearly that isn't going to work," the sensei said. Moments later, he stood behind me, tying a long black piece of fabric over my eyes.

"Now we can start," he declared, and I readied myself again.

"Alexandra, I want you to picture where I am." His voice traveled from my left to right side and around my back. "Try to estimate how far away I am by the sound of my voice. Can you tell?"

I pointed to a spot near my left side and asked, "Why are you on your knees?"

"Good, Alexandra, good!" He moved again, this time directly in front of me. I waited for him to speak. A rush of air came at my face and I involuntarily threw up a hand. Something hard met with my good hand and I pushed it away. Itosu's ankle. Apparently I wasn't the only one using kicks that day.

"Now this time when you are sensing my location, I want you to find me and do a forward kick toward my center."

"With the blindfold on?"

"Yes. That is the lesson today, to gain more spatial awareness. Every fight will not be in a well-lit gym or outside in the bright sun. You need to be able to do it blind."

I scratched at the blindfold over my eyes and listened. I tuned out the treadmills in the background and a few other people sparring on the other side of the gym. My ears were only in tune with Itosu. I couldn't see his arm movements, but I felt each step he took on the mat and listened for any sound near me. When I was sure he was standing directly in front of me, I lifted my leg and kicked. My foot only met with air and I almost lost my footing. I pulled down the blindfold. Itosu stood about ten feet away from me.

We tried it a few more times until I could sense him within a few feet. "Okay, this last time I still want you blind and I want you to continue to fight me after the initial kick," the sensei said. "Can you do that?"

"Sure." My body tensed. I wasn't ready to do a pushup with my left hand, let alone fight an opponent.

Itosu moved around me several times before he stopped. I had a funny image in my head of him leaping and crouching in circles around me. I blocked his first kick with one of my own. Then he was behind me. I spun around to block him, but not before his hand met my shoulder. He didn't stop. I felt the air change again, this time on my left side. I threw up my arm to make the block, forgetting about my wrist. It hit his forearm and I yelped in pain.

I waited for the next kick or punch. It never came, so I pulled off the blindfold. Itosu stood directly in front of me, his eyes on the wrist I had cradled against my body. He reached for my forearm. "What is wrong with your hand?"

"Oh, nothing." I chewed on my tongue. I was caught.

He turned my arm over. The movement pulled on the strained muscles again. I sucked in a quick breath at the pain. "Alexandra, this isn't nothing." Itosu started to bend my wrist back and I pulled it away. He found my arm and pressed lightly at the radius bone right where my hand attached to my wrist. I winced and yanked my arm back again.

The disapproving look in his eyes reached into me. I knew I could easily make something up about how I injured my wrist, but I was tired of lying. The air in the gymnasium seemed to press in on me. I had to get as far from here as possible.

"No, it's fine. Really." I tried to relax my arm against my side. "I've got to get ready for class, anyway." I bowed to Itosu and bounded from the gym, leaving my jacket behind. My wrist throbbed as I ran up the stairs. The pounding in my chest increased until I got to my dorm room and fell onto my green fur blanket on my bed. I buried my head in my pillow.

What is wrong with me? Lately I seemed to be running from everything but getting nowhere. I should have been getting ready for class, studying for an upcoming test, or doing the overflowing pile of laundry in the corner of the room. I was supposed to be planning how I would get the Van Gogh painting in the Louvre, but all I could picture in my head was another Van Gogh—the one I desperately needed, the one on which I had rested all my hope. The one that could bring my brother back.

Daly had promised to confront Elijah again before Golkov moved him, but said he wouldn't mention the painting. Deep down I knew it wouldn't matter. Elijah had insisted he would only work with me and would only help my brother if I brought the painting. Somehow I had to get to Elijah again. There had to be something else he would accept in exchange for helping Tanner.

"Alex?"

I lifted my head. Casey sat on her bed with sheets of white paper spread out in a grid on her bedspread.

"What are you doing here?" I asked. "I thought you had Stats at nine."

"I thought you had Russian at nine." The clock on the wall showed we had only ten minutes before our classes started. Neither of us moved.

"I'm skipping." Casey moved her finger up and down the columns and rows of papers. She chose one, held it up for a second, and then crumpled it up and tossed it across the room. It landed a few inches from the garbage can, next to about fifteen or twenty other wads of paper.

"What's going on?" I asked.

She chewed on a blue-painted fingernail. "I had this idea and I've been trying to work it out on my own, but I'm thinking I will need a team again to pull this one off."

"A team?" For some reason, the word shifted my mood and I hopped from my bed. "Are you planning another—"

"Prank, yes. But this is more than a hot-pink arm on a statue, or tricking a professor into thinking his class has been moved to the cadaver room. This one will be . . . epic." Casey threw out her arms. A rush of air caused a few papers to fly off the bed onto the floor.

"So who's involved this time?" I asked.

"Well, see, that's the thing. This one is big enough that I wouldn't want any of the girls on the floor joining in, in case it goes south."

I slid from my bed and picked up the papers. Each one had a geometric figure on it—a rectangle, a square, an L-shape, a T-shape, and one that looked like a Z or an S made of small cubes. I walked over and handed them to her. She set them in the empty spots on the bed and rearranged them a few times. The changing movements jogged a memory of a favorite game to my mind, but I wasn't sure how Tetris had anything to do with a prank.

"I think I've got the logistics figured out. I bribed a bunch of guys at the Tockwotton Studio to build me wooden frames, and I borrowed a bunch of Christmas lights from facilities management."

"Borrowed?"

"I'll return everything later. Maybe." Casey smiled wickedly.

I put my good hand on my hip. "Uh-huh."

"Don't worry, I'll just buy new ones if there's any damage." She played with one of her large hoop earrings, which matched the blue polish on her fingernails.

"Why do you need Christmas lights? Christmas was a month ago."

"You'll see. I can't give you all the details now—that would ruin all the fun. I've got to work out a few kinks." She stopped shuffling the papers around and stacked them in a neat pile.

"How can I help?" I asked.

"You sure you want to be involved? This one could be grounds for suspension if we get caught."

"Are you kidding me?" *This is exactly what I need right now—a distraction.* "I'm totally in."

"I don't want to involve too many people, but I'm going to need someone who's pretty techno-savvy." She paused. "Hey, what about that guy who bedazzled your phone?"

I laughed and nodded. "Yeah, I think I can convince him to help out." An idea started rolling around in my mind. *Casey and Millard . . . hmm.* "I might have to promise him something in return for his help."

"At this point, I'll do anything to make this happen." She sprang from the bed and opened one of our shared closets.

"What happened to all our shoes?" I peered inside to find the closet brimming with bags and boxes of cords, Christmas lights, and what looked like circuit boards. Casey was definitely going to need Millard.

"Sorry, I kind of rearranged things over the weekend," she said. "Our shoes are under my bed now. All the accessories are at the bottom of the other closet."

"Forgiven." I sat on my bed again, not in the mood to attend my

Russian class or be tutored by the professor. "So how do I fit into the plan?"

"Well, you know how you're pretty fast on your feet?"

"Yes." This was getting stranger by the minute.

She gave me a sly grin that showed a dimple on one of her cheeks. "How do you feel about breaking and entering?"

15

———

LOATHSOME

You could just use the handle. I raised my hand to the apartment door and knocked three times. I would have called except I still didn't have my new phone or Millard's number, and I wasn't about to call Daly even though my mind had recorded his number long ago. I wasn't sure either of them had left The Company yet, and since I was avoiding headquarters, Golkov, and Itosu, this was the only way to communicate.

Casey and I had spent the rest of the day getting more Christmas lights and wood for Tockwotton Studio. She still hadn't told me where or when this prank would take place, and I didn't care as long as it helped me ignore the rest of the world. I texted an apology to William from Casey's phone, saying I wasn't feeling well, which was true. Eventually I would have to face it all again, but now all that mattered was enlisting Millard to Casey's cause and maybe getting my new phone. I really hoped Daly was still at The Company.

My hope vanished when he answered his door. "I knew you couldn't stay away forever. I'll have you know that Golkov thinks you are spending the day with your father." Daly leaned against the door-frame in a pair of jeans, and a red T-shirt that hugged his biceps. "Sensei ignored me when I tried to give him a story about your wrist and why you ran off from your session this morning. You seem to be doing a lot of that lately."

"Doing what?" I shoved my hand in the pocket of my jacket.

"Running away. Why did you do that?"

"I just . . . I needed some time to recoup from everything."

"Okay." He didn't sound convinced.

"So is Millard here?" I looked over his shoulder.

"Millard?"

"Yeah, is he home? I need to ask him something."

Daly rubbed the back of his neck. "Um, no. He ran out to get some late dinner. Do you want to come in?"

"Okay, fine. But I'm really here to see Millard."

I ignored the hurt look in Daly's eyes. He pushed the door open farther and let me in. I sat on one of the gray leather couches, and he took a seat at the other.

"So . . . what do you need to see Millard about?"

"It's a secret."

"A secret?" Daly leaned forward and rested his elbows on his knees. "That sounds . . . secretive."

"Exactly." I crossed my legs and tapped the toe of my shoe on the mirrored coffee table.

"And you're not going to tell me about it? If this has something to do with Elijah, I think you'd better come clean. Millard told me you asked for your own bug detector with audio jammer like mine. I'm not letting you near Elijah again."

"Letting me? Are you some kind of boss over me now?" I stared past Daly to the dark sky. The waning moon's light spilled over the edge of the balcony outside and through the glass doors directly behind him, illuminating the edges of his dark hair.

"Alexandra, no. I'm just . . . we'll figure this out. There has to be another way to help Tanner."

Without the Van Gogh in tow, I was afraid to talk to Elijah and wasn't sure what to say. The memory of my mom and her trust in him was real. Maybe Elijah would understand and still be willing to help.

I took a deep breath. "How much longer do you think Millard will be?" I looked to the front door. "You know what? I can just come back later." I stood. Thinking about Tanner brought memories into focus I couldn't face right then, not when I had schematics of the Louvre running through my mind.

"Alexandra, wait." Daly caught my arm. His touch melted some of my willpower. "We'll figure something out, I promise." His face reflected so much confidence. My rapid pulse vibrated through my skin and against his hand. *What is happening to me?* I pulled away and took a few steps back. *William. I have William.*

Daly moved closer.

"Please don't," I whispered.

"You can't tell me you don't feel it." The warmth in his eyes reached into me.

I shook my head. "Don't you remember after Moscow? The kiss?" My voice came out quiet and shaky.

"Do you remember?"

The memory hurled itself to the front of my mind until it felt real, like I was standing there in the skiff of snow outside Marston Hall just two months before.

"Alexandra, wait," Daly had called after me as I left for Golkov's office. He'd stood in front of me, like he was doing now in his apartment. In the memory, he said, "I just . . ." He'd concentrated on his shiny leather shoes. "Oh, what the heck." The fire in his eyes had been real, and watching it this time in slow motion, I saw hope on his face as he kissed me on the lips in the memory.

I had said, "Eew" and pulled back. I hadn't thought of him that way—I wasn't in love with him. Daly had been like an older brother to me. A protector. A friend.

In the memory, he spoke to me again. "Hold that thought." He'd wrapped his arms around me and pulled me into a gentler kiss. I hadn't returned the passion he had shown in that kiss. But watching the memory now, my heart raced.

The colors in the memory were more vivid than real life. "Seriously, James, gross!" I had shoved him back. I slowed down the moment to see even the slightest reaction on his face.

That's when everything changed.

In the memory, I saw the hurt in his deep-brown eyes, for just the briefest of moments before he said, "I've been wanting to do that since the first time I saw you, but now . . ." His eye twitched in slow motion, and while I knew what he would say in the memory, this time I noticed how his eyes wanted to tell me something different. "Now I don't know why," he said. At the time I had believed him when he added, "That was somewhat loathsome, wasn't it?"

In the flashback, I finally saw the lie in his words. I knew him so well now. I recognized the tightness in his lips when he was embarrassed, and the tiny twitch in his right eye when he wasn't telling the whole truth.

In the memory, I had stumbled back and fallen into the snow.

Now, in the present time in Daly's apartment, I stumbled back and he caught my wrist—the bad one. I cried out in pain and the memory from last November disappeared.

"I'm so sorry. I forgot about your arm," he said.

The pain in my arm wasn't nearly as bad as the agony ripping at my heart. I had William. I wanted to be with William. "I . . . I can't." I waved Daly off and escaped from the apartment. I rushed past a surprised Millard, who almost dropped the two pizza boxes he carried. I didn't want to wait for the elevator so I ran down the twenty-six flights of stairs into the lobby.

"Are you okay, Ms. Laxer?" asked the doorman as I bolted through the open door.

Ignoring him, I rushed out the door, then ran down the street to my car. I drove around Providence for a while before recognizing where my mind was pulling me. Soon I was standing at the door at 455 Hattery Road.

The nurse answered my knock. "Oh, it's you." She held open the door with one hand, rubbing her eyes with the other. "Last time I forgot to give you this." She held out a silver key on a chain. "You are welcome to stop by anytime, though I should warn you that he gets a bath every Tuesday and Friday morning around eight."

"Thank you," I said. "Can I see him now?"

"Yes, yes, of course. I'll be right over here if you need anything." She motioned to another room off the hallway, then went inside and closed the door.

I wiped at my cheeks and entered Tanner's room. Everything was the same as before, except he wore a blue shirt underneath the plaid comforter.

I fell into the armchair next to him.

"So how's your day going?" I asked with a half cry, half laugh. I knew he couldn't hear me, yet it didn't matter.

"Mine's been a bowl of peaches." I watched Tanner's chest rise and fall. It was almost like he was just sleeping in his bedroom, except for the pressure cuff and the tubes running from underneath his blanket.

"I'm a spy." I leaned forward and touched his arm. "I mean, it's not the CIA or anything and I'm not supposed to tell anyone, but I figure you're my brother so it doesn't count."

I paused as if waiting for his response.

"Yeah, yeah. I know. You thought I'd end up being some boring teacher or physicist." I stopped for a moment. "Brown really is everything I'd hoped it would be, and more. You would love my roommate, Casey. She makes some of her clothes and she's the mastermind behind these crazy pranks on campus that would make your high school ones look like children's games. The one where you wrote "EHS" in gas on Wenatchee High's lawn was epic, but the detention and community service afterward—not so much."

I mussed Tanner's hair in the front and smoothed it forward like he usually wore it. "You should probably tell the nurse not to use a comb. It makes your hair look like you actually brush it. You wouldn't want the girls busting down the doors here." I thought about all his girlfriends in junior high and high school. Tanner had never let any relationship get too serious. His heart was set on his dreams of playing football. I looked down at his now-skinny arms and wondered if he would ever play ball again.

My emotions bubbled to the surface. "You suck, you know that.

You really suck!" I leaned closer and gazed at my brother's peaceful face. "Actually, I suck, Tanner. I'm an awful person. I could almost justify lying to Casey and William about the stuff I've done for The Company. Of course I can't tell everyone I'm a spy, because it could risk the missions and the good we can do, and endanger people. But now? Now, I'm even lying to The Company. This Russian guy, Ivan, he's the Red Eye leader. He's worse than Beau Schmidt. Do you remember how that kid used to tease me to no end about my freckles and being skinny, like there was something wrong with having long legs and no hips?" I pulled Tanner's blanket up a little higher and folded it down at the top like Mom always had when she tucked us in at night.

"Anyway, this Ivan guy is really bad, Tanner. Like mobster bad. I'm in a situation I can't get out of, and if I don't do what he says, he's going to hurt the people I care about, including you. He wants me to steal a painting. In the Louvre, of all places. Do you remember how we went there when I was seven and we totally got lost in the Egyptian antiquities wing?

"Yes, it was 'we.' I definitely wouldn't have gotten lost without you distracting me. I still carry a map in my head of how we made our way back to Mom and Dad. I can't look at a Sphinx again without picturing you posing next to the large one with that tape smashing your nose. You and the Sphinx looked like twins. Where did you get tape in a museum, anyway? What an adventure."

I sighed. "I've got another problem, which I know may seem miniscule after the part about Ivan. You're probably going to say I don't need a guy, and that's true. I hadn't looked for it. In fact, I ran away from it—several times. But I don't know what to do. Things were going fine with William, and then Daly showed up and had to act all . . ." I got up and paced the room.

"But that's the problem. I don't know how I feel anymore." I stopped at the window and parted the metal blinds. The window faced an empty alleyway I could barely make out in the dark.

"Tanner, you don't get it." I let out an exasperated huff. "No, you're right. I don't want to know how I really feel because if I do, I'll hurt someone." I returned to sit on the chair. "And if I hurt one of them, I'll lose one of them." I rested my hand on Tanner's arm.

"I can't bear to lose anyone else. Does that make sense?" My brother's chest rose and fell slowly in response. I watched it for a few minutes until mine followed the same rhythm. When we were teenagers, I would go in his bedroom at night when I needed to talk, and he often confided in me, too. We didn't have all the answers, but just being there for each other and having a sounding board helped a lot.

Now that my mind had calmed, the throbbing at my wrist returned. "I know, Tanner. I will get the wrist looked at. Maybe I was using the pain as a distraction too. But I don't need to anymore." A new resolve surfaced from within me.

"You've always been there for me, Bro. Even when you couldn't be. You've reminded me what I still need to fight for. Thank you." I stood up and patted his leg. "I know what I have to do."

16

FOOL WITH A CHANCE

"I have to see him," I said the words even before the door to Golkov's university office closed behind me.

He set down his silver pen. "Alexandra?"

"You have to know what I'm talking about. I just went to Elijah's cell, but the guards wouldn't let me past this time."

"I'm sorry, but you can't see him." Golkov stood up, blocking the view of the Rembrandt painting on his wall—the painting my mother had given him years before.

"At one point we both considered Elijah a friend. Yes, he's made bad choices and he deserves to be punished, but I need to talk to him one last time. Please." Tanner had given me the strength to keep my voice strong and steady, despite what I felt inside. I wouldn't let my brother down again.

Golkov shook his head. "You can't see Elijah because he's gone, Alexandra."

I gasped. "What do you mean he's gone? Then why were the guards there?"

"He's been moved to another secure location until his trial and sentencing. The guards are a ruse. Which I believe has worked." The professor moved around his desk and leaned against the counter that held the puzzles I'd solved for him.

"Then tell me where he is and I'll go there myself."

"It's not that simple anymore. My friend at the CIA supervised his transfer. He's being moved to one of their black sites."

"Those actually exist?" I huffed. "Of course they do. Where?"

"Even if I knew where it was, I couldn't share that with you."

"You don't understand, Golkov. I have to talk to him!" Now the desperation was coming out in my voice.

"Why don't you help me understand, Alexandra?"

I could tell him, couldn't I? No. He wouldn't understand. Tanner's coma and Elijah's claim to be able to save him sounded crazy even in my head. Maybe I was fooling myself, but I didn't care. I would rather be a fool with a chance than a realist with no hope.

I moved closer to Golkov's desk. "In our business, we tell lies and keep secrets. In other areas of life, these things are looked down on." I took a deep breath, my own words weighing on me. "But I remember what you said to me once. You said that keeping secrets from the world isn't keeping them in the dark. Some of the secrets we keep are a protection—not armor for ourselves, the keepers, but a shield we hold up around the people we care about."

Golkov nodded, a thoughtfulness showing in his blue eyes. A clarity started forming in my own mind.

"I know not everything we do falls into that category," I continued. "But I've understood for a while now what my mom did in not telling me about her involvement with The Company.

Sometimes we have to dig trenches for the ones we love. We may not be able to take the guns from our enemies, but we can stop the bullets from hitting their targets. And if we're good, really good, the ones we protect won't even know they're under attack."

A crease formed on Golkov's forehead. "That is correct, Alexandra, but you must also know that some secrets should be told. Lies can destroy relationships." He picked up the last puzzle I had solved, the three separate metal pieces of the Hanayama equa cast. "That is the hardest part of our job, knowing when to share" —he slid one metal piece into the other in one swift movement until the center gyroscope began to turn within the circle— "and when to be silent." With one hand he held up the puzzle. Putting it back together would have been no easy feat for me, and yet he had done it in seconds. I wondered how quickly he could solve all of the puzzles on his counter and on top of his cupboard. Faster than me?

I stared at the metal shape in his hand and then past it into his kind eyes. "Professor Golkov, it's really important that I see Elijah one more time. Can you trust me?"

Golkov placed his elbows up on his desk and rested his chin on his hands. He studied my face. "Of course, Alexandra. I'll always trust you."

"Then I need you to get me to Elijah. And I need to talk with him alone."

Family protected one another, trusted one another. And Golkov and I were like family.

He let out a long breath. "I'll make a call."

"THANK YOU, ROSE," I said to Tanner's nurse as she wrapped waterproof gauze around my wrist. I had stopped by to visit my brother on my way to the airport. "Why do you have all this stuff here anyway?" I stared down at the bandages and casting materials she had laid out on the coffee table in the cramped living room.

"I like to be ready for anything, and I might have noticed how you were holding your arm the last time you were here. You seem like the stubborn type who would have to be dragged to a doctor's office. Luckily, your wrist should heal quickly. I would have recommended a splint, but in your case I think anything easily removable would be, well, removed."

I laughed a little. She barely knew me, yet she had picked up on the traits I tried to hide the most. "I'm glad you're here taking care of Tanner. I couldn't have chosen a better nurse."

"I'm not doing this out of the kindness of my heart, though that handsome face of your brother's does make it easy. I'm getting paid quite well for my work here. In fact, it means I can pay for my last year of medical school." Rose wrapped the final bit of gauze between my thumb and pointer finger. Using a pair of bandage scissors, she trimmed the gauze down.

"You're going to be a doctor? Wait, who is paying you to take care of my brother?"

"Elijah found me last June and offered to pay off my school loans if I signed a contract to take care of Tanner for a year. I couldn't pass it up."

At my loud gasp, Rose said, "I assumed you knew."

My mind raced through everything I knew about Elijah. He worked for the CIA doing medical research as a doctor. He did some kind of work for my mom and she trusted him. He was my driver in Russia. He visited me in Providence and gave me clues that he was a double agent, working for The Company and Red Eye. Now I'd learned he was paying for my brother's care. But why?

"What color do you want?" Rose held up two rolls of fiberglass casting tape, one red and one black. "I've got a few more colors in my bag if you want—"

"Black. Definitely black."

"Okay." She dropped the red roll on the table and dipped the black one in a bowl of water. After a few seconds, she unrolled the end and started wrapping the tape around the gauze at my wrist.

"Have you met him? Elijah?"

"Of course. He came in weekly until about two months ago," Rose replied. "He's only been in once since then, but his payments and the supplies always arrive on time."

I debated whether or not to tell her that she probably wouldn't see Elijah again. "What did you think of him?" I finally asked.

"Well, I guess he kind of reminds me of my father, except the accent, of course. Elijah was always nice to me. He even offered to help me to get into a good hospital once I start my residency. I guess he has some connections." She rolled another layer of tape around my wrist. I could feel the resin hardening.

"Did he ever tell you why Tanner was here? Did he explain how my brother got here?"

"His chart mentioned the car accident. And from what Elijah did say, he pulled a lot of strings to get him here. I'm not allowed to talk to anyone about your brother. Until I met you, I didn't even know his name. I thought he must be some Ukrainian diplomat's son in witness protection or something."

"Ukrainian?" I held my hand flat while Rose tucked the edge of the gauze between layers of tape and continued back down over my wrist. She rolled the gauze in at the bottom, about halfway from my wrist to my elbow. Then she ran her hand over the entire black cast, adding a little bit of water from the bowl over one rough edge.

"Yes. I just assumed that because of where he's from."

"Elijah's from Ukraine?" I had always wondered about his accent, but had assumed that like Golkov, he had come from Russia. If Elijah wasn't Russian, why was he involved with Red Eye? Russians and Ukrainians weren't the best of allies.

"As far as I know he's Ukrainian," Rose replied. "He told me he lived on the East Coast of the U.S. for several years while going to medical school. I can't remember where. I do recall him saying his parents were still there and that he moved back for his medical residency." She started to gather her things on the coffee table.

"Anything else?"

Rose looked at me funny. "Um, I don't know. He must have a wife or family."

"Why do you say that?" I poked the cast with my finger. It was already hard to the touch.

"I guess it was how he treated Tanner and me. And, well, for some reason I just felt I could count on Elijah—like I could my father, you know? Even though Tanner is in a coma, Elijah always talked with him like he was awake. I even caught him once talking about football."

I smiled. That's how I'd remembered Elijah before Moscow. What had changed? There had to be an explanation.

"Oh, by the way, another nurse started coming just yesterday. She gave me Elijah's name and said she would be replacing the nurse who comes on my days off. Her name is Anya if you ever come by and I'm not here. You'll recognize her by her beautiful red hair."

"Okay." I wondered how a new nurse was starting without Elijah there to take care of the details.

"Well, you're all set. I'm sure Tanner appreciated you coming by again."

"Thanks, Rose. You've been such a big help." I held up my neatly casted wrist.

I was ready. It was time to get answers.

17

COERCIVE

A stubby man led me down a seemingly endless corridor. The lights on the walls were so bright I almost forgot we were two floors underground. "Is this your first time to Langley?" he asked me.

"Yes." I'd heard about Langley on some TV dramas but had no idea if that information was accurate. We definitely hadn't crossed any big CIA seal before getting on the elevator. In fact, I hadn't seen a CIA insignia anywhere, from Providence to the helicopter ride over Washington DC, to the front doors of the plain white building near the Air Force base where we landed.

"You must have some pretty good connections with the man upstairs," my guide said. "They don't usually let anyone down here unless they are transferring the prisoners to the airbase."

"I guess," I replied. All I knew was that Golkov had made a call and that Elijah, who hadn't yet left the country, would remain at Langley until my visit.

Finally, we stopped at a door. The man inserted a key into the electronic panel, rose up on his toes for a retina scan, and then input a series of numbers. The red light on the panel disappeared and a green light blinked. The door opened.

We stepped inside a small room with a woman seated at a desk. She nodded to the man, who then led me past her. Vertical metal bars like those in a prison stood between us and another hallway, this one short and narrow. The man input a number on another keypad, and the bars slid open. We stepped into the hallway and there were three doors in front of us. He pointed to the center one and said, "He's in there. I'll beep you in once I'm on the other side of the bars."

I watched the man return to where the woman sat. He pushed a few buttons and the bars slammed shut. He nodded to the woman, who typed something into her computer. The man then pressed another button near the bars. I stepped in front of the middle door just before it clicked open.

Everything was white, from the walls to the sink and toilet to the tiny cot on the far side of the room. Elijah sat on the cot with his hands in his lap but didn't turn to face me. I stared at the profile of the man who might have the power to save my brother. I wasn't sure if I wanted to yell or cry.

"Alexandra," Elijah said with quiet earnestness. His shoulders relaxed as if he had expected someone else.

"How were you going to help my brother?" I moved across the room until I could look Elijah in the eye. I stopped when he shifted to face me straight on.

"Don't worry. It doesn't hurt anymore. Just a scratch, really." He turned so I could see the other side of his head. A diagonal cut ran from the edge of one eyebrow, down behind his ear, to the base of his neck. Stitches held the skin together every few millimeters. There had to be at least thirty or forty stitches.

I moved close and noticed the preciseness of the cut. My mind flashed to Elijah sitting next to me at the hotel in St. Petersburg after he had jumped into the Kruyokov Canal to save me.

I found his eyes now in the white room. The cruel gaze was gone. This was the man I remembered. "What happened, Elijah?"

"Apparently the CIA's bug-detection equipment is better than The Company's. They found the chip here." He touched the side of his head. "A line ran from it into my ear canal. They had to cut wide to make sure there was nothing more."

"What kind of chip?"

"The kind Red Eye uses to track your movement and transmit what you say. It is attached to pain receptors at the base of your skull." Elijah shivered and rubbed his hands together. The Company ring was missing from his finger.

Everything started to make sense, including his refusal to explain his coded messages about being a double agent. His anger in The Company interrogation room. His trying to kill me. Red Eye had made him do it all.

"Is it gone now?" I asked. "All of it?"

"Yes." He closed his eyes as if in pain, then opened them. "I'm so sorry, Alexandra. I didn't want you involved, but they knew someone from The Company had taken the case back in St. Petersburg—the one with the plans for a biological weapon, the plans you burned before jumping in the canal. "They found me after I dropped you at the airport. After they inserted the chip, I thought I would still have the strength to withstand their mind control. But they gave me no choice, no agency." He dropped his head into his hands.

"It's okay, Elijah. I think I'm starting to understand." I touched his back.

He pushed away from the bed. "No, Alexandra. It's not okay. I feel so ashamed. I wasn't in my right mind at the warehouse." He paced in front of me. "Before I saw you at the museum in Providence and gave you those passages about being a double agent, it was only Red Eye threats against me—pain forced upon me. But after I arrived in Moscow, I found out they had her. It pushed me over the edge. I would have done anything to save her."

"Elijah, who? Who did they have?"

"My fiancé. She was living in Russia, near the Kremlin. We met while I worked at the hospital in Ukraine, and she followed me to Omsk when I worked at the hospital there. I hadn't contacted her in weeks, but Ivan somehow found her."

"Oh, Elijah, I'm so sorry." I rose from the bed. "I wish I would have known—"

"How can you even look at me? I tried to kill you. I was trained as a doctor who is supposed to save lives, and I nearly took yours." Trembling, he faced the wall.

I placed my hand on his shoulder. "It's okay. Really."

Elijah turned around. His bloodshot blue eyes rimmed with tears. "I did all of it to save her and now . . . now they have probably—" He shook his head. "They forced me to tell you to get that painting. I thought the only way to get you to do it was to involve Tanner. I'm sorry for that. I knew your mom would have wanted me to protect him. I was going to tell you about him. But I didn't want you to get your hopes up until . . . Now everything is lost, and it's all my fault. I'm going to some CIA prison and I wasn't able to do what I needed for Tanner. The Van Gogh is probably lost forever. It's too late." Elijah sat down on his cot and put his head in his hands again. "Anya is gone too."

"I got the Van Gogh," I said after several seconds of silence.

Elijah lifted his head.

"Well, kind of," I admitted with a sigh. "I located it and took it from a mansion in Barcelona, but Red Eye found me before I could get it to you."

"They have it? Red Eye has the Van Gogh?" Elijah's gaze brightened and then dimmed again. "It doesn't matter. They would know the chip has been removed and destroyed. Anya is gone."

My mind flashed to my visit to Tanner the day before. Something the nurse said. I watched the conversation for a minute until I knew what had sparked the thought. "Does your fiancée have red hair?"

"Yes. How did you know?" Elijah scooted forward on the cot.

"I can't be sure, but the nurse watching Tanner told me another nurse had just arrived. She said her name was Anya and that she had red hair. She also said Anya had mentioned you."

Hope brightened Elijah's expression. "I didn't tell anyone else about Tanner. That means . . . that means Red Eye kept their promise.

They let her go." Elijah chuckled and looked like he might cry. "She's alive . . . she's okay."

"There has to be a way to get you out of here," I said. "Can't you just tell them everything you told me? I can vouch for you, and I'm sure Golkov will too."

Elijah's lips tightened. "I already told Golkov all about Red Eye's hold over me. After they found the bug, he came to visit me, and I was finally able to come clean about what happened in Moscow. Until that point, Red Eye's threats were weighing on me. I knew they would hear everything I said and punish Anya for it." Elijah shifted on the bed. "I had tried to protect The Company, even with that chip in my head. I knew my location in Rhode Island was transmitted, but I stayed away from headquarters at Brown University until Mr. Daly brought me in. I still don't think our office location was compromised. I'm sure Millard's jamming technology prevented the GPS in my head from working. The comms link was intact, though. Every time I tried to say something Red Eye didn't like, they . . ." A visible shudder ran through Elijah's body.

"Why didn't you write it down or give me clues like you did with Shakespeare before the Moscow mission?" I asked.

Elijah shook his head. "I couldn't think straight. They were messing with my brain. And I couldn't take any chances with Anya. I had to protect her."

"You told all of this to Golkov?"

"Yes." Elijah stared at the blank white wall.

"Then why are you . . ."

He faced me again, his eyes hollow.

"Golkov didn't believe you?" I couldn't hide my surprise. Elijah and Golkov had worked together for at least as long as my mother had worked for The Company. I assumed they had been friends.

"I wouldn't have believed me either. When I did what I did, I lost all trust in me. Whether or not the chip was inside me, I tried to push you from that roof. That's all Golkov sees, and rightly so. Coercion isn't an excuse."

"But blackmail is." More than anyone, I knew what blackmail could make a person do. "I will make this right, Elijah. I promise."

"You don't owe me anything, Alexandra. I tried to kill you, and you still found the Van Gogh. You might have saved Anya. I will always be in your debt and will help you in any way I can."

"Actually, I'm not worried about me." I thought back to something Elijah had said earlier. "Wait. Does Golkov know about Tanner? Does he know he's alive?"

"Yes, of course. Golkov was the one who sent for me while I was working in Omsk. He asked me to find a way to help your brother. That's why I came to the hospital after the accident."

I let it sink in for a moment. "Golkov has known about Tanner all this time?" *Why didn't he tell me?* I fisted my good hand at my side.

"You can't blame him," Elijah said. "He didn't want to give you hope until he knew if something could be done. It's the same reason I didn't tell you sooner."

I swallowed back my anger at Golkov. "Were you telling the truth when you said you could help Tanner?"

"Yes, I think I can. My study was never completed because the CIA shut down the project due to the high cost, but I kept the research. We were trying to find ways to extract information from terrorists through electrical stimulation of different regions of the brain. What they didn't realize was that some of the research helped me wake up unresponsive portions of the brain in comatose or stroke patients. It's an intricate process that requires cranial surgery. I've already scanned Tanner's brain. Anya was helping me to prepare to map it before I was captured. She has the research, but she's no surgeon."

I knelt in front of Elijah. "I want you to do it."

"There's a chance it won't work, Alexandra. He might lose his memories. He might not even survive the surgery."

"I know Tanner. He would take the chance. If things were reversed, I would want him to do the same for me."

"I'll do whatever I can."

"I know you will."

Elijah looked around his small room. "I can't do anything if I'm locked up."

"I'll need some time, but I'll find a way to get you out of here."

He looked down at my casted wrist. "Did Ivan do that?"

"No." I stood and smiled. "I did this one all by myself."

18

THE SHIELD

"Hey, you got flowers." Casey grabbed my hand as I entered our dorm room.

"Oh," I said. Golkov hadn't been in either office when I returned from Langley, and I'd made no headway at getting Elijah released.

"Wow, you'd think a girl would be a little more excited about a gift from a guy." Casey leaned over the large bouquet on my desk and sniffed. "Ahh."

I ignored the flowers and pulled open the closet doors. In all the rush to get to Elijah and fly back, I hadn't changed clothes in two days and was beginning to smell like it. I hadn't attended any classes all week, either. I wanted to fall on my bed and sleep away the exhaustion that pulled at my shoulders, but there was no time to rest.

"Well, if you're not going to read the card, I am." Casey snatched the card out of the bouquet and ripped open the envelope.

"I don't want to know what it says." I yanked off my shirt, grabbed the first one I saw in the closet, and pulled it over my head. I had other things to worry about, like how to sneak into the Louvre archives and how to get Elijah's name cleared.

I turned to see Casey's eyebrows cinched together. "Alex, these aren't from William." She studied the card again and gasped. "Oh my gosh! They're from that other guy. The one that works for Golkov. What's his name?"

"Daly?" I pulled on a clean pair of black leggings.

"No, no. His first name?"

"James."

My roommate took a few steps back and tumbled onto her bed, her eyes never leaving the card. "Um, no. That's not it either. The other guy that works for Golkov, then. The one I'm meeting later today to help with my prank. The techie one?"

"Millard?" I zipped up my knee-high boot.

"Is that his first or last name?"

"I . . . I don't know. That's all we ever call him." I zipped my other boot. I couldn't believe I didn't know Millard's first name.

"Well, I guess you'll know now. You must have made some impression on him." She held out the card to me. "At least read what the poor guy has to say and let him down easy."

I stood up and accepted the card, wondering why Millard would send me flowers.

Dear Alexandra,

It was so lovely to meet with you the other night. I love your appreciation for priceless works of art. I think you'd agree with me that some things are irreplaceable. Until we meet again.

Ivan

P.S. Why didn't you tell me Tanner was so quiet?

The card fell from my hand and fluttered to the floor. Ivan had found me. That wasn't the worst of it. He had found Tanner, too. If he had located us, it meant he . . . My mind flashed to my father, William, Daly, Golkov—everyone I knew at Brown and cared about. *No. No.* My chest rose and fell rapidly. Memories of everyone I cared about flew through my mind. I stumbled back to my bed.

"Alex?" Casey's voice sounded far away, as if she was in another room or was just a memory. "Alex?" I watched as her hand squeezed my shoulder, but I couldn't feel it. "It's not that bad, is it? I can talk to him if you don't want to. I'm sure it will be fine."

"No," I managed, shaking myself back to reality. I jumped up. "I have to go. I have to go." I grabbed my leather jacket and raced from the room.

William. I have to find William. It was 4:45 on a Wednesday, so he would be in class. I cut across the college green, which was covered in about four or five inches of snow. The cold wind bit at my cheeks as I ran down the sidewalk to Prospect Street. I glanced behind me several times to be sure no one was following me. The sun disappeared behind the Rochambeau House when I reached the front. *Please be in class. Please be in class.*

I yanked open the heavy front doors of the building and hurried down the hall, slipping a few times from the snow on my boots. Not caring who might be watching, I slid to a stop at his classroom door and burst inside.

William's eyes and mouth opened wide. "*Un minuto, clase. Por favor, leen pagina cuarenta y dos.*" He moved awkwardly to the exit and ushered me out, then closed the door behind us in the empty hallway.

"Alex," he said in a low voice, "what are you—"

I wrapped my arms around him and squeezed as hard as I could.

"What's going—" I stopped his words with a deep kiss that should have thawed any last bit of the cold from outside. Except my heart wasn't in it. All I could think about was Ivan's words on the card. *Some things are irreplaceable.*

William pulled away a bit to gaze into my eyes. "Not that I mind that kind of interruption—in fact, feel free anytime." He cupped his warm hands around my face. "But is everything okay?"

"Yes. Yes, I think so. Yes." I pulled him into another hug. "I'm just so glad you're here." After another minute, I let go. "Sorry. You can go back to your class."

"You've sorta been MIA all week. Dinner? After class?"

"I wish I could. I have to go. I'll explain later."

"Okay." He reached out for my hand and found my cast. He shook his head and laughed softly. "Yes, you do have some explaining to do. I'll see you."

"See you." William opened the door and stepped inside. I turned to leave, but not before a few whistles escaped the classroom. My cheeks burned as I made my way to the exit.

I tried to call my father on the courtesy phone at Rochambeau House. There was no answer, but his use of technology, or lack thereof, gave me hope he might be there. I looped around the building a few times to make sure I wasn't being followed, then flew up the yellow-painted stairs of the Peter Green House. I didn't stop until I reached the third floor. I paused outside my father's office, took a deep breath, and entered. He sat in his large office chair with his feet up on his desk and his frowzy mop of hair peeking from behind the thick black book in his hands. He lowered it and removed the reading glasses from his nose.

"Alexandra? Is it Sunday again already?" He set his book down on a pile of papers and placed the glasses on top.

"No, it's Wednesday. I just . . . I was nearby and just wanted to say hi."

"Well, hi." He stood up and walked to an overflowing bookcase. He picked up a book and started back to his desk. I crossed the room and intercepted him with a hug.

"Um . . ." he said, his body stiff for a second. Then he relaxed and hugged me back.

"I love you, Dad." I squeezed his broad shoulders. "I'm so glad you came to Brown with me."

He pulled back. "I thought you came with me."

He wasn't wrong, but he wasn't exactly right either. I'd been accepted to Brown before the accident and had been leaning toward leaving Washington to attend the East Coast school.

"I'm glad we came together." I smiled at him.

"Me too." He slipped from my arms and went to his chair, then opened the book in his hand. "Anything I can do for you?" He started to put his glasses on.

"Nope." I glanced at a family portrait hanging crookedly on the wall. Tanner's fifteen-year-old face smiled at me. Somehow he'd managed to get through his teens without passing through that awkward stage. His handsome face hadn't changed much since then.

I opened my mouth but quickly closed it again. My father had a right to know his son was alive. But I couldn't tell him, not until I knew whether Tanner could ever come back to us.

Some things are irreplaceable.

Was Ivan threatening to hurt my defenseless brother? The thought almost dropped me to the floor.

My father cleared his throat. "Okay, well, I'll see you Sunday."

I nodded. "See you Sunday." I closed the door softly before sprinting down the stairs and out of the house.

I DIDN'T RUN down the sidewalk once I got out of my car in downtown Providence. My energy had been sapped away. Ivan knew who I was, where I lived, and worst of all, who I loved. He had me in a choke-hold, yet my instincts told me that he wouldn't press me further as long as I cooperated—as long as I got his precious painting. Still, I had to be sure Tanner was okay, that this mission I was going on—alone—wouldn't be for nothing. I wanted to hurry by The Company headquarters to check on Daly and Golkov and everyone there, but with Ivan watching me, I couldn't. As far as I knew, Ivan had no idea I worked for a spy organization located in the basement of Brown University, and I wanted to keep it that way. Later, when it was dark, I would make sure no one was following me and then sneak into head-quarters.

I stopped in front of the apartment on Hattery Road and let myself in with the key Rose had given me. A silence loomed over the hallway until a floorboard creaked under the weight of my foot. My heart jerked in my chest.

Maybe my intuition was wrong. Maybe Ivan had done something. As I reached Tanner's door, a click sounded behind me. I turned as a nurse in pajamas emerged from a bedroom. Her auburn hair fell over her shoulders in tangled strands. She wiped at her face with the sleeve of her shirt. She might have erased her tears, but her red eyes and blotchy face hid nothing. The image of Elijah in the CIA holding cell pushed to the front of my mind.

"Anya?" My hand still rested on the doorknob. Tanner's face flared into my vision—not in the coma, but from a memory.

"Rose wasn't lying," the nurse said. "You do look like him. Alexandra, right?"

Anya's words barely reached my brain as the memory of my brother overtook me.

TANNER'S closed bedroom door signaled not only his need to keep people out, but also his barricade within. I didn't want to start a war, so I knocked.

"Yeah?" he said.

"Can I come in?"

"Whatever."

I let myself into his room and was surprised at the lack of clutter. Even his bed was made. I'd never seen his covers pulled tight over the mattress or the pillows in place. I raised an eyebrow.

He peered over his shoulder at me and then turned back to his laptop on the desk in front of him. "Don't get used to it."

"I didn't even know you had a desk." I plopped onto his bed and smoothed out the blue comforter.

My brother swiveled around in his office chair and faced me. "What do you want, Lexie?" The crease between his eyebrows looked foreign on his face, as did the redness around his eyes.

"Sorry, I just thought . . ."

"You thought what? That you'd come in here and we'd talk about how hard life is for you?" His icy tone brought me to my feet.

"What's that supposed to mean?" I crossed my arms in front of me. "You'll never get it, Lexie. School is a breeze for you. You go to college already, and I'm older than you." He slammed his laptop closed. "It's not so easy for the rest of us."

"It might be different for me, but I still have to work. I work hard!"

"Whatever." Tanner pounded his fist on the wood of his desk. "You can see the answers in your mind. You've never had to stress about grades. You've never had to do . . ." He shook his head.

I was about to yell at him and explain how I still had to solve calculus problems or write English papers. Seeing examples or having the book or notes in your head didn't make it as simple as he thought. But the droop of his shoulders stopped the words forming on my lips. I made myself take a deep breath before I spoke.

"Had to do what, Tanner? What did you have to do?"

"Terrible. I'm terrible." He rubbed at his head with both hands. "I needed an A on the test. The scout told me they didn't just want a player who conquered the field. They wanted someone smart off the field too."

I took a step closer and put a hand on his arm. "What did you do?"

"I cheated."

"What?" I couldn't believe what he was telling me.

"I had a C– in French, Lexie. I went to talk to the teacher and the test was just sitting there in his office. I had my phone in my hand and I took pictures of the pages. You don't understand the pressure I've been under lately with football and my other classes and worrying about Mom . . ." Tanner's voice trailed off.

I wanted to ask him again about the secret I knew he was keeping from me, but this wasn't the time.

"The answers weren't even on the test. I just had no idea what to study and wanted somewhere to start."

This was my brother—my best friend who always did the right thing. He might have acted cocky sometimes, but the idea that he would cheat was beyond shocking. "Tanner . . ."

"I know what you're thinking, Lexie. But I didn't have a choice."

"There's always a choice. No matter what pressures you are under, you decide how to respond. No one else does that for you."

Facing the wall again, my brother rested his elbows on his desk and let his head fall into his hands. "I didn't have anybody to turn to."

"You could have come to me. I would have helped you study. We could have done this together."

"You're already gone. You might be still here, but the moment you *decided to run off to some Ivy League school, you made your choice and I wasn't a part of it."*

"What are you talking about?" I moved to the side of his desk so he couldn't hide his face from me.

"Those thick envelopes from Harvard and Brown. You're already in."

"Did you also see the one from WSU?"

"What?" Tanner looked up at me with glossy eyes.

"I'm not going to the East Coast. I'm staying here. Well, not exactly staying here. I'm going with you. To WSU. This fall."

His bright smile lasted about three seconds before it faltered. "No. I can't let you do that. How are you supposed to cure cancer or invent time travel at a state school? You have to go to the best school so that—"

"Other schools will always offer master's degrees and PhD's. And there will be amazing professors at any school."

"Mom and Dad are never--"

"Already taken care of. This is happening, Tanner, whether you want it to or not." I placed my hands on my hips. "I'm going with you."

He sat for a moment, a mixture of emotions playing on his face. Then in one swift motion, my tough brother with his broad shoulders and muscular arms jumped from his chair and tackled me in a hug. He lifted me off my feet for several seconds before placing me on the floor and releasing me. His goofy grin faded and he raised his chin slightly, determination in his gaze.

"I have to go to the school early tomorrow," he said.

"Why?"

"Because you were right."

"I usually am." I grinned slyly.

"I do have a choice." Tanner moved to his chair and picked up his school bag. "I'm going to talk to my teacher. I've got to tell him what I did. Maybe he'll let me make up for it somehow. I will make this right." He unzipped his bag and pulled out his French textbook, then set it on his desk and started scanning pages, his back to me.

"So I'm guessing no homemade brownies for movie night?" I said.

"No, not tonight. Maybe Monday." His gaze remained on the pages of his book.

I'd always admired Tanner's confidence and athletic talent, but as I watched him poring over his book, those qualities weren't what made me proud. It was his penitent nature and his courage to face up to his mistakes. In my mind, that made him brave. I hoped I could be that courageous someday.

I sat on the edge of his bed again and used my foot to spin his chair toward me. "All right. Give me that textbook. If you haven't guessed it by now, I'm pretty good with them."

"Are you going in?" Anya pointed to Tanner's door.

"Yes, sorry." I had dropped my hand from the knob, so I reached for it again. "Wait," I called out to her. "I have to tell you something." She stopped in the hall. "I know who you are."

Her red-rimmed eyes widened. "Please don't—"

"It's okay. I know Elijah too. Not as well as you probably do, but he's my friend."

Anya took a step forward. "I've been trying to reach him, but he won't answer his phone," she said quickly. "He warned me something might happen, but I just thought he was being overly cautious after all the extra security measures we had to take at the hospital in Omsk." She paused to take a breath. "I didn't realize he had a good reason for being so discreet. When those people came and kidnapped me last fall . . ." She choked on the words. "Have you heard from him? Elijah?"

I wasn't sure what information I could share with Anya and wished I had asked Elijah more questions. I had no idea if she knew about The Company or Red Eye or any of it. I decided to err on the side of caution. "He's safe, but he can't contact anyone right now. I know he would have talked to you if he could."

"How do you know?"

"I spoke with him yesterday, but he's no longer able to contact anyone."

"Yesterday? So they don't have him?" She tucked her bright hair behind her ear.

"No. He's okay. It's just—"

"Is there something I can do?"

"No," I said a little too quickly. "I mean, he wants you to stay safe. I can't tell you where he is now, but he's coming back." *He has to come back.* "I promise you'll be the first to know when he does."

"Okay." Anya nodded. "He said to trust you. He always trusted your mother."

"You knew my mother?" My voice broke.

"No, but Elijah always talked highly of her. I never understood how they came to work together with her work in art and his work in medicine. I guess some people are just drawn together, no matter how different they are." I had a feeling she wasn't just talking about Elijah and my mother anymore.

"Thank you. Thank you for helping my brother."

Anya yawned and gave a tiny smile. "You're welcome." She motioned with her head toward Tanner's door. "Let me know if you need anything. I'll be here."

I nodded and entered his room. A wave of relief spread through me at the sight of my brother lying in the bed with his chest rising and falling in a slow rhythm. I closed the door and moved to the cushioned armchair next to his bed. Nothing had changed since I'd seen him two days before, except now my hands were trembling.

"I don't know if I can do this." I scooted the chair closer to Tanner's bed. "Maybe I'm not strong enough."

I watched his face, so relaxed, so peaceful. He had gone to his teacher all on his own, nearly sacrificing his scholarship to WSU. The teacher had given him a failing grade on the test and required him to take an even harder one to make up for it, but Tanner had persevered with a strength I envied. Even now, lying in a bed with his pale skin and thin frame, he gave off an air of power and courage.

"I need you." I pressed my hand to his and enfolded his fingers in mine. "I can't do this alone anymore." I stayed like that for a while, wishing he could squeeze my hand back to let me know he understood. All I felt was my own pulse against his skin and the cool metal of The Company ring around my finger.

"I know I can trust them. I just . . . I can't involve them in this, especially not Daly, now that . . ." I didn't finish the thought because I wasn't sure if he and the others at The Company were still safe.

"Tanner, I'm sorry. I need to check on them." I let go of his hand. "I'll be back soon."

19

ALONE

I circled around campus three times before parking my car in a lot several blocks from my dorm. The sun had already set as I cut across campus and entered two other buildings, then made my way into Marston Hall, checking over my shoulder to make sure no one was following me. I hurried up the stairs.

I peeked in the window of Golkov's university office, but no one was there. An ache clutched at my gut as I took the steps three at a time on my way down the stairs. The lobby was empty when I rounded the corner and stood in front of the door to the basement. I could have used the back entrance but felt safer staying in the building. I picked up my pace when I reached the shiny concrete floor at the bottom of the stairs. The retina scan seemed to take several seconds longer than usual. I had entered The Company headquarters just a few days ago, but it felt like months.

Once inside, I let out a breath. A few employees moved from office to office, while others typed away at their computers like everything was normal. I squinted through the small glass offices, but couldn't see into Golkov's until I reached his door.

Daly looked up when I entered. His eyes held questions, but the grin on his face sent a wave of relief over me. *He's okay.*

"Alexandra, what brings you here on a Wednesday night?" Golkov asked. "We were just wrapping things up here. Did you have another session with Itosu? He didn't say anything when he came by a few minutes ago." The professor stretched his arms behind him. "Hmm. Maybe I need to schedule some time with him. These old bones of mine could use a workout."

I wanted to confront Golkov, to yell at him for hiding Tanner from me, but I couldn't. He wasn't forgiven, but all that mattered in that moment was that Golkov wasn't in Ivan's grasp. A feeling of gratitude overcame me and I had to blink back tears. Everyone was okay—William, my father, Daly, Golkov, and Itosu. I moved a few feet into the office and focused on slowing my breathing.

Wait. "Where's Millard?" A frantic feeling seized me again. *No, not him.* I looked at Daly.

"I just left him. That's why I came to see Golkov. Millard thinks he's found a way to get a computer chip into contact lenses. I let him know there's no way I'm going to be a test subject again. I'm barely getting the feeling back in my bottom lip from his underwater breathing apparatus. Who needs a laser underwater anyway?"

"You would be surprised," Golkov said.

Daly laughed. "Really? I've got to hear about this one."

Their conversation should have relaxed me, especially since everyone was safe, but it didn't. Ivan and his threats still loomed in my mind. My world was coming apart, and Golkov and Daly couldn't see it. I stood up straight. I wouldn't *let* them see it. I would be the shield. Tanner had protected me as we grew up, always standing up for me in my awkward days where he could have easily fallen in with teasing his sister. My mom had shielded me from her dangerous life. Even my father had been my protector by moving across the United States with me. My friends at The Company had been there for me.

Now it was my turn.

"I need some time." I swallowed. *Be brave. Be courageous like Tanner when he faced his teacher and admitted to his mistake.*

Daly and Golkov stared at me in obvious confusion.

I reached for the ring on my finger. I hadn't taken it off even when the nurse had insisted as she put on my cast. "I need some time away to figure things out." I eased the ring off my hand and set it on Golkov's desk. "It's not anything either of you have done." The words flowed out of me with perfect ease, because lying was second nature to me now. *I'm doing this to protect them,* I told myself, but deep down I knew it wasn't the only reason. Golkov had kept a secret from me. It shouldn't matter now that I had learned Tanner was alive, but it still hurt. "I just need to take a step back from everything and decide where I want my life to go."

Daly started to speak, but I cut him off with my hand in the air. "Please. This is something I have to do."

Golkov rose from his leather chair. "All operatives need a break every now and again. Why don't you take a few weeks off?" He picked up the ring from his desk and held it out to me. I knew what he was saying—take a few weeks off and return ready to start again. Accepting the ring would confirm his belief in me and my role in his organization. But maybe Golkov and Daly were wrong. Maybe I just couldn't commit to everything The Company asked of me.

I took a few steps back without meeting Golkov's gaze. "I have to go." I turned for the door.

"Alexandra?" Daly called out to me. He wasn't just saying my name. He was wondering if my leaving The Company was synonymous with leaving him. Scenes from the ballroom in Barcelona flew through my mind—his wide smile, the feel of his hand on the small of my back, his confidence in me. My fingers paused on Golkov's door for just a moment before I walked out of the office. Looking back would have been an answer to Daly, and I wasn't ready for that kind of commitment either.

I STOPPED outside at the bottom of the stairs to make sure I'd stuffed my car keys in my pocket. Glancing up at my dorm room window, I realized I should have waited until Casey got home. The note I'd left had been vague—*I'll be gone a few days. Feel free to finish my Oreos*

under the bed—but it was all I had. If anyone came by, I didn't want them to think anything was out of the ordinary.

I couldn't give Ivan more reasons to taunt me with his threats. The Van Gogh painting couldn't wait for me any longer.

I lifted my overstuffed backpack over my shoulder and scanned the dark campus. Only a few students were making their way down the sidewalks. The cold air bit especially hard against my skin. I decided to take the long way to my car, looping through campus a few times, just in case someone was following me. There had been no signs of Ivan or anyone I recognized from Red Eye, but that didn't mean they weren't there.

I had just rounded Wayland House when I heard Daly shout my name.

Maybe if I keep walking, he'll give up.

"Alex, wait!" His voice was nearer.

I stopped, knowing he'd chase me down if I didn't.

"What's going on?" He stopped beside me and took a few breaths. "What was that back there?"

"Just what I said. I need time, okay?" I started to turn but his hand caught my shoulder.

"Tell me what's really going on. I hear you talked to Elijah again. What did he say? Did you tell him Red Eye got the painting?"

I moved back and Daly's hand fell away. "It doesn't matter."

"Yes, it does. I saw your face back there. I thought you trusted me now. What aren't you telling me?"

I did trust him. We made a good team. *If he went on this mission with me, there would be no stopping us.*

My internal debate was cut short as Ivan's words from Barcelona echoed through my brain. *Remember what is at stake.*

I remembered.

I had been right the week before in Golkov's office. I'd told him we sometimes have to dig trenches around the ones we love to keep the enemy away. And if we're good, really good, the ones we protect won't even know they're under attack.

I had to protect Daly.

"James," I said softly. "I know you want to help, but the best thing you can do for me right now is to let me go."

"I'm not going to just let you go when I know you're hurting." He reached for both my hands, cast and all. Neither of us wore gloves, and his skin felt warm against my fingers. "We are going to find a way to help Tanner." His powerful gaze held mine for several seconds until I remembered where I was headed and what I had to do.

"I have to—"

"Alex?" William cut me off. He stood five yards away, his face a mixture of surprise and rage. He looked between Daly and me before I realized Daly was still holding my hands. I pulled away.

"William, before you say anything, you have to know this isn't what it looks like. He's just a colleague. A friend."

I waited for him to confront me, to yell, but he just stood there. Finally, after several seconds, he walked away. I felt sick inside.

Suddenly remembering Daly was still there, I turned around.

"Just a colleague? A friend? Is that all I am?" The betrayal in his eyes matched William's.

"I don't know anything." I shifted my bag higher on my shoulder. No, that wasn't true. I did know something. Thousands of miles away there was a painting. The only thing I knew with absolute surety was that I had to steal it. "I have to go." I started to move down the path.

"If you keep running away, eventually it'll work," Daly called to me.

I whirled around. "What will work?"

"You'll run so fast and far that no one will be able to reach you. You'll finally be alone."

"Maybe that's exactly what I want." I held my bag against me and began to run. It wasn't until I reached my car several minutes later that I let the tears fall.

20

THE LOUVRE

Trying to avoid the surveillance cameras hidden throughout the square, I kept my head down. No one could know what I was about to do, and if I could help it, no one would ever know. Not my father, not William, not Daly, and especially not The Company. If this was going to work—if there was going to be any chance of saving my brother and everyone I knew—it would be all about timing.

I pulled up the collar of my tan trench coat, recently purchased at a Paris boutique along with a red pencil skirt and a beige silk blouse. I'd left my running shoes in my tiny hotel room, trading them for a pair of nude pumps that were fairly comfortable despite the high heels. In a hospital emergency room, I'd managed to convince a nurse to cut off my cast. My arm hadn't healed, but the black cast would've drawn too much attention.

It wasn't my first time at the Louvre; our whole family had gone to Paris when I was seven. Yet as I walked on the street next to the Seine River, everything seemed different than the movies that had played in my head for a decade.

I crossed the courtyard and headed for the glass pyramid in the center. Rising over fifty feet in the air, it stood above the main entrance to the Louvre. The pyramid's modern lines contrasted with the classic columns of the palace surrounding the square. I followed the crowd through the line and used the ticket I had purchased at a kiosk earlier that day. As I made my way through the Louvre's glass doors, I tried to forget how this unsanctioned mission was draining my small savings account.

I found my way down the marble stairs to the lower ground floor and spun around to get my bearings. Voices spoke in tongues I didn't recognize. People passed by in a tornado of unrecognizable faces. The place was crowded, yet I felt alone.

My first task was to find the archives where paintings were restored. Like the mansion in Barcelona, I wasn't sure where the painting in question was located, but I did have every available map imprinted in my mind. I'd spent hours studying the maps and had identified eight possible locations for the archives. Many of the maps marked sections of the museum as "closed." A closure would make sense if there was a temporary renovation or new exhibit being set up, but even the maps from twenty or thirty years ago showed some "closed" spaces that hadn't been opened since. I decided to start at the top of the museum and work my way down. It might take me all day to cover 600,000 square feet.

At the Sully Wing, I took the stairs to the second floor, then wove my way quickly through the Richelieu Wing, letting the paintings from Germany, Flanders, and the Netherlands blur past me in rich colors and ornate frames. Back in the Sully Wing, I looped through the hall, stopping only once in the room that housed the paintings of Georges de la Tour. The courtesan's eyes in *The Cheat with the Ace of Diamonds* caught me off guard, and I paused to study the master-piece. I sympathized with the poor young gambler being cheated out of his money by the courtesan and her two companions. At the same time, because one of the cheaters' cards faced me, I felt like I was in on the crime. It was as if de la Tour knew who I was and was aware of my own illegal activity.

Besides one section under renovation, I had no luck finding any doors or hidden spaces on the second floor. I moved to the first floor of the Sully Wing. My eyes passed over the Greek sculptures and Egyptian artifacts, searching behind them for closed doors and locked rooms. At one point I thought I'd discovered a possibility until a man in a gray vest opened the door using a magnetic card. A peek inside, just before the door closed, revealed a small room filled with shelves of cleaning supplies. The man emerged a few minutes later with a rolling cart and mop.

I almost waited to enter the Denon Wing, to save my favorite part of the museum until last, but there was a chance I wouldn't make it there if I found the archives first. If I had to complete a mission I was forced into, I might as well see the one painting my mother cherished more than any other.

The French called her *La Joconde,* the Italians referred to her as *La Gioconda,* but I knew her as the *Mona Lisa.* The subject of the painting had never been officially identified, though many claimed she was Lisa Gherardini, the wife of Francesco del Giocondo. Her face, and more notably her enigmatic smile, had been the topic of countless articles and documentaries, all of which raced through my brain in rapid succession. As her face took the forefront in my mind, I realized something. No one would ever know who La Joconde was or the reason for her subtle smile. Like me, the *Mona Lisa* had a secret, one that most people would never know.

I stood in the opening of the Salle des États as museum guests pressed past me to view the masterpiece—all 21 by 30 inches of it. Despite the noise of the crowd, there was a reverence to the room. I couldn't see her face from the doorway so I moved into the room.

My breath suspended in my throat. It couldn't be. I blinked several times, but it didn't erase him from my sight.

"William?" I knew he couldn't hear me from across the room, and yet I couldn't help saying his name again. When his eyes met mine his face lit up, but he didn't budge. The crowd between us thickened until he and I stood on opposite sides of the room. Each of us stood there as if waiting for the other to take the first step.

At that moment I realized the pieces of my compartmentalized life had finally converged. There was no longer Alex, the Brown

University student, and Alex, the covert spy. William was there in front of me while I was on a mission. He wasn't a part of this side of me. Yet he was standing right here in the Louvre with the *Mona Lisa* looking over his shoulder.

My insides twisted and turned. Half of me wanted to grab him by his navy-blue blazer and pull him into my arms, thankful to recognize someone in this lonely place. The other half of me wanted to turn and run away, to keep him from this portion of my life. Once he knew, there would be no turning back.

He began to snake through the crowd. I still couldn't move. *William is here.*

"Wow, this place is amazing! Did you see the *Mona Lisa*? The *Mona Lisa!*" His voice drowned out the cacophony of languages around me. It was the first time all day I had heard someone speak in my native tongue. To my ears it seemed like the lull of ocean waves.

"You're here," I said when William stood a few feet from me.

"Of course I'm here. I couldn't leave things like that. I shouldn't have walked away."

I flashed to the last time I saw him, to the storm of betrayal in his eyes. I didn't understand his enthusiasm now and wondered why he wasn't still angry at me.

"I should have trusted you. I'm sorry." He held out his hand. I grasped it, knowing I should be the one apologizing. I was keeping secrets from him. I hadn't told him about Daly coming to Barcelona with me. Hadn't told him about Tanner. Hadn't told him what I really did for Golkov.

Those weren't the only things I was keeping from William. The biggest secret of all had less to do with Daly, Tanner, and The Company, and more to do with me. Because today I wasn't being a spy to stop a terrorist, solve a crime, or help my country. In less than six hours I would become a thief to help a terrorist. Even worse, I was doing it to help Red Eye, the organization that had threatened not just the life of my family or friends, but also a country I loved.

"Alex?" William pulled me off to the side of the room, next to a painting.

"How did you know I was here?" I asked him. "How did you get here?" I leaned into him so he could hear my voice over the crowd.

"What do you mean? I got your text and the ticket you left me. Your driver even picked me up from the airport. He's probably around here somewhere."

"My driver?" A sick feeling came over me. I couldn't have sent a text. I'd never gotten a new phone from Millard, and I hadn't even transferred my phone number to my new burner phone.

"Yeah. He drove me to the museum. He's the one who told me you'd be here now. I'm supposed to tell you to meet back at the Triumphal Arch at midnight. Though I don't know why so late. I thought the museum closed at ten." William looked to his right. "We can probably tell him a different time. He was in the Grand . . . Oh wait, there he is now." William let go of my arm and pointed over my shoulder to the archway I'd just stepped through. "What's his name again?"

"Ivan." I forced myself to turn and face the man who had set my life upside down. *My phone.* That's how he'd found me in Providence. He must have used my fingerprint while I was knocked out in Barcelona to gain access to my phone's contents. He had known who I was the entire time.

Ivan's face appeared less threatening in the light of the museum than in Barcelona in the dark street outside the mansion and in the interrogation room. His smile might have seemed jovial to people around us, but I knew the heart behind it—a heart made of solid stone as cold as the marble flooring in the Louvre's Grand Hallway. That icy heart was set on a painting that was probably housed forty feet below us. He could have had me steal any painting in this museum, yet he wanted that one. But why would Ivan risk his identity and the possible association with my attempt to steal the Van Gogh?

"Are you okay?" William squeezed my hand and stepped in front of me. The pressure brought me back to reality. Ivan still stood about twenty feet away, watching me. His expression told me more than any conversation could have. He was going to do whatever it took to get what he wanted. He already had all the leverage he needed over me.

But I'd had enough. Ivan could do whatever he wanted with me, but I wasn't going to let him mess with William, or anyone else I cared about. I needed a new plan.

"I'm fine." I turned to William, knowing Ivan's eyes still rested on me. "You said you trusted me, right?"

William nodded, and a brown curl fell over his eye. He released my fingers and I thought he was going to brush the hair away like he usually did. Instead, he placed his hands on the sides of my waist and slid them slowly until they reached around me and rested on my lower back. "I don't think I'll ever entirely understand everything about you, but I do trust you, Alex, more than anyone I've ever known."

"Good." My heartbeat picked up. I put my arms around him and pulled him into me until my lips brushed his ear. "Then I need you to do exactly what I say."

WILLIAM and I paused in front of a painting. "This one is interesting. The dramatic colors kind of remind me of . . ."

"Van Gogh," I said.

"No, I was kind of thinking David."

"Oh." I closed my eyes and tried to slow my breathing. I hadn't been looking at the painting, hadn't really appreciated any artwork we'd stopped at in the last half hour. My eidetic mind had been reading through any and every document I'd ever seen on the Louvre, including maps, security protocols, and the Prefecture de Policia de Paris. If this new plan was going to work, I had to be certain how any outside force would respond.

I felt Ivan's eyes on me as William and I walked into Napoleon III's drawing room. Any other time the ornately carved woodwork shining with gold leaf would've had me gushing. Instead, I kept glancing around, searching for the entrance to the archives and waiting for the right time to give William the signal. Dotting the room were gold-painted chairs with plush-velvet seats in a purple damask fit for royalty. The drapes on every wall should have given the room a feeling of warmth, but all I felt was the cold stare following me to the center of the room.

"I can't believe a king used this room. I'd be too distracted from the ceiling to ever look down," William said. He continued to comment as we walked about the crowded room. I had to give him credit for acting the part of the enthusiastic tourist, though I had a feeling he didn't have to act too much.

He stopped as we rounded the room and threw his arm out to halt me as well. "What's he doing here?" William whispered.

I followed his gaze to the opposite corner of the room near a large window. Sunlight poured through the glass and onto the profile of a tall, dark-haired man.

Daly.

There was something regal about his stance, as if he rightly belonged in Napoleon III's living quarters from over 160 years ago. *No, Daly shouldn't be here.* I felt the blood drain from my face. *Did Ivan bring him here too?*

Daly's eyes found mine through the crowd. In slow motion, he moved his head about an inch one way and then the other. Anyone watching the exchange probably wouldn't have noticed the movement, but I knew what it meant. I wasn't supposed to acknowledge his presence.

William stepped in front of me and asked with a set jaw, "Did you know he was here?"

"No," I whispered, staring past William's glare to an ornate mirror on the wall close to Daly. The reflection showed Ivan standing behind us near the entrance of the room. He stood with his arms folded, his eyes focused on William.

"First he interrupts our date. Then he thinks he can hold your hands. Now he . . . Wait, he's the colleague, isn't he? He's the one you danced with in—"

"William." I brought my hands up on either side of his face and leaned into him. He was going to ruin the plan. I had to get his focus off of Daly. So I kissed William. The fluttery feeling that always came with our kisses never came, but I still pressed my lips to his. I needed time—time to figure out my next move.

I opened my eyes to find Daly still at the curtains. I couldn't describe his expression or how it made me feel. All I knew was that everything about this moment was entirely wrong. I wasn't supposed to be kissing William in a crowded room. Ivan wasn't supposed to be hovering over our every move, and Daly wasn't supposed to be there. Whether or not Ivan knew who he was, I couldn't involve Daly in this. I had to protect him. And William. That's what cemented my plan and pulled me back from the kiss.

"I want to see the *Mona Lisa* again." Though we still stood close, I said it loudly enough that anyone in the room could hear.

William didn't ask questions. From the corner of my eye, I watched Daly move through the crowd and head out the door on the other side of the room. Ivan remained by the entrance door as we returned the way we had come. I grabbed William's hand and pulled him quickly past the man he thought was our guide and driver.

I didn't concentrate on the exterior of Napoleon III's apartments as we passed through the courtyard that was now enclosed at the top with one of the mini glass pyramids, letting natural light embrace the sculpted art in the square. I ignored the paintings and sculptures we'd already seen on the way back through the Grand Gallery.

Because of the crowds, we had to pause for a minute near the *Winged Victory of Samothrace*. My eyes memorized the beautiful lines of the marble sculpture of the goddess Nike that rose over ten feet above us. Though the majestic figure was missing both arms and had no head, something about the body and the angel wings gave the illusion it was about to take flight. It was made of stone and yet still appeared free. Right then I would have given anything to represent strength, speed, and victory like she did.

William squeezed my hand, his anger at seeing Daly stilled for the moment. I knew William wanted to ask me a million questions, none of which I could answer. I just hoped he would do what I had asked of him despite that.

Ivan still trailed us as we jogged past a small staircase leading to the ground level. My body ached to race down those stairs and out the museum doors. It would have been no use. I had to get William to a place where Ivan couldn't follow. Daly had disappeared. For some reason, the thought of him being far away from Ivan relieved me so much that by the time we reached the Grand Gallery, my body relaxed—until we neared the doorway to the Salle de États, where the *Mona Lisa* hung.

Daly was leaning against a marble wall inset. When he saw us, he slipped down the hallway, following the signs to the *Mona Lisa*. William and I moved in his direction with the crowd. Somehow Ivan managed to stay within about ten feet of us, and he gave me a smug grin each time I glanced back.

With the workday over, the size of the crowd increased. Ivan's presence pressed in on me so much I could barely breathe. I still wasn't sure how I could pull any of this off. I'd walked the grounds and through every hallway. I'd read all the Louvre articles and books I could find. I'd watched countless documentaries. My mind was now an interactive map of every painting, sculpture, and artifact the museum had ever carried, but I still didn't know exactly where *Portrait of Dr. Gachet* was located, how I would get my hands on it, or how I was going to remove it from the museum.

The only thing I knew for sure was that this was a solo mission. I'd told Golkov that some secrets were best hidden. Today confirmed that. I wouldn't put William in harm's way. And I couldn't let Daly get involved, no matter how good his intentions were. I would build a fortification around them and protect them. I would be the shield.

It's now or never. I pulled on William's arm as we crossed the threshold into the *Mona Lisa* room. "Change of plan," I whispered. "Do it to him." I motioned across the room near Giordano's painting *Adoration of the Shepherds.* William's wide eyes were soon replaced by a narrowing glance when he saw the person I pointed to.

William strutted in the direction of the painting. In the direction of Daly. I stuffed my shaking hands into my coat pockets and pretended to study *The Marriage of Cana* painting to my right. Though it was the largest painting in the Louvre, all my attention zeroed in on William. My body tensed as Ivan stepped past me, following only a few strides behind William. *This better work.*

William didn't stop when he came to Daly. In fact he didn't even slow down as he walked briskly to *Mona Lisa*. His shoulder collided with Daly's so forcefully that Daly whipped to the side. *That had to hurt.* Itching to stand between Daly and William, I moved in their direction, but stopped in the center of the room. I had to let the plan play out. Ivan had stopped and stood off to the side in the crowd, only a few feet from the arched wood railing around the *Mona Lisa*.

Daly's eyes met William's in a moment of confusion and then anger. He brushed off the sleeve of his suit jacket as if William had tainted it with his touch.

"Excuse you," Daly said loudly.

A smile twitched at William's lips. "Excuse yourself. You were in my way."

"Your way? Seriously, what is wrong with you?" Daly looked William up and down. "Why don't you take your pleated pants and polyester vest and find a chess match or something."

William stepped forward. "Why don't you find a place you're actually wanted and stop stalking Alex? It's like you can't even take a hint."

I chewed on the inside of my cheek. William was supposed to be making something up to pick a fight, yet his words sounded real.

"What's that supposed to mean?" Daly twisted a cuff link at his wrist.

The crowd in the room had now encircled the two handsome men arguing with each other. It didn't matter that both spoke in English and half of the audience probably couldn't understand the words. Famous paintings had nothing on a brewing fight.

William jutted out his chest like he was trying to appear bigger than Daly, who had broader shoulders and an inch or two of height on him. "It means exactly what I said it means. She might work with you, but she's with me."

I stuffed my hands farther into my pockets and glanced around at the crowd. Only Ivan's eyes met mine. I couldn't tell if he was confused or angry or both.

"You're wrong." Daly moved until he and William were less than an arm's length apart. "If you knew anything about her, you'd understand that the only reason she is still with you is because she doesn't want to hurt you." He stabbed his finger into William's chest, and William batted his hand away.

I stood there dumbfounded. *Did Daly really just say that?*

"You have no right to think you know anything about . . ." William's voice wavered. This wasn't just an act for him. I started in their direction. This had been a stupid plan—I had to stop it. William turned his head to the side and found me. Our eyes locked for one second before he took a deep breath, a new determination in his gaze. "I know Alex." His chin rose as he spoke.

"If you did, you'd realize she doesn't want you here." Daly said the words with an antagonizing glare, yet his tone held pity.

William's body tensed and I thought he was going to say something more. Instead, his arm came back and he swung his fist right at Daly's face. I gasped and pushed my way to the front of the crowd. The punch caught Daly off guard and he stumbled back a few feet. He reached up to wipe at the corner of his mouth with his thumb. It came back red with blood.

"You did not just do that." He straightened and glared at William.

I finally made it to the front of their audience, and Daly noticed me. He eyed William again and turned to me again like he was waiting for me to intervene. I didn't move. He stared at me for one more second before he raised a thick eyebrow and smirked. Then he lunged forward, his knuckles meeting with William's jaw.

William stumbled to the side until his shoulder hit the wall, shaking several of the paintings hanging there. He got his footing and rammed his body into Daly. They both flew back into the crowd. A man caught Daly, who then pushed himself into William again. I'd seen plenty of fights at The Company and had participated in many of them. None looked as ragged as this one. William and Daly smashed into each other and threw punches. At one point, I swear I saw Daly grin. William was not as skilled a fighter, but his stamina kept him going. A chorus of yells, all in French, came from behind us. The guards were coming. Just as I had anticipated.

Daly was too busy shoving William against the railing in front of the *Mona Lisa* to hear the screams of "*Arêtez-vous!*" and "Stop!" from museum security. William was far too distracted as he kneed Daly in the stomach to notice the approach of the four guards. It wasn't until one of them grabbed Daly's shoulders and pulled him and William apart that the fighting stopped. Sweat dripped down from the curls on William's forehead. His eyes were still narrowed at Daly, the color of his irises a piercing blue against his red face, but he didn't struggle against the guards who had his arms pulled behind him.

Daly, on the other hand, yanked and twisted in the guards' hands. "Let me go," he yelled and tried to wrench away from the third guard now grasping his arms from behind. The strange thing was that I knew he could have freed himself from their clutches if he really wanted to. He was holding back, but why?

"We are sorry for the disturbance," said a museum worker in a blue vest. "We take the destruction of property very seriously at the Louvre." Two more blue-vested employees inspected the paintings and wall where Daly and William had been wrestling. Another worker in business attire ran his hands over the railing. "Which is why these culprits will be turned over to the proper authorities."

Exactly as planned. The security guards would take Daly and William to their holding office until the Prefecture de Policia de Paris arrived. Then the police would transport Daly and William to their station and detain them overnight. *Protect* them overnight.

Ivan's eyes bore into me as the guards escorted William out the door. Ivan couldn't get to him now and he knew it.

William nodded at me as he passed. Of course he didn't understand why I'd asked him to do what I did, but he had trusted me enough to make it happen anyway.

Daly continued to fight the guards, who were now dragging him across the floor. As he neared me, he jerked out of their grasp and toppled into me, sending us both to the floor. With his head next to mine, he whispered, "Do what needs to be done."

My heart raced within my chest as his hand found mine and he slipped something small and thin into my palm. Guards pulled him off me and he continued to struggle against them, or at least made a show of doing so, as they dragged him from the room. A museum worker helped me to my feet and apologized for Daly's behavior.

With blood zipping through my veins, I left the room and found the closest restroom. I assumed Ivan wouldn't dare follow with so many people around. Once I had locked myself in a stall, I looked down at the plastic rectangle Daly had placed in my hand. It was a museum employee key card. The black magnetic strip caught the fluorescent light above me. I wasn't sure how much Daly knew, but he had given me exactly what I needed—a way in.

21

A BLESSING IN DISGUISE

In the history of the Louvre, only one noteworthy theft had taken place. That heist made the *Mona Lisa* famous. The Italian handyman who stole Leonardo da Vinci's masterpiece worked for the museum, making protective glass cases. He had the perfect cover. When Vincenzo Peruggia was ready to escape with the *Mona Lisa* rolled up and tucked under his coat, a plumber had unknowingly helped him by letting him out a side exit. A plumber's key had been the answer to the thief's problem.

Nearly a hundred years later, I slipped my own problem-solving key card into my bra, along with the burner phone I'd purchased. Next, I pulled off my tan trench coat and draped it over the bathroom sink, then grabbed the rubber band from my wrist and pulled my hair back in a messy bun. I reached into the coat pocket and removed the thick, black-rimmed glasses I'd bought from a street vendor. I slid them on and looked from side to side in the mirror. The glasses aged me a few years and made me look like a professional, as did the red skirt and beige blouse I'd hidden under the coat.

Now for the finishing touch. From the inside pocket of my coat, I carefully removed the jet-black wig Casey had bought for me last Halloween, but that I'd refused to wear. I stretched it over my head as tightly as I could with my injured wrist, and tucked all my loose strands of blond hair inside. The woman who stared back at me in the mirror with cropped bangs and a bob of shiny black hair was not me. Seventeen-year-old Alexandra Stewart no longer existed. I clipped my fake ID badge to my blouse.

"My name is Irina Karaskova from the Rejnikov Museum in Moscow," I practiced with a thick Russian accent. "Thank you for allowing me this opportunity." Irina smiled at me in the mirror. I was ready. She was ready.

I half expected Ivan to be waiting outside the bathroom when I walked out over an hour after I'd entered. I was glad he wasn't. William and Daly were safe. For now. The rest of my friends and family back in Providence would only be kept safe if I completed this unsanctioned mission.

As I found my way down the hallway, a chill ran over my skin, but it wasn't something my trench coat, disposed of in the bathroom garbage can, could have changed. Then I realized that even if Ivan was still in the museum, it didn't matter. He wouldn't recognize me as I strutted down the hallway with my shoulders back and my eyes forward. Anyone who looked at me would see a dark-haired museum curator who must have been down those halls so many times that the artwork no longer caught her attention.

Following the schematics in my head to the Denon Wing exit, I strode down the stairs to the ground floor. Instead of studying the sculptures of Venus de Milo or Psyche and Cupid, I examined the walls for doors that might lead to the archives. It took me nearly an hour to loop through that floor, with no luck.

Finally, there was only one place I hadn't checked. I found my way to the basement just as my watch read 9:45. I moved slower down the hallway this time, even though the crowds had thinned. I needed time to rehearse.

A voice over the intercom told museum guests to find an exit because the Louvre was closing. Over the next ten minutes, I counted nineteen museum curators, all with ID badges, coming from the same direction. They didn't wear the vests or the security uniforms the other Louvre workers wore. If the curators' ID badges hadn't given them away, their business attire and staunch expressions would have—that and the videos and photos of museum personnel that had been playing on a loop in my head. It made sense that they were all leaving around the same time. I just needed to find out where they came from.

I scratched at my scalp through the wig and continued forward. After nearly five minutes of walking, I saw two unmarked doors about ten feet apart, each with a rectangular panel and card reader on the wall next to the doorknob. I also found a black-uniformed security guard standing directly between the two doors. Everything inside me screamed for me to turn around or walk past. What if the card didn't work? What if the security guard knew I wasn't supposed to be down there?

My mind flashed to everyone I loved and cared about. If I did this I could protect them from Red Eye, yet doing this was crossing a line I might never come back from. The things I'd done before as an agent had been on the side of right or at least in a gray area I could justify. But this was all the way on the other side.

Yet I had to do it.

I put on my Mona Lisa smile, pulled out the magnetic card, and made a beeline for the door on the right.

"Bonjour."

The security guard looked in my direction and squinted at my name badge. His eyes lit up and a tiny smile broke out on his face. "I hear the Rejnikov has the Rembrandt, the one that was stolen," he said. "Have you seen it?"

I wanted to tell him my mother had been the one to recover the painting and that I had been in the very room where it now hung. I wanted to explain that her life's work had been to preserve art and share it with the world. But this wasn't the time for a walk down memory lane. "Yes. Yes. It was my job to authenticate it, which is why . . ." My hands started to tremble.

"You authenticated *The Storm on the Sea of Galilee*? Is it as impressive in person? I hope we will have it on loan in the future."

"It is quite a find. As I was saying, Monsieur Barbaret has asked me to come to your museum to authenticate another painting." I tapped my foot impatiently.

"Director Barbaret?" The security guard looked to his left and right and took a step forward. He spoke in a low voice, even though the hallway was empty. "So it's true. Do they really have a . . ."

"I'm not at liberty to say," I cut him off. "All I know is I have a job to do."

"Yes, of course." The security guard scooted back to his post and nodded at me.

I slid the key card through the card reader. *This had better work*. A red light flashed and the door made two low beeping noises. My heart sank.

"Sometimes those cards can be a little temperamental. Here, let me help you." The guard reached for my card and rubbed it a few times on his sleeve. He slid it through the reader again. The red light and low beeps came again. "Huh? Have you used it before?"

"No, it was just given to me."

"Hmm. Maybe they didn't activate it. Or maybe it's the reader. Let me try my card." The security guard slid his through. The reader also showed a red light. He cleaned his card on his sleeve and tried it again. It still didn't work. "I'm sorry, Mademoiselle" —he squinted at my badge— "Mademoiselle Karaskova. The machine seems to be malfunctioning. I'm going to have to call this in." He put his hand on a radio at his belt.

I extended my hand. If he called someone, my chances of getting through that door were gone. "Wait. Let me try mine one more time." I reached for my card and wiped the magnetic strip with my finger, then slid the card through the reader as quickly as possible. A green light blinked and a higher-toned beep sounded. I pulled open the door.

"Looks like you're okay to enter after all." The security guard returned his card to his pocket. "Good luck with the painting. I can see it will be in good hands."

I breathed a sigh of relief when the door shut behind me. Daly had gotten me in. Actually, I had a feeling Millard had altered the card to copy the signature of the one swiped just before it, so my card would work the second time. My team had helped me after all. Now it was my turn.

I had expected a dark basement room filled with piles of chaos. Instead, I walked into a pristine white hallway lit with lights that seemed to simulate daylight. My heels clicked on the white marble floor as I made my way down the corridor. It opened to a large room about forty feet wide and sixty feet long. A few smaller hallways and rooms came off one side of the room. I counted thirteen curators or restorers still occupying the room, each concentrating on the work in front of him or her. Sculptures dotted the room, some covered in cloth, others in various stages of the cleaning process. Marble-topped tables held artifacts from different times and places, anything from vases to weapons and clothing. Large frames and canvases leaned against a wall at the back of the room. I would have to walk past all the employees before I even got near the painting I needed.

Words from The Manual jumped into my mind. *"A spy blends into his or her environment. Being covert is less about hiding and more about belonging. You are not playing a part. You are your cover."*

Just act like you are supposed to be here, I told myself. I adjusted my glasses, put my shoulders back, and strutted across the floor. Two workers looked up from the sculptures they were cleaning. I nodded at them and they promptly returned to their work.

I found my way to a group of paintings leaning against the wall. All of them were much larger than the *Portrait of Dr. Gachet,* but I stopped and began leafing through them just to be sure. About halfway through, I stopped. The Louvre would never allow a painting worth nearly a hundred million dollars to just lean against a wall with several others. No, it would be locked away or in its own special .

. . I scanned the back wall, past a carousel of paintings, to a small table in the corner of the room. A flat package wrapped in brown paper sat alone on the white marble tabletop. I moved carefully in that direction, hoping to go unnoticed. I felt the tiny cameras hanging from each wall follow me across the floor. I chewed on the inside of my lip. The unmarked package on the table measured about two feet in both directions. I reached for the tape holding the acid-free paper in place. Would they really leave a priceless painting sitting out on the table?

"So you're the one they hired to restore it?"

I nearly jumped out of my shoes. A man in his thirties with slick, dark brown hair came to stand beside me.

"You speak French?" he asked, his eyes focused on my badge.

"A little," I replied in French. I'd managed to work my way through the conversation with the guard outside, but only barely. Though I understood quite a bit, I'd only studied the French language for about three weeks and knew my pronunciation and comprehension had much to be desired. At least some of the rules and Latin bases were the same as Spanish.

"Don't worry," the man said in Russian. "I speak Russian very well. I served a mission in Siberia many years ago. You'd be surprised how many Russians find their way to the Louvre."

And Americans that just happen to be spies who can impersonate Russian curators. "Yes." I started to open the paper. The crinkling resonated through the air. I sensed more eyes on me now.

"Do you mind if I take a look?" The man stepped forward. "I am Avery Le Beau." He put out his hand, which was covered with a blue glove. He pulled his hand back. "Sorry. I supervise all the sculpture restoration here." He removed the glove and extended his hand again. I shook it quickly and returned to folding back the paper from the painting. He leaned in closer to me. "And don't listen if you hear the others call me stone face. I don't smile while I work, but I do when my companion isn't an ancient man of marble." He smiled at me with a set of perfectly white teeth. Despite the agitation in my gut, I returned the smile.

The second layer of paper revealed the gold-framed oil painting *Portrait of Dr. Gachet.*

"It is quite a masterpiece," Mr. Le Beau said in a quiet voice, fit for church.

"Yes, it is." I didn't have to pretend to be in awe over the painting lying on the table. It wasn't the subject that enthralled me as much as knowing that it was one of Vincent van Gogh's last paintings. I picked up a pair of white cotton gloves from the table and slid them on. My hand hovered over the gold-leaf frame like the polar ends of a magnet, an invisible force keeping me from the connection. If I touched the painting, I wouldn't be able to let go. This painting's value wasn't monetary for me. It was a bargaining chip—a chip I desperately needed. I was beginning to understand how Elijah felt when he was forced to make the decision he did to save his fiancé. If becoming a felon was the river I had to cross to save my loved ones, I would swim into its depths, no matter how the water raged.

I stood straight again. "I wonder if he had any idea when he painted it that his works would become such a legacy." I lifted the painting and studied it more closely.

"If he knew billions of people would view it and write about it, maybe he wouldn't have even started, or at least he would have worked on it until it was perfect."

"It *is* perfect." I took a breath. Van Gogh had created over eight hundred paintings in his lifetime, but his doctor's portrait told more about Van Gogh than many of his other works. This small piece of art carried emotions that might be missed if someone hadn't read about him as I had. I saw Van Gogh's depression in Dr. Gachet's melancholy expression and the subdued colors. I felt the artists' mental torment in the harsh contrast of the deliberate, dashed strokes of the paint brush. The bright yellow books and foxglove flower on the table in front of Dr. Gachet were a hint of hope that Van Gogh had seemingly never found in his own life. The artist had painted his heart on the canvas. "I'd like to think he would have remained true to himself," I commented finally.

"Hmm." Le Beau thumbed a wedding band on his ring finger. "I heard they were searching for the right person to restore the painting.

They wouldn't trust just anyone with it. How did Damien find you?" Le Beau drew out the question like he was envious.

My mind flipped through memories so fast it was a wonder my hands didn't vibrate. Louvre personnel charts, online resumes, and newspaper articles jumped to the surface. There was no Damien in my brain's library. I lowered the painting to the table.

I rehearsed my next few words carefully in my mind before I faced Le Beau. "Jean Luc requested me." My tone took on a sharp edge when I said the first name of the museum curator over Dutch works of art. "He heard about my restoration of the Rembrandt at the Rejnikov." I pointed to my name badge.

Le Beau took a step back. "Yes, yes of course, he did."

"And I'm sure he would want me to get to work as soon as possible." Le Beau's apologetic smile didn't stop my fingers from tapping on the tabletop.

"Sorry. It's been a long day." He looked at his watch. "Why are you here so late? Everyone else is leaving now."

"This masterpiece has been hidden for far too long." I turned the painting over to reveal the aged wood and yellowed paper backing. "In addition, I must be back at the Rejnikov by Monday. So if you'll excuse me . . ." I reached to a shelf that held more protective gloves, cotton swabs, cleaners, varnish, and tools.

"Yes, I'll leave you to your work." He skittered back to his sculpture.

I grabbed a container of neutralizing liquid and some cotton swabs. After swapping my cotton gloves for nitrile ones, I dipped the swab into the liquid and pretended I knew what I was doing. After all, I was Irina Karaskova, much-sought-after art restorer. I rolled the swab on the back edge of the canvas. I might have done my research, but I wasn't willing to sacrifice the painting to keep my cover. I just needed to pretend long enough to empty the room.

My hand started to cramp from the slow movement across the back of the canvas. Every few minutes, I grabbed a new cotton swab and dipped it in the liquid. I resisted the urge to look over my shoulder as footsteps moved, papers rustled, and keys jangled. From my calculations, three or four people still remained in the room with me. I didn't have much time. If I correctly understood Ivan's message to William, Ivan was giving me until midnight before he would make good on his threats.

On the shelves, I found a thin metal file with a pointed tip that would slide under the staples and nails holding the canvas to the canvas frame. The wood squealed as I pried off the first staple, but I kept on working. If anyone came to look over my shoulder, I could say I was re-stretching the canvas and hope they didn't ask more questions. I couldn't get some of the nails with the file. I searched the tool shelf and finally found a small hammer to pry them loose. A few of the nail heads were so old they broke off in the process, but I managed to pull the painting off the back of the canvas frame and remove the thin metal brackets holding it to the exterior frame. No doubt Ivan would have preferred to keep the canvas in the frame, but I couldn't walk out of the Louvre with a framed painting in tow. A rolled-up canvas, on the other hand, would be easier to conceal.

I cautiously peered over my shoulder. I still wasn't alone. Why weren't these people getting off work at a reasonable hour and letting me escape with the painting? It was nearly eleven-thirty. I couldn't stay here any longer.

I lifted the canvas out of the frame and carefully peeled back the frayed yellowed edges of the painting. I held my breath as I removed the frame that had held the canvas taut for nearly 125 years. The frame stuck in one corner and I used my finger to pry it loose. My insides cried out in horror to the sound of cracking paint. I pulled off my nitrile gloves and replaced them with the cotton ones. With one hand under the painting, I carefully turned the canvas over. As I inspected Van Gogh's masterpiece, tension left my shoulders. I didn't see any cracks besides the kind that came with age. I closed my eyes.

Could I really turn this painting over to Ivan? What would Tanner do? I let my mind flood with memories of the brother I knew before he lay comatose in a bed. His brazen smile in my memories was so annoyingly lovable that I couldn't help but grin while standing over the *Portrait of Dr. Gachet,* a man who would forever be etched with a gloomy expression. A similar expression engulfed my mind, an uncharacteristic one of Tanner. Before I could stop it, my mind sucked me into a memory of him the day before the accident.

I SLAMMED *my bedroom door so hard the paintings in the hallway trembled against the wall. I heaved off my backpack and threw it into a chair before collapsing onto my bed. My hands gripped at my comforter. I yanked my furry green blanket from the foot of my bed and put it to my face. I screamed into the soft fabric and let the threads capture my anger. I still couldn't believe what Tanner had done. He had made a decision that affected my life, and I had to find out about it in a letter?*

A soft knock came to my door. "Lexie?" Tanner said.

"Leave me alone!" I yelled at the door.

"Just let me in. I have to explain."

"Go away." Once more I buried my face in the blanket, which smelled faintly of smoke, even though I'd washed it after we'd roasted marshmallows the weekend before. My mind flashed to a memory of my family around the campfire, their faces dancing with firelight. We had tried to do one of those scary ghost stories where each person had a minute to carry the storyline before the next person picked up where he or she left off. Our ghost story went from frightening to comedic in less than five minutes. Feelings of togetherness and happiness and love flooded through me like they had that night, and just like that, they washed away my anger at my brother. My eidetic memory had betrayed me once again.

"Please hear me out." Tanner's gentle voice, muffled through the door, reminded me that he would never intentionally hurt me. Maybe I should give him a chance after all.

"Fine," I said hollowly. I didn't get up from my bed but glanced toward the door as Tanner solemnly made his way inside my room. He ran his hands over his light blond hair and looked at the carpet.

"Why did you do it, Tanner? Why did you tell the dean that I had accepted a scholarship to Brown University? I don't even want to live in Providence. I want to live with you." I scooted back and hugged my blanket against my chest.

"I know you were willing to give it up, Lexie, and I love you for that. But I couldn't let you sacrifice your dream just so I could live mine."

"*I wasn't giving anything up.*" My voice was starting to rise again. "*You should have just told me.*"

"*I tried to, but you wouldn't listen, even when—*"

"*I would have listened.*"

Tanner shook his head and sat on the edge of my bed. "*Like you're doing right now? Every time I brought up college, you would interrupt to list the classes and road trips we could take together. I never once heard you talk about classes you wanted to take, or your major and the things you would study. Not like you did when you mentioned one of those Ivy League schools.*"

I pushed my blanket aside, not wanting to admit he had a point. "*I would still get to do that . . . later.*"

"*See, that's the thing, Lexie. You were going to put four years of your life on hold. When I saw you had thrown away a folder with the Brown University logo, I realized I couldn't let you do it, even if it meant we'd have to live on opposite sides of the country.*"

"*But I wanted—*"

"*No, Lexie. Deep down, you really didn't. You act like going to different schools would break up our family or something. But no matter how far apart we are, we'll always be brother and sister. We're going to call, video chat, and visit each other way too much. We'll both come home on holidays. Honestly, you'll probably get sick of me.*"

"*No, I won't.*" I used a corner of my blanket to wipe at my face.

"*I know I said you are strong enough to take care of yourself,*" Tanner went on, "*and even though that's true, you'll never have to do it all alone. There's always going to be an annoying person to have your back, or tell you you're making a stupid decision, or yank your ponytail.*" He reached out to pull my hair, but I rolled out of his reach.

I hated that he was right. "*But it's too late, Tanner. I never accepted the Brown University scholarship. You shouldn't have told WSU that.*"

His face twisted into a wry grin. "*Well, actually . . .*"

"*Tanner, what did you do?*"

He put his hands behind his head and lay back on my bed. "*It wasn't like I had to do any code-breaking or sleuthing, though I'd be pretty good at it.*"

"What did you do?" I asked again.

"I just had to create a student account and register you for classes."

"You did what?" I jumped from the bed.

"Russian 301, Physics, Calculus, World History, and English Lit." My brother held up one finger at a time as he listed the classes.

I stared at him for a full ten seconds with my mouth open and my hands on my hips. "Russian?" I finally said.

"Mom's idea. She probably wants someone to perfect her parents' language. Though, honestly, I thought you were already fluent, what with that brain of yours and all."

"Mom knows about this too?"

"And Dad. He's the one who made me add World History."

My mind reeled, and not just with constantly playing memories. My whole family had gone behind my back to accept a scholarship, change my college plans, and schedule classes for me.

And I loved them for it.

My face felt hot and tears threatened to spill onto my cheeks. I turned to look at my wall that held framed puzzles I'd completed and a bulletin board that overflowed with quotes and pictures.

"Lexie, please don't be mad." Tanner stood by my side now.

I shook my head. My blurry vision made the quotes on my board indecipherable, though my mind held a readable copy. Phrases about perseverance and friendship and trust and family were pinned next to smiling faces of everyone close to me. I wasn't upset at Tanner anymore. I was just upset that things had to change.

"I'm sorry I didn't ask," he said.

"I would have talked you out of it," I choked out the words.

"I know." He put an arm around my shoulder.

"So Brown University, huh?"

"I hear you can make up your own major at Brown. I wonder what they would call a major where you study karate, art history, Russian, math, running, and puzzles. Hmm . . ."

"I guess I'll have to see for myself." I shrugged out of Tanner's arm and straightened a picture on my board. It was my brother and me at the beach when we were kids. My family was correct—going to Brown was the best

course for me. I think I'd known that for a while, but it took Tanner to help me see it. It must have been hard for him to admit it too, since he had really wanted me to join him at WSU.

"You know you're never really going to be on your own, Lexie. No matter how many miles between us, we're family. And we'll always be there for you." He patted my back. "Even if you're being self-sacrificing and stupid."

"Hey!"

"I only speak the truth." He tugged my ponytail before darting out of the room.

22

——————

CHOKEHOLD

I set the Van Gogh on the counter and smoothed the back of my wig, feeling the lump of a ponytail beneath it. I knew now what Tanner would do. I just wasn't sure if there was time, and I couldn't make it happen in here with a few employees still within earshot. There probably wasn't a cell signal this far underground anyway.

My eyes scanned the shelves until they rested on a cardboard tube leaning on the wall. It was a bit longer than I needed—about two and a half feet—but it would work. I grabbed the tube, along with a large sheet of brown paper. If I leaned over the table just right, the cameras wouldn't pick up what I was doing. I slowly rolled up the painted canvas with the brushstrokes on the outside to prevent cracking. I wrapped the brown paper around the rolled-up painting, slid it into the tube, and topped it with the plastic lid.

After removing my cotton gloves, I searched the surrounding area again for props. I found a few manila envelopes, one more cardboard tube, a stack of folders, and a thick manual with the title *Sixteenth-Century Renaissance Pigments*. I piled the items on top of each other and set the tubes on top. One tube under my arm might look suspicious, but a group of items I could barely carry was a distraction to help me keep my cover.

I re-tucked my blouse into my skirt, adjusted my glasses, and hoisted the pile of items into my arms. If looking ridiculous was my plan, I was following it to a T. A curator holding an ancient-looking African statue looked up from his bifocals before he continued using a pointed tool to clean the artifact. As far as I could tell, no one else in the restoration room even glanced in my direction.

The items in my arms weighed less than ten pounds, but the awkwardness of the props made it hard to reach for my magnetic card on the way out the door. My chin held the cardboard tubes while I found the card and slid it through the reader. The door beeped again with no problem. *Thank you, Daly and Millard.*

"Mademoiselle Karaskova, I wondered if you would make it out before shift change." The guard's broad smile caught me by surprise. I was carrying a painting worth more than maybe even the *Mona Lisa.* The cardboard tube pressed against my chest. "Did you see it?" he asked. "The Van Gogh? Is it really just behind this door?"

I leaned toward the guard and spoke low in his ear. "It's close, very close." I stepped back and cleared my throat. "But you didn't hear anything about it from me."

"No, no, of course not." The guard winked.

I nodded at him and proceeded down the empty hall.

The closer I got to my escape, the more Tanner's words filled my mind. I had to be true to myself. He had known that attending WSU wasn't my dream. It wasn't who I was. And neither was this. The weight of the painting in my arms pulled on me. I wasn't a thief. I couldn't support a terrorist organization. I stopped at the glass door of the pyramid exit. Only two inches of glass stood between the Alex that Ivan wanted me to be and the Alex I knew I should be. I had a choice.

I adjusted the pile in my hands to reach for my burner phone. There was one person I could always count on. I just had to trust in him, which I should have done from the start.

I dialed the number. It rang only once before Golkov's groggy voice answered from an ocean away. "Hello?" It must have been nearly six in the morning in Providence.

"Hi, Professor. It's me."

"Alexandra? What can I do for you?" His grandfatherly tone eased a bit of the tightness gripping my stomach.

"Do you still have contacts in the CIA?" I asked.

"Yes." I could almost see him rubbing at his gray beard.

"In Paris?"

"Possibly. Alexandra, what is this about?"

"I need your help."

I STILL CARRIED a cardboard tube under my arm when L'Arc de Triomphe du Carrousel came into view. I'd left the rest of my props on a bench just inside the pyramid exit door. Directly under the keystone of the center arch stood Ivan with his hands behind his back, his silhouette a dark shadow against the lights of the Jardin des Tuileries. With midnight approaching, only a few straggling tourists occupied the square. At least that is how it would appear to an onlooker untrained in surveillance detection. As I passed by the inverted pyramid, in my periphery I caught two men hiding behind a tree. Another four waited on either side of the Louvre building. I counted at least eight more in the tall bushes of the gardens. A woman in all black crouched atop the sixty-foot archway, hiding between two horse statues.

I crossed the street and didn't stop until I was close enough to see Ivan's haunting eyes.

"So nice of you to make it." He held up his wrist to reveal a gold watch. "And just in time, I'd say. You're smart—I'll give you that. After that little stunt in the *Mona Lisa* room, I thought this night might end a little differently. What would have happened if you hadn't . . ." He adjusted the handkerchief in his pocket and smoothed the front of his suit. "No matter now. I can see that you have the painting."

Four dark-suited men emerged from behind the stone of the

inner archway. Another two appeared from each of the outer arch openings. All eight men had guns pointing in my direction.

Icy wind bit through my silk shirt as I gripped the cardboard tube in my hands. An elbow pressed into my back, forcing me within a few feet of the man who had been my puppeteer for weeks. Every decision I'd made since our encounter in Barcelona had been because he'd been yanking my strings. No, not just since Barcelona. Since Moscow, since Ivan had done the same thing to Elijah.

Ivan put out his hand and held it open. His hawk-like stare—those eyes I somehow knew—terrified me to the core. On the outside, I was the image of composure, the perfect spy. Inwardly, my strength held by a straining thread. Suddenly I wished I was wearing one of Millard's earpieces, with Daly's voice guiding and reassuring me.

Another elbow jab from behind thrust me into Ivan, who grabbed for the tube before I fell to my knees on the cold concrete. My glasses toppled from my face.

"Make sure she's clean," Ivan yelled at one of his thugs, who shoved me to the ground, face down. With a knee on my back, the man proceeded to frisk me. I rehearsed a move Itosu had taught me before I remembered the guns right above me.

The plastic top of the cardboard tube bounced to the ground near my head. I winced as a Red Eye operative forcefully finished patting me down.

"What is this?" The violence in Ivan's voice pummeled my eardrums. I knew what he was staring at inside the tube, and it wasn't the *Portrait of Dr. Gachet.* Ivan dropped the empty tube and kicked it away. I prepared myself for what was coming.

"You stupid, stupid girl." His fingers dug into my neck as he yanked my face in his direction. The Red Eye operative at my back rammed his knee deeper into my spine. "Where's the painting?"

"Where it should be," I managed to rasp out before I coughed against the sidewalk. Ivan ripped the wig off my head. I screamed as the bobby pins tore out strands of my hair.

With my disguise gone, I was no longer Irina Karaskova. I was just Alex. And that was exactly who I needed to be.

The guard at my back lifted the knee that held me down. Ivan bent over and yanked hard on my real hair until my face was only inches from his. "You don't realize the mistake you've made."

A hazy memory flashed in front of my vision. I concentrated on it through the blurriness. My memories were always crystal-clear copies of everything I saw. If a scene from my past was hazy, it meant the original moment was too. Pain sliced through my shoulder and the side of my head. Somehow I realized the agony wasn't happening to me while in the middle of Paris. It was in the memory. Whenever I recalled the crash that had taken away my mom and possibly my brother, everything felt raw and exposed just like I was experiencing it for the first time. Why was that memory coming at me now?

"Or maybe you do understand what I'm capable of."

My eyes blurred as Ivan jerked me all the way to my feet and dragged me to the archway. He pressed my back against the stone. Finally, I broke through the fog shrouding the memory.

"You . . . you were there." The air from my lungs scratched at my throat. The car accident in Washington had knocked me unconscious, but I had awakened briefly before the ambulance arrived. I remembered the eyes now staring me down. I'd seen them the day of the crash. *Ivan was there.*

"I know who you are, Alexandra. I've always known." He dug his fingers into my shoulders. "You are going to tell me exactly where that painting is, or everyone you care about will meet the same fate as I gave your mother."

"No!" I screamed as I kneed him in the groin. Twice. He grunted and fell back a few feet. "No," I yelled again. *It was an accident. It had to be an accident. Why would anyone intentionally hurt my mother and my brother and me?*

I pushed away from the arch and propelled my body into Ivan, not caring about the guns aimed in my direction. All I could think about was that my mom was gone and my brother lay in a coma and it wasn't an accident. It was Ivan's fault. It was Red Eye's fault. I wanted Ivan to feel some of the pain I had felt over the last eight months.

Itosu's words about conquering a much larger opponent echoed in my mind. *Can't walk, can't fight. Can't see, can't fight. Can't breathe, can't fight.* I rammed my head into Ivan's nose. A burst of pain shot through the middle of my forehead. He screamed. I knew his guards would be on me in any second. I thrust my elbow into his neck, right into his Adam's apple, and wrapped my other arm behind his neck and squeezed with every ounce of energy in me. Ivan struggled against me, but I wouldn't relax my hold. It would take less than thirty seconds for him to pass out.

Something hard hit the side of my head and I lost my grip as pain seared through me. Strong arms pulled me away from Ivan, who wheezed and coughed for several seconds. The men gripped my shoulders and held my arms behind me. Ivan reached under the back of his jacket and pulled out something dark and shiny. When my vision cleared, I recognized the gun in his hands from one of The Company manuals. A Russian PSS captive piston pistol. It would be so silent that no one would hear it go off. No gun-powder residue would show on me or on his hands. It was the perfect weapon for a discreet spy.

He pointed it right at my heart.

"I didn't" —he coughed— "want it to end like this." He gripped his gun now with two hands and shoved the barrel into my chest. My body felt numb against the cold metal. My mind had numbed too. No flashbacks, no memories, nothing.

"You have a great deal of potential." Ivan removed a handkerchief from his pocket and wiped at the blood streaming from his nose. "I'll give you one last chance, Alexandra. Maybe we can still come to an arrangement." He bent his head from one side to the other, stretching his neck. A bright red mark had formed where my elbow had been. "You are going to go with one of my men and retrieve the Van Gogh. Then no one else will get hurt tonight."

"Why us?" I asked flatly. "Why her? What did my mother do to deserve that?"

Ivan's eyes narrowed, and a laugh shook him, making the gun move against my chest. He let out a loud guffaw. "It's like—how do you say?—déjà vu. She was so much like you." Ivan pressed the gun harder into me. "But she ruined it all by giving the Rembrandt to that stupid museum, instead of me. I don't accept broken promises."

"No," I whispered. Ivan had blackmailed my mother, too. That was why she had left the letter for me in the back of the Rembrandt painting in Golkov's office. She knew that going against Ivan's wishes would put her in danger. But she had done the right thing. She had been true to herself. "No." I raised my head and stared into those icy eyes. "I won't help you."

"I should have known you were your mother's daughter." Ivan's finger curled around the gun's trigger. I closed my eyes. If he shot me, seeing wouldn't matter, but my instincts told me not to record this moment. Somehow I could be free if my eidetic mind didn't capture its last moments.

I waited for several seconds, my eyes squeezed shut. If I concentrated hard enough, I could reach past the sounds of Ivan's breathing to hear the flow of the Seine River. The rush of water increased in my ears, and for a second I thought the river was getting nearer. Except it wasn't the sound of river rapids that was reaching my ears. It was shuffling feet closing in on us. Above me, the sound of ripping cloth or someone sliding down rope vibrated through the air. Still, I waited. I didn't dare open my eyes.

Ivan's men started yelling, yet I remained still like the marble statues I'd been among all day. When the metal pistol fell away from my chest, I finally opened my eyes. A woman in black held Ivan's gun. Golkov had come through with his CIA contacts, and they had gotten here just in time.

Ivan's shock couldn't overshadow the anger simmering behind his eyes. He launched into me, knocking me to the ground. My skirt ripped as I wrapped my legs around his middle and dug my chin into his neck, just like I had done with Daly weeks before. In under five seconds, Ivan slumped over and I pushed him off me.

I rose to my feet and tucked my blouse into the skirt that now exposed part of my thigh. I smoothed my hair and saw my shoes on the ground about ten feet away, next to the woman holding Ivan's gun. She handed the weapon to a man next to her, who slid it into a plastic bag.

"Ms. Laxer, my name is Julia Helm. Yuri Golkov is a good friend of mine." She picked up my shoes and handed them to me. Several strands of nearly black hair had escaped her ponytail. Though her physique was that of a fit twenty-year-old, she looked to be about my dad's age.

I bent over and slid on my shoes. "Thank you." My voice wavered as I looked down at Ivan's still body. The only movement was his chest rising and falling.

Ms. Helm motioned at me toward the Jardin des Tuileries. I followed her into the garden, away from the chaos of CIA agents and Red Eye operatives. "That was quite a chokehold back there. They don't teach that one at Langley."

"I learned it from . . ." I stopped myself from blurting out Itosu's name or mentioning The Company.

"Don't worry, Ms. Laxer. I'm not here to question who you are or what you do for Yuri Golkov. As far as I'm concerned, an anonymous tip came in as to the whereabouts of one of the most-sought-after Russian terrorists. We have captured him and over twenty of his operatives." As Ms. Helm looked over her shoulder, I followed her line of sight. Red Eye operatives were being ushered from the Louvre grounds in unmarked cars. Two men carried a handcuffed and unconscious Ivan and placed him in the back of one of the cars. "I have a feeling these arrests will give us the information we need to take down this organization straight to its foundation. Over the past three months, we've used the information supplied to us from their headquarters where the explosion took place last November. We've taken out several of his operatives all throughout the continent."

"You know about the warehouse in Moscow?"

Ms. Helm eyed me curiously. "Apparently you do as well."

"I was there." The words plowed out of my mouth before I could stop them.

Her eyes widened. "The information we gathered from the building's remains and the operatives we captured was key in our first steps to taking down this organization." She continued to study me. "Have you considered working for the CIA? We are always looking for fresh young recruits with keen minds. And with the combative skills you displayed tonight, it seems like the job would be right up your alley."

I scooted forward and put my hand out to shake hers. "Thank you, Ms. Helm, for everything. But I already have a job and I need to get back to it now."

"I see." She reached into her jacket pocket and pulled out a card. "Well, if you ever decide you want a change, let me know."

I accepted the card. "I will. And again, thank you for the rescue tonight."

Ms. Helm put a hand on my shoulder. "None of us can take down the enemy on our own. We all need backup—we all need people we can trust."

It was true. I shouldn't have tried to complete a mission alone. Fortunately, Daly had been there for me, and Golkov had rescued me. But I had a feeling Ms. Helm wasn't just talking about missions.

As I got up from the bench, Ms. Helm dropped her hand and smiled at me. "Besides, I should be the one thanking you. We have the head of Red Eye in custody. Without you drawing him out, I don't know how long it would have taken us to find him. If we can ever return the favor, let us know."

I smiled and took a few steps forward before I stopped and turned around. "Actually, there are a couple things you can do for me."

"Yes?" She stood up.

"How's your relationship with the Prefecture de Policia de Paris?"

Ms. Helm's eyes scrutinized me before one side of her lips lifted.

My mind flashed to Daly and William and their altercation in the Louvre earlier that day. "I have two innocent friends who helped me tonight and they could use their own rescue."

"Done. What's the second thing?"

"There's a man being held at Langley. A prisoner. He was black-mailed into making some pretty bad choices, but he's a good man. He doesn't deserve to be placed in a black-site prison."

"How do you know about those?" she said quietly as if someone might be listening in.

"I know a lot about the CIA."

"I'm beginning to see that." Ms. Helm stepped toward me. "Tell you what, I will get your two friends freed and work on getting the CIA prisoner released if everything checks out. If I follow through, I want your help on something too."

"Okay," I said warily.

"I have a mission coming up that needs someone like you. How would you feel about joining the CIA on it? Temporarily, of course."

I would have promised anything to see Elijah released. I put out my hand to shake hers. "It's a deal."

23

ANYMORE

I paced across my room. Images from Barcelona and Paris had plagued me since I returned to Providence the night before. I'd come to a decision, and it was time to keep a promise I'd made to myself on the flight home.

Casey stirred in her bed. "Alex? You're back. How was your trip?" She yawned and sat up.

"Exhausting." *And tense and terrifying and dangerous.* "I'm glad to be back."

"I'm glad too. We have so much work to do for the—"

"Hey, Case, do you think we could talk later? There's something I really have to do."

"Sure. Need any help?" The concern on her face didn't help the nervous pit in my stomach.

"No." I pulled on my jacket. "We'll chat later, okay?"

"Okay." She lay back down. "I'm going to get a few more hours of sleep. We're going to be up pretty late tonight."

I wasn't sure what Casey had planned, but I didn't stop to ask for details. If I waited any longer, my anxiety would overtake my courage. *I have to do this.*

The walk across campus passed too quickly. I thought if I walked instead of driving, it would give me a few more minutes to pull myself together, but I wasn't ready. I paused outside William's door with my hand frozen in the air, but before I found the fortitude to knock, the front door swung open. Dr. Red stepped in my direction, but changed his trajectory when he saw me, bumping into the porch railing.

"Oh . . . sorry, Al-ex," he stuttered. "Didn't see . . . I mean . . ." Now his face matched his name.

"It's okay. I was just about to knock. No worries."

His shoulders relaxed. "So, Paris, huh?"

"Yeah." I played with some chipped paint on the railing.

"You okay? I can't believe a crazy guy was stalking you."

"Me neither." I tucked my hair behind my ear and shivered, glad he was buying the story Ms. Helm had come up with.

"I can't believe he actually drove William to the Louvre. That guy sure did take 'creepy stalker' to a whole new level."

I took a deep breath. I couldn't think about this right now—couldn't think about Ivan.

"Shoot! Sorry, Alex. You probably don't want to talk about this. William's always telling me I need to work on my tact. No wonder I don't—"

"Hey," I interrupted, "is William here?"

"Uh, yeah. He's upstairs, probably writing about his eight-hour stay in a French prison, for his memoir or something." Dr. Red cupped his hands around his mouth and yelled through the doorway, "William, your girlfriend's here!" He turned back to me. "Listen, I gotta get to rounds at the hospital. Again, I'm sorry. Glad you made it back safe."

"Thanks."

Leaving the door open, Dr. Red ran down the porch steps and raced away on the sidewalk.

I peered inside the house to find William standing at the bottom of the stairs. His expression was a mix of surprise, relief, and uncertainty. I stepped over the threshold and shut the door behind me.

"I tried to call you," he said.

"Sorry. I need to get a new phone." I leaned against the door. "I also wasn't ready to talk to anyone." William wasn't the only person I'd been avoiding.

Still standing by the stairs, he asked, "What happened in Paris?"

"You already know—"

"It makes no sense. Who was he? Why was he following you?"

"I can't . . . I don't—" I inhaled through my nose. "It doesn't matter. It's over now." A jumble of scenes blurred my vision as my mind rewound on high speed through Paris, Ivan, Red Eye. If my brain had a delete button, I would've erased all those memories.

William crossed the room and wiped a tear from my cheek. "Hey, it's okay." He gave me a warm smile. "You don't have to talk about it now."

Now? No. Not now, not ever. I swallowed. I had come here on a mission.

The softness around his eyes made my resolve falter. *I can't do this to him.* I straightened. If I truly cared about him, I had no choice. If the Louvre had taught me anything, it was that I couldn't compartmentalize my life. I couldn't be one person in one situation, and one in another. Not only was it unfair to people I cared about, it was dangerous too. William could never be a part of one side of my life. That meant I could no longer let him be a part of the other side.

"Alex?" William's voice wavered, his smile fading.

I swallowed away the ache in my throat. "I'm sorry." I stared over his shoulder at the molding around the kitchen door behind him. I couldn't look him in the eyes.

"For what?" he asked.

For the Louvre. For getting you involved in something you don't even know you're a part of. For putting you in harm's way. For what I'm about to do.

Lying had become so easy for me that I could beat a lie detector. But lying to William, someone I cared about a great deal, felt impossible. I stepped around him into the living room.

For lies to be the most convincing, they must be founded in truth.

He reached for my arm and turned me around. I placed my hand over his and pushed it off, but he caught my fingers with his.

"I can't do this anymore," I said. "It's too . . . complicated, too . . . hard." I pulled my hand away.

"It's okay. You're strong. You can get through anything. I've seen it." William's voice was solid and even. He didn't get it. Why couldn't he hear what I was trying to say?

"No, William." I shook my head and took a step back. "I can't do *this*." I used my hand to motion between us.

Finally I met his gaze. His thick brow furrowed and then relaxed as hurt reached his eyes.

"Alex, what are you saying?"

I wanted so badly to look away, but I knew he wouldn't believe me if I didn't face him. "I can't be with you." The truth of the statement burned in my chest. I took in a breath that closed off before it reached my lungs. I wouldn't cry.

"You don't mean that." He moved toward me. I inched back until my legs touched the arm of the couch.

"I can't . . . there's just . . . You have your Fulbright, and I have my life here. Can't you see that it's never going to work?"

William's lips tightened, and I noticed a tiny white scar on the side of his mouth, just a few millimeters long.

"I'm sorry. I can't do it." I shook my head, then forced out the words I never wanted to say. "We can't be together."

"No." He moved close to me. "*No puedes hacerlo. Te amo.*" The richness of his words reached into me. He loved me. His hand brushed my chin until it rested on my cheek. Another warm hand cupped my other cheek. I held my breath.

I couldn't let him be a part of the Alex who lied and pretended and broke laws and hurt others, the Alex who would put him in danger every day we were together. Daly had been right. William didn't know me because I couldn't *let* him know me. Like my mom, I would do anything to keep the ones I cared about safe.

"I know you love me too," William said. He pulled me into a kiss, his hands caressing the sides of my face. I had no strength, nothing left within me to push him away. In many ways I wanted to give in to the kiss, to give up my dangerous life for a normal one that involved going to classes and hanging out with the perfect boyfriend. Safe and secure.

I let his lips linger on mine for a second longer, just one last time. A goodbye kiss. A farewell.

A memory flashed in my mind of the first time I met William after tripping over him in the Barus-Holley hallway. Next, my mind flashed to Blackstone Park, where we first kissed as snowflakes fell around us. Then my mind exploded with scenes from the Louvre and seeing William next to the *Mona Lisa*. The beautiful lines of the painting had forever changed in my mind. Now all I saw were the cracks and layers of varnish. Suddenly the face of Ivan burned through the canvas of the painting. I gasped and placed my hands on William's chest, pushing him away.

"You're leaving soon. We both know that. I can't go. My life is here. This is my home." My brain flashed to Daly, my father, Tanner, Golkov, Millard, and Casey. One thing I knew for certain was that I couldn't imagine leaving any of them, even for William.

"We can make it work," he said. The fierceness in his gaze almost cracked my willpower as he moved near me again.

"No, William. No." There was only one way I could do this, and I'd had plenty of practice. I let the sound of ocean waves from my memory rush in my ears. "I can't be with you because I want to be with someone else." It was easier to say than I thought it would be.

This time William stepped back. Seeing the pain on his face was harder than any mission I had been on, harder than facing Ivan and Red Eye, even harder than letting go of my mom and Tanner.

"That's not true." The strain in William's voice told me he wasn't sure he believed his own words.

I knew he was thinking of the moment when he saw me with Daly at the back of Wayland House. The memory might not have been as clear as what I watched in my own head, but I could tell it was just as real for William. And maybe it was worse this time because I wasn't trying to explain it away.

In my head, I concentrated on the gentle curve of the distant skyline at Cannon Beach, how it appeared so smooth from a distance, so peaceful. "Yes, it's true." I sidestepped away from the couch, away from William. "I think I should go."

He caught the sleeve of my jacket and blocked my path to the door. "Then tell me you don't care about me. Tell me that this" —he used his free hand to motion between us, like I had done earlier— "has meant nothing to you." Beneath the pleading of his words, I sensed a bitterness rising in him.

I felt the sand at my toes and a cool wave lap over my ankles. "I don't love you anymore." As the words escaped my lips, I wished I could take them back. Not because of the lie I was masking with ocean waves, but because I'd let the word "anymore" slip in. As part of my lie, I'd admitted the truth. I had loved him.

But I didn't now. The realization struck me so hard that tears began to burn at my eyes and run down my cheeks in a torrent of confused emotions. *I have to leave.* I could take down a man twice my size, but I couldn't face William's pain. I had to save myself from that memory replaying on a loop. I shook my sleeve from his grasp and pushed past him to the door.

"You're really going to just go?" he asked quietly.

I glanced over my shoulder to find him with his arms crossed and expression solemn. Though there were only a few feet between us, his face told me it was a chasm. I turned away again and closed my eyes. I should have just opened the front door and escaped, but my hand paused on the knob.

"I have to," I whispered, squeezing my eyes shut tighter as if I could push away the memories of William passing through my mind. Suddenly, another face and another series of memories played like a movie, overshadowing William's playful smile. I knew then why the lies I thought I was telling him had come so easily.

I hadn't just been lying to William. I had lied to myself. I didn't have to go. I didn't have to keep him from the other part of my life. I had given Tanner that advice when he cheated on his high school test, but now the words really rang true in my own life. *"There's always a choice. No matter what pressures you are under, you decide how to respond. No one else does that for you."*

William and I stood there silently for what must have been at least two minutes, unsaid words floating in the air between us.

"You know what the worst part is?" he said finally, his voice fracturing the movies in my head. "You didn't even ask me to stay."

I opened my eyes and turned just enough to see his dejected countenance. I had gotten through to him. He knew what I was only now learning myself. I had chosen to leave him even before he had accepted the Fulbright and planned to go to Mexico. My choice had started when I kept back a significant part of my life. My choice had begun when I shared everything—my eidetic memory, the accident, my brother, my hopes and dreams—with someone else.

"I would have stayed. I would have . . . for you." This time he whispered the words.

My heart broke. I wanted to say something, but William turned and walked away. The old stairs of the house cried out with each step he took up to the second floor. His footfalls resonated through the ceiling above me as he continued down the hallway. I didn't move until the sound of his bedroom door closing pressed against my chest. It was over. We were over.

I opened the door and walked outside. The rush of icy winter air bit at the tears on my face. Recalling ocean waves or Itosu's meditation techniques couldn't help me now. I slammed the door and flew down the stairs. My feet pounded the sidewalk until the burning of my lungs overpowered the ache in my heart.

I kept running until I reached Marston Hall, only pausing long enough for the retina scanner to admit me into The Company headquarters. I propelled myself down the hallway and didn't stop until I reached the gym and stood over Itosu, who sat cross-legged near the corner of the room.

"Have you been taking it easy on me in training?" I asked.

The hint of a smile came to his lips, but I ignored it.

"Have you?" I asked again, this time more forcefully.

"One doesn't expect a tadpole to jump." Itosu rose up to his feet, and even though he was about my height, his confident posture towered over me.

"I'm not a tadpole." I ripped off my leather jacket and threw it against the wall. My new hot-pink cast probably didn't help me appear serious.

"I see." Itosu ran a hand over his cropped dark hair.

"You're supposed to train me to face my enemies. So train me. Give me a fight I can't win." I tapped my foot impatiently.

"First, you change into your workout attire. When you come back, I will do what you ask."

"Fine," I huffed, then marched into the changing room. Arguing with the sensei would be pointless. If he would bring me a fight that would distract me from everything else, I could wear my workout clothes. I pulled off my jeans and long-sleeved shirt and stuffed them into my locker before I put on The Company workout attire. I shut the thick locker door so hard I was pretty sure Itosu could hear it through the wall.

I pulled my hair up in a high ponytail and exited the dressing room. "Okay, I'm ready for our . . ." I stopped short. Itosu stood in the center of the fighting circle. About twenty operatives, some in suits and the rest in their workout clothes, formed a U-shape around the edge of the room. This audience wasn't what had my heartbeat roaring through my chest.

Itosu wasn't alone in the center of the circle. Daly stood next to him with his hands in ready position. I hadn't seen him since the Louvre. He wore his workout attire and a dazzling smile that almost broke through my mood.

I rolled my eyes. "I said I wanted a real fight, Itosu."

Daly hopped back and forth from one foot to another. I'd fought him before and knew he was an excellent fighter, but seeing him bounce in front of me like a boxer felt like an insult.

Itosu bowed slightly. "You said you wanted a fight you couldn't win. This is one of those fights."

I put my hands on my hips. "I've beaten Daly before. Even if I wore a blindfold I could get him on his back."

Daly stopped bouncing and his smile widened. "If I remember

correctly, I was the one who got you on your back first during our sparring match."

My mind flashed to that initial match over two months ago. I'd gotten him on his back, but only after he'd managed to pin me on mine while straddling my hips with his legs, his hands pressing mine into the floor. The memory made me blush, but I managed to say in a matter-of-fact tone, "We both know you cheated."

"You hit me on the head with a cookie sheet," Daly shot back.

"You called me a witch."

"Well, you had a broom and I just needed to—"

Itosu cleared his throat loudly. "Alexandra, if you thought your only opponent was Mr. Daly, you are mistaken." Itosu raised his hands in front of him. "You asked me not to hold back. Neither of *us* will."

I looked between the two men. I was angry, but not at either of them. My emotions simply needed an outlet. Daly stared at me intently. He knew about my left jab and my affinity for Disney songs, but I wondered if he remembered that I knew him too. I could read him better than all the books I could see in my head. It wasn't just his scenes playing through my mind, either. The cocky grin that often spread across his face didn't come from a superiority complex as I'd once assumed. He actually only smiled like that around the people he cared about—it was his way of showing his confidence in the relationship. He could just say my name and I knew by the inflection in his voice what he meant before the rest of the words flowed. Even as he watched me now with one eyebrow hovering a centimeter lower than the other, I saw a glint of compassion in his eyes. He wanted to ask me what was wrong. He could tell there was more going on with me than just wanting to train with Itosu. More than what happened at the Louvre. More than anxiety over a brother I could lose again.

I approached the center of the padded floor, stopping about ten feet from both of my opponents. Then I glanced up and noticed Golkov standing across the gym at the top of the stairs. Though I couldn't see his expression, the stance of his body and the tilt of his head reminded me that I had a lot of explaining to do. I wasn't sure how much he knew about my escapade in Paris, but after my phone call to him for CIA help, he would certainly have questions. Ivan's arrest and the subsequent downfall of Red Eye wouldn't have gotten past Golkov's radar, either. I should have already been at his door. But I still hadn't forgiven him for hiding Tanner from me. And I wasn't ready to accept back The Company ring.

My emotional roller coaster with William that morning weighed on my heart and flashed through my mind. But the only way to get through this was to move forward. I couldn't erase the memories moving almost constantly across my vision. The thing was—I didn't want to anymore. There was nothing more precious than the movies of my mom playing on repeat in the synapses of my brain. I could never give up those car rides with Tanner as we belted out country songs I knew he hated, or argued over who knew more about football. Brown University, working with my new friends at The Company, Casey, even my good times with William. There was so much I wanted to keep. I would keep every memory that haunted me as long as I could hold onto the good memories.

With a shake of my head, I returned my focus to the fight. I stood in ready position, with one foot back and my arms out in front of me. Itosu was correct. I might not be able to win this fight, but I'd have a lot of fun making a new memory.

24

FAITH

I tried to walk by Golkov's office unnoticed, but he called my name through the open door. Slowly, I turned around, smoothing a few strands of my still-damp hair from the sparring match. Itosu and Daly had won, of course, but I'd gotten Daly on his back first this time. With the handicap of a cast on my wrist.

"Can we talk for a moment?" Golkov motioned for me to enter his office.

I remained planted where I stood, not sure what to say. "Tanner" was the only word that came out.

Golkov's eyes went wide, and suddenly I realized Daly hadn't told him I knew about my brother. The professor peered down at the dark marble floor. I'd never seen him look ashamed before.

"My brother was alive and you didn't tell me." I let my emotions flow out into my words. "I thought we were like family. You don't hide things like that from your . . ." My thoughts circled about and stopped right where they began. I couldn't judge Golkov for doing the same thing I was doing to my own father.

He looked up at me. "I wanted to tell you. That day in my office, when I said that some secrets should be shared. I was going to tell you, but you were so focused on seeing Elijah."

"Because he was going to help Tanner. He was always going to help Tanner."

Golkov leaned against the glass window beside his door, a pained expression on his face. "I heard what Elijah said. I'm sorry I didn't believe him. I guess I let my regard for you cloud my assessment of the situation. None of it made sense, and I should have questioned it more. He was an ally and friend for nearly twelve years."

I let out a sigh. "I didn't understand either. When I learned about the chip and about Red Eye blackmailing him, it was too late. If I'd told you or Daly I had to get the painting, Ivan would have exposed The Company or hurt you. I couldn't let him do that."

Golkov rubbed his beard. "I'm sorry you went through all of that on your own."

I took a few steps forward. "I wasn't on my own. I had all of you right here." I touched the side of my head.

Golkov's posture seemed lighter now. "I will do my best to see that Elijah is released. It will take some time for everyone around here to understand, but I will make this right."

"It's okay. You don't have to—"

"No, Alexandra. I do. Hopefully Elijah will be able forgive me for my—"

"No, what I mean is that he's already on his way here."

A crease formed on Golkov's forehead. "How would you know that? He was being transported to the black site."

"Your contact at the CIA, Julia Helm, said she owed me a favor for helping catch Ivan and Red Eye." I didn't mention my promise to join the CIA on a mission. It felt like a betrayal to Golkov, and I still wasn't exactly sure what it would entail.

"You've been talking with the CIA?"

"He should arrive in Providence sometime later today. I just have to go take a Chinese quiz first."

"Hmm." A tiny smile, nearly hidden under Golkov's beard, reached his lips. "You just got back from a mission where you made it to the Louvre archives, nearly out the door of a high-security museum with a priceless Van Gogh painting, and brought down a large Russian terrorist organization. And now you're on your way to take a Chinese quiz before you meet with a man that might possibly save your brother."

"Yep."

Golkov chuckled, shook his head, and muttered something under his breath.

"What?"

He put a hand on my shoulder. "You are just so much more than I expected."

"Um, thanks." I played with the zipper of my jacket. "Well, I should probably go."

"Yes, I don't want to keep you." He withdrew his hand. "Oh, and good job with Mr. Daly today. I like to see him flat on his back every now and again."

"Yeah. Me too." I started down the corridor.

While I walked, I replayed our conversation. When I got to the end, I slowed down the memory and watched Golkov's lips after he laughed. If I concentrated really hard, his words became clearer. I couldn't be sure, but it sounded like he said, "And the student surpasses the teacher."

ANYA STOOD in the hallway when I entered the apartment on Hattery Road. She put her finger to her lips and motioned toward Tanner's room.

"Elijah just got here," she whispered. Her radiant face brightened even further when she smiled. We both quietly moved to the open doorway. An unconscious Tanner still lay peacefully in his bed. Elijah stood next to him with his back to us.

". . . long road ahead of you," Elijah was saying in his thick Ukrainian accent. "But I know I can do this—we can do this." He took a deep breath. "You'll be up and playing football in no time. I'll bet you'll even be able to beat that sister of yours in a race." His shoulders started to slope downward.

"I'm sorry for what I did to your sister. You don't know how sorry." Elijah placed a hand at his forehead. I couldn't see his face, but I imagined his anguished expression as I moved into the room and stood beside him.

"Tanner understands," I said quietly. "I understand."

Elijah turned to me with his piercing blue eyes. "I'll need a few weeks to prepare, but I'm willing to perform the surgery if you're certain."

I watched memories of my brother up and moving before I let my gaze rest on his comatose form. This wasn't the real Tanner. "It's what he would want."

"Anya and I will work out the logistics and details." Elijah held out a hand and she joined him on the other side. "But there is one more thing I need from you."

"What is that?"

Elijah turned and took my hand. "Faith."

I nodded. That was something I could give.

25

MISSION TETRIS

Though it wasn't snowing, a gust of wind blew a handful of flakes down from a leafless tree above me. They fluttered to the sidewalk, so light and free. I lifted my face to the sky and savored the peace of campus at night. As Itosu had taught me, I drew in a deep breath, pulling in the air slowly to fill my lungs and expand my abdomen. Scenes from Moscow, Barcelona, and the Louvre filtered through my mind in an echo of colors. The dark moments hadn't disappeared, but I saw the memories in a new light. My choices had changed me, and because things hadn't been easy, I had grown stronger.

I'd made it. I released the breath and smiled. With Ivan caught, Red Eye gone, and a chance for Tanner, my smile was real for the first time in what seemed like forever. Everyone I loved was safe.

I opened my eyes to find Daly standing there in black pants and a leather jacket. His gaze was fixed on me in such a way that a wave of heat traveled through my body.

"You doing better now?" He moved closer.

I nodded. While I couldn't put my feelings into words, I knew having him there wasn't entirely unpleasant. In fact, his presence somehow made me feel whole and complete.

It wasn't until he stood a few feet away that I noticed his slightly swollen lower lip and a small, horizontal cut running between his lip and chin.

I stared at the wound. "Did I do that?"

"Do what?"

I touched his chin softly, suddenly realizing this was the first time my skin had met with his—if you don't count fist punches. Or Barcelona. My face flushed as our dance played through my mind. I pulled my fingers away. *What am I doing?*

"This?" Daly motioned to the cut. "It's nothing. You should see the other guy." He brought his hand up and skimmed his thumb over my battle wound near my left temple. I didn't move as he cupped the side of my face. The throbbing of my head mysteriously moved to my heart.

A warm smile reached his lips. All I could think about was how near we stood and how I wished we were even closer. If I tilted forward, something dangerous might happen. If I tilted back, nothing would happen. Torn between both options I remained still, balancing on a scale between danger and the life I'd known before.

"What are you doing here?" I said breathlessly.

"What do you mean?" Daly's breath warmed my face.

"I mean, here on campus."

"Millard said you needed me."

"Millard?"

Casey bounced up the path next to Daly, who immediately dropped his hand from my face. She looked between us.

Figuring it was too late to pretend I didn't know him, I said, "This is Daly—"

He stepped in her direction. "Casey and I have already met." He reached out his hand to her.

I stared at him slack-jawed as he lifted her hand to his lips. It wasn't just the idea that they already knew each other that shocked me, it was the deep voice Daly had used, with a British accent.

"Hi, handsome," Casey gushed as he kissed her hand.

My stomach twisted in knots.

"I still can't believe you and J. R. are roommates," she said.

"J. R.?" I looked at Daly and her, thoroughly baffled.

"Yes, J. R. and I are like family." Daly still spoke in an accent that sounded so real, I wouldn't have guessed he was American. He zipped his black jacket all the way to the top.

"You guys ready for this?" Millard came up beside me with a cardboard box full of wires.

"J. R., why don't you tell us exactly what you need us to do first?" Daly said to Millard.

Millard raised an eyebrow at Daly, probably confused at his accent, then looked at Casey and me. "Casey's the one with the plan," he told Daly. "I'm just here for the programming and wiring."

Millard's eyes lingered on Casey, who played with her black pearl earring. Then she pointed to Daly and me. "I need you two on foot duty. Most of the frames are in the Sciences Library basement and will need to be brought up, starting at the seventh floor. I stored the last twenty in our dorm closet and under our beds. Snag those last when the RA is asleep." She pulled some black cloth from her backpack. "You'll need these." She handed a ski mask to Daly and one to me. I stared at mine in confusion. *What is going on?*

"J. R., I need you with me on the fourth floor. I got the wood shop to install two frames per window on the first two floors like we talked about." Casey turned back to Daly and me. "We are going five windows across, which means the two of you will be placing in eighty more frames. The straps are hooked to each frame. All you have to do is attach them to the Velcro, which is already on the metal surrounding the windows."

"How did you get the Velcro in place?" Millard asked.

A Cheshire grin overtook Casey's face. "You'd be surprised what you can get a guy to do with the promise of a date."

Millard narrowed his eyes. "A date?"

Casey squeezed his arm. "Don't worry. I only had to agree to one date. But Alex is booked solid for the next four weekends."

"What?" I yelled. A passerby, who I recognized as a student in my

Chinese 202 class, paused and stared at our group before quickly moving down the sidewalk toward Macmillan Hall.

Millard set his box on the sidewalk. "I'll get each relay hooked to the cables, and then we can start pulling the rest of the wires through the dumbwaiter shafts and connecting to those floors. I hope those Christmas lights don't overload the power grid. Sending voltages over long distances is always tricky."

I looked up at the Sciences Library. The rows and columns of windows sparked a memory of Casey sitting with a grid of papers displayed across her bed. Geometric shapes, each made up of four blocks, had been printed on each page. I was beginning to understand. We were recreating her Tetris grid in 3-D in Christmas lights on the side of the library. It would be the biggest Tetris game ever.

"You said it would take months to pull off this prank." I stared at my roommate.

"Alex, it's been nearly a month. And with J. R.'s genius, he got all fourteen custom circuit boards built and ready in under a week. We've just been waiting for the rest of the frames."

"Wrapping the frames in Christmas lights took the longest. My fingers are still sore from Friday night." Millard held up a hand, and Casey did the same. They wiggled their fingers at each other and laughed until their eyes locked and their fingers intertwined.

Unable to hold back a smile, I turned to Daly, who was grinning at the flirtatious couple in front of us. I waited about ten seconds before I said, "So . . . when do we start?"

"Oh, sorry." Casey dropped her hand and bit the corner of her lip. The obvious attraction between her and Millard gave me a sweet satisfaction. I'd had a feeling they'd hit it off.

"You'll need these too." Millard reached into his box and pulled out two pairs of sunglasses.

"Yeah, once the lights go out, those will be a lifesaver." Casey grabbed another pair from the top of the box and slipped them into her coat pocket.

"I've always wanted a pair of night-vision glasses." Daly put the glasses on and looked around, then removed them and slid them into his jacket pocket.

"You're taking all the campus lights out again?" I flashed to the first prank I'd helped Casey with the year before, the one involving the statue of Caesar Augustus and a roll of hot-pink duct tape.

"Nope. Just the Sciences Library lights and the sidewalks around it." She looked at a paper in her hand. "We need several hours to set this up, and we don't want the security guards to suspect anything."

"Luckily, the campus maintenance manager emailed all employees to let them know the electrical at the library was being serviced tonight." Millard winked at Casey.

"It's a quarter to nine now. Let's meet back here at midnight. That gives you about twenty minutes per floor. Think you can do that?" Casey looked at Daly and me.

"Yes," we said at the same time.

Millard picked up his box and handed it to Daly, who had already put his ski mask on his head like a winter hat, with the face part rolled up at his forehead.

"Where are your masks?" I motioned to Millard and Casey.

"You guys are the ones sneaking in through the back and into the basement." Casey motioned to the walkway behind the library. "We're going through the front door. No one will suspect a couple just grabbing a book before the library closes."

I tucked my night-vision glasses into my back pocket and donned my ski mask. I shrugged at Casey. "I guess we're ready."

"Hmm." She squinted her eyes at me.

"What?" I put a hand on my hip.

"You could totally pass as a spy." She turned up my jacket collar. "That is if you didn't have that cast on your arm. Spies are too cool to break bones."

Millard's eyes went wide and Daly started coughing next to me, only some of his coughs resembled laughs. Casey grabbed Millard's hand and pulled him forward, then turned back to Daly and me. "We're going to make Brown University history."

I smiled as they moved down the sidewalk. I wasn't sure about history, but we'd be making a memory—a good one this time.

Daly nudged my shoulder. "You ready to do this thing with me?"

I looked up to find his eyes asking about more than just our present situation.

"Yes." I rose up on my toes and pulled his mask over his face, but not before I saw his cocky smile. "First we have a mission to complete."

Dear *Van Gogh Gone* Reader,

Thank you for going on Alexandra's journey with me! I hope you loved reading the story as much as I loved writing it. Readers keep authors in business, so I appreciate your support.

If you enjoyed *Remembrandt* or *Van Gogh Gone,* please consider leaving a review on Goodreads.com, Amazon.com, or any online store you purchase through. Reviews and word of mouth are what keep an author writing. Let me know if you leave a review, and I'll send you a signed bookmark! As another thank you to my readers, I wrote and recorded a song (yes, I sang!) that accompanies the series. You can listen to "Remembrandt Song" and download your free copy online (https://soundcloud.com/author-robin-king).

I also love to attend book clubs, conferences, and school assemblies. Please email me at authorrobinking@gmail.com to schedule your event.

If you would like to keep up to date on my books, author events, or giveaways, please join my newsletter at https://linktr.ee/author robinking or check out my website at www.authorrobinking.com.

Thanks again,

Robin

ACKNOWLEDGMENTS

When I was younger, I hated to write. Thankfully I had parents and leaders who encouraged me to put my thoughts down in a journal. If it wasn't for their astuteness, *Van Gogh Gone* wouldn't exist.

I also couldn't have done this without the best writing group on the planet, Riveting Writers. Your guidance and push to keep writing have been my saving grace. One day we will all be NYT bestsellers.

Thanks go out to my beta readers—Mary, Brooke, Amy, Raelynn, Rebecca, Cheryl, Carina, Jen, Jessica, and Mom. Your suggestions were key to making the book so much better! You all deserve lots of chocolate and a good book.

A shout-out goes to my first editor, Linda, for pointing out my writing flaws, while still letting me keep my favorite parts. Walnut Springs Press is lucky to have you!

I'm grateful to my siblings, Jason, Whitney, Wendy, Aaron, David, Jared, Devin, and Shae. There may or may not be characters in this book who have some of your attributes. I'm not saying which one of you influenced the character Ivan.

I want to thank my dad, who could have totally been a spy if he'd wanted to. You taught me that I can do anything if I put the work into it. I get that now.

I don't think thanks are enough for my mom. You were my alpha reader, beta reader, and personal editor. Out of everyone, you have been the biggest support and have spent the most time reading my stuff. One day, I'll write a Regency romance just for you.

Instead of thanking them, I should be asking for forgiveness from my family. I've been on my computer way too much, and hope you'll forgive me for it. Does an acknowledgment make up for it? Jeff, Henry, Elijah, Trevor, Charly, Alana, and Olive—look, all your names are in a book!

Last of all, thanks to my amazing friends who helped me get the cover of the book I wanted. Summer (summernocolephoto.com), you did such a great job photographing our model. Jen (classycosmetics.com), your makeup skills are perfection. Bryn (copperrobin.com), you are a hair goddess. And to my model, Marli, thanks for being the perfect "Alex." You make the cover unforgettable.

ALSO BY ROBIN KING

ROMANTIC SUSPENSE

Remembrandt (The Art of Espionage #1)

Van Gogh Gone (The Art of Espionage #2)

Memory of Monet (The Art of Espionage #3)

CHILDREN'S BOOKS

Postcards from Pinky

Find out about upcoming books at www.authorrobinking.com.

Remembrandt Song

A photograph holds a thousand words, a memory even more.
A catalog of all events waiting in a drawer.
They play within my mind—who, what, and where.
I don't walk down memory lane, I live there.

Like a Rembrandt painting, will the edges of the memory begin to
fade?
And I wonder, how long before I've lost the ones I've made?
Etched within my mind are things I can't let go.
But I know some things are better left forgotten.

The eyes—they see the experiences I face.
Memories of the past haunt me in my place. Remembrance of the
pain and grief flood my tattered mind.
Where is the hope I long to find?

Like a Rembrandt painting, will the edges of the memory begin to
fade?
And I wonder, how long before I've lost the ones I've made?
Etched within my mind are things I can't let go.
But I know some things are better left forgotten.

Balancing two different lives, one simple and secure.
Safe used to be ideal, but now I'm not so sure.
My other life is dangerous, with secrets, risks, and thrill.
The adventure calms the memories, makes my mind go still.
This is the life I chose, I can't run away.
He's the only reason I want to stay.

Like a Rembrandt painting, will the edges of the memory begin to
fade?

And I wonder, how long before I lose the good ones that I made?
Etched within my mind are things I won't let go.
And I know some things are best if not forgotten.
Yes, I know some things are best if not forgotten.

(Listen to the song sung by the author at
www.soundcloud.com/author-robin-king)

ABOUT THE AUTHOR

Robin M. King received her bachelor's degree in education from Brigham Young University and has been instructing children and young adults for over twenty years. When she's not writing or helping her students remember the quadratic formula, she leads a clandestine life as a wife and a mother of six. Don't tell anyone, but Robin's also a marathoner, photographer, singer, seamstress, baker, and household appliance repairman. You can find her online at www.authorrobinking.com and on social media @robinkingauthor.

Robin's first novel, *Remembrandt* (2014), introduces readers to Alexandra Stewart's world of cryptic codes and covert missions, followed by *Van Gogh Gone*. Read the 3rd book in Remembrandt series, *Memory of Monet* now.